W9-BBV-046

THE ONE THING WORTH HAVING

The One Thing Worth Having

by

LONA B. KENNÉY

Allen, Bennington
Publishers
Garnerville, N. Y.

LIBRARY OF CONGRESS
CATALOG CARD NO. 81-83207
ISBN 0-937884-02-0 (hardcover)
    0-937884-03-0 (paper)

Published by ALLEN, BENNINGTON
Garnerville, N. Y. 10923

DISTRIBUTED BY
Associated Booksellers Inc.
P.O. Box 6361
147 McKinley Ave.
Bridgeport, Conn. 06606
203-366-5494

MANUFACTURED IN THE UNITED STATES OF AMERICA

"Youth is the one thing worth having."

OSCAR WILDE, *The Picture of Dorian Gray*

*To all victims of youth-worshiping
society*

THE ONE THING WORTH HAVING

One

Doriana lay flat on her back, trying to guess the time. It was impossible to tell with heavily bandaged eyes. The hospital had quieted down, so maybe it was late evening or even night. She was no longer nauseated, and had virtually no pain, but she was as thirsty as if she had crossed the Sahara.

It was no doubt Dr. Tamashiro's orders not to let her have anything by mouth during the first few hours after the operation, and Dr. Tamashiro's orders were followed strictly. That much she learned from the start, when, over her loud protests, they scrubbed her face, including her nose, with harsh green soap and water and then painted it with half-strength iodine. This was so different from her relationship with Dr. Orgood, whom she could generally charm into quite a few things. Things like having Seconal instead of Nembutal, or being painted with colorless Zephiran instead of a colored disinfectant like iodine or Metaphen. And the mood in the operating suite when Dr. Tamashiro operated differed vastly from the casual atmosphere in which Dr. Orgood's assistant told his interminable tales, and all that Doriana heard during Dr. Tamashiro's hour-long operation were brief and sharp orders like "Ehrhardt clamp," "Lester forceps," "Dermatome. . . ."

Gradually she drifted back into a state of semiconsciousness, filled with troubling visions of her early childhood on her native French Riviera. . . . She was six years old, standing in the living room of her parents' modest cottage in Nice, holding on to her young mother's skirt, and looking up at her prematurely aged, deeply lined face, which so shockingly contrasted with the radiant blonde beauty of her picture on the mantel. She could hear her mother's laments at having

1

incomprehensibly been cheated of something rightfully hers, of something precious without which life was worthless and meaningless—her youth.

"Please don't cry, *maman chérie,* please don't cry," she was pleading, trying to comfort her mother, her own eyes welling up with tears. . . .

She moaned, and her own plaintive voice brought her back to reality. She tossed, felt a sharp pain in her eyelids, and completely awakened, still haunted by her reverie.

She was not a little girl anymore, and her poor, unhappy mother had died many, many years ago, leaving her a legacy of destructive anxieties whose significance she had only recently fully realized, along with her true understanding of her mother's frightful transformation that must have set in after her pregnancy and shortly following her husband's sailing for a five-year-term in Indochina, where as a government agronomist he hoped to put away a few thousand francs for the family's future.

And as year succeeded year, at the approach of his return, apparently dreading the terrible moment of having to face him and perhaps lose him forever, her mother became more and more agitated, talking incessantly about the experimental new science of plastic surgery, which was so hopelessly out of her reach. . . . She couldn't understand her mother's terror at the time, not only because she was too young, but also because even though she had only hazy, disconnected memories of her father, she thought that this kind giant, whose happy laughter, while he was bouncing her on his knee, still rang in her ears, couldn't hurt anyone. And now she also reflected sadly that many things might perhaps have turned out differently for her mother, had she been born only half a century later, in the era of hormonal therapy and highly developed plastic surgery, and that she herself would not have been cursed with such a youth complex, fed by later experiences like the time when she was barely eighteen and just getting a start in pictures.

"All your talent is in your gorgeous boobs, a sexy behind

and your youth, kid. And that will last you only a few short years," a boorish movie director in Hollywood had told her in front of everybody who happened to be on the set. . . .

She was still unquenchably thirsty.

"Nurse," she called, "Nurse." This was the one drawback of a private room—being isolated with no one to hear you in moments like this. This private room had been hard to get on such short notice.

"There's a critical shortage of hospital beds," Dr. Tamashiro's secretary had argued. "Or hadn't Ms. Delor heard?"

The recollection of this rebuke had almost made her as uncomfortable as when her own secretary, Noelle, had mimicked this telephone conversation for her. But she shrugged it off. First of all, she had won her private room, and anyway she had made up her mind to go back home at the earliest possible moment, and wouldn't let anybody stop her, not even if Dr. Tamashiro said that she would have to stay put on her back for forty-eight hours. Hugh was away again, this time on business, somewhere in Wyoming, and he might call. And the unsophisticated Noelle might blurt out that she was at the hospital, and scare Hugh who would jet right back and find her with her eyes still swollen and bruised. It was ridiculous of course that she tried to keep this trip to Shangri-la from her husband. Sooner or later he'd find out anyway. Well, let it be later, if she could help it.

It was not only Dr. Tamashiro's authoritative orders that might interfere with her plans, she thought. The operation she just underwent was so different from the regular face-lifting performed by Dr. Orgood. Maybe only the first lift was the real operation, with deep cuts in front and behind her ears, that pulled out the beginning of potential jowls and erased the lines of sadness with which smiles paradoxically mark up the human face, and more cuts inside the hairline over the temples to pull out future crow's feet around the eyes and to smooth even more the fine skin over her high cheekbones. The subsequent "freshening up," as Dr. Orgood labeled it, was not as complicated. It involved perhaps the same incisions, but far less separation of the skin from the underlying subcutaneous tissue, and she was able to leave the hospital the following day. But it proved far more complicated after a lid operation. She couldn't remove the bandages from her eyes and possibly risk ugly scars.

She thought she felt her eyelids under the dressing dry and itchy, and it again reminded her of how thirsty she was. She groped for the buzzer and felt the electric bed control that automatically cranked the bed into all desired positions, but could not find the bell where it was supposed to be, clamped to the side of her sheet. She raised her arm, trying to reach the cord pull of the overhead intercom with the nurses' office down the hall, but it eluded her as well.

"Nurse, N-u-r-s-e!" she called again.

"What can I do for you?" a man's voice inquired.

It was not the same uncultured voice of the male attendant she had heard before falling asleep after a belated Demerol shot they had given her, not before surgery as prescribed by the doctor, but after the operation. And there was no servility of somebody hoping for a good tip in the man's tone.

"Please give me a drink of water. I'm parched," she said groggily.

She heard him move about silently, pour the water from the thermos pitcher, then felt the glass straw against her lips and greedily sipped the ice water. She heard his soft laughter that he was evidently trying to keep down, for it sounded somewhat uneven as if someone were twiddling with the volume control of a television or radio set.

"Who are you?" she asked.

"I don't think I ought to tell you just yet," the man said, chuckling, "since I know who you are, and that gives me an advantage."

She was so taken aback that momentarily she remained speechless. She had registered under an assumed name, but obviously the ruse had not worked.

"Don't get angry, Miss Delor," the man said. "It's not

such a good idea after plastic surgery to have blood rush to your head, no matter what." He laughed again.

"Who are you?" she repeated, trying to sharpen her wits.

"I'm just a resident," he said.

"I'd like another drink of water, Doctor."

She heard his soft-stepping feet move around the bed and the water gurgle from the pitcher into the glass again, but when she puckered her lips, instead of the sipper she expected, she felt firm lips pressed against hers. The kiss was brief, and she heard his voice at her ear, while a strong restrained hand held her down.

"You'd better not fight me. Eye sutures are so fine that any undue strain may burst them. Your dressing may come off and you might disfigure yourself permanently."

She felt cold panic. This resident was a madman. Was what he was saying meant as a threat? If he really was unbalanced he might rip off her bandages. No, he won't, for then she could identify him. She ought to play dumb and keep on talking, make him talk, until the nurse returned. She could not reach for the bedside phone, but perhaps she might finally locate the buzzer to light the bulb outside her door or find the intercom cord. . . .

"Don't bother trying to locate the buzzer. I moved it out of your reach," he said, covering her cold hand with his that felt very warm.

She made herself calm down. This resident was right. It was foolish of her to flush so violently and perhaps cause more discoloration than necessary. Dr. Tamashiro had said the skin around the eyes would remain red and bruised for some time following surgery. She did not quite believe his last minute warning. Somewhere between his gloomy prognosis and the overly optimistic prediction of his young associate that she would forget about the operation as soon as the stitches came out, there should be some reasonable time period after which she might appear in public without her dark glasses. In any case she had an easy explanation ready. Cy Winters, her manager, would have to concoct a press release about a mishap on the East Side Highway. . . .

She abruptly became aware that the resident was still talking to her.

"Besides, you really needn't fret," he was saying, "because except for me nobody here has any idea of who you are. And I know it only because I would recognize you anywhere, any time, and in any getup. I've seen every single one of your old movies at least twice."

Then once more his lips were against hers, and maybe because she was still so tired after the operation, and felt so helpless realizing that any struggle was futile, she let him kiss her without resisting and allowed his hard lips to part hers, and as seconds passed, stretching interminably, she felt short of breath and groaned, and he let her go, and only then did she become aware that he had pulled off the covers and her hospital gown and was cupping her nude breast.

"Let me go, you're crazy!" she said, although she suddenly knew that he was not, at least not in the literal sense. But how could a physician associated with such a renowned teaching hospital allow himself to act like this and risk his career? One word from her. . . .

While his hand kept stroking her breasts, she felt his other hand over her bandage, as if to restrain her from moving.

"You have the body of a girl," he continued. "And yet, I was only a twelve-year-old kid when I saw you in 'Repossessed.' You played a nympho. It was the first time, before I even knew what having sex was, that I had ever had a man-size erection. From then on I had them not only each time I saw you in movies, but even when I simply thought of you. And I masturbated till I ached. And when I was older, every time I laid a broad I pretended it was you, and when I succeeded at it, I was the most goddam potent guy anywhere. Even now . . . want to feel?"

"You are crazy," she said again. But although she was terrified, there was neither anger nor indignation in her voice. Perhaps it was the unreality of this situation; and the unreality of this doctor whom she had never seen and who suddenly did not talk or behave like one. But mostly it was the effect of the drugs she had received.

"Sure I'm crazy, crazy about you," he said. "And I would be even crazier if I let this opportunity of having you slip through my fingers."

It was not only what he was saying that made her recognize the sound of an impatiently unzipped fly. She had heard this familiar sound so many times before at Arlen's. A slave to a split second, so important in his TV newsman's job, he always rushed things as soon as she crossed the threshold of his bachelor apartment, without giving her a chance to undress.

She managed not to betray her terror when he pulled the sheet all the way down to her feet. She had to stall for time.

"But this would be criminal assault, and you know it," she said. "Is that what you want, Doctor? To ruin your career, your whole life? The nurse will be back any second."

"The nurse won't show before I leave," he said, forcing his hand between her thighs, and trying to arouse her with his prying fingers.

"Please let me go, please," she begged in a near scream.

"Shuddup!" he raged in a whisper, but let go of her, and for a second she thought that he had responded to her plea.

I'm a goddam fool, he thought. I've wasted so many precious minutes talking instead of simply getting into her, and perhaps finally getting her out of my system. Maybe it was still not too late. . . .

She felt his body pinning her to the bed, and forgetting about the delicate stitches that might burst any second, struggling under him to prevent him from penetrating her, she thought that he was terribly heavy, that he must be a tall man, as tall as Hugh. And when she despaired that she was unable to continue struggling a second longer, she felt a sudden relief from his weight, and took a deep breath. Then the evidently carelessly thrown sheet ballooned over her and slowly settled down in cool waves.

He was no longer restraining her head, and raising it

slightly from the soft pillow into which it had sunk deeply during the struggle, she heard loudly speaking voices in the corridor, and his soft swearing. Presently the door clicked open.

"I'm just leaving, Nurse," he said, and she heard the door close.

"I went for your prescription," the nurse announced cheerfully, approaching the bed. "Dr. Tamashiro said you could have a shot any time you needed it."

"I need one now," Doriana said. So the nightmare was over. She felt drained and inhumanly tired. But somehow the nurse's cheerfulness irritated her. The idiot was out getting a prescription while she was nearly raped in her hospital bed. "Who was this doctor?"

"What doctor?"

"The one you just passed on your way in."

"Wasn't that your brother?" There was alarm in the nurse's voice now. "I had just stepped out the door when your brother came. I told him it was after nine P.M., but he insisted he had some very urgent family matter to discuss with you and not to disturb you two for awhile. Is something wrong?"

Doriana was trying to decide what to say. Her tormentor was unmistakably not a resident at all, and if the nurse were to alert the hospital police, maybe they could stop him at the gate. But then there would be an investigation and the press would get hold of the scandal and. . . .

"No," she said. "There's nothing wrong, although he was not my brother really. He was an insurance investigator." God, how exhausted she was.

"Honestly! What some people won't do for—"

"Forget it. Please give me a shot. Just don't leave the room again. Not even for a second."

"Don't worry, I won't." There was again that bright note in the nurse's voice.

Poor girl, Doriana thought without acrimony. She must

have been scared stiff when she realized that she had been hoodwinked.

The sting of the hypodermic needle made her wince but didn't interfere with her thoughts. For in her muddled mind something the intruder had said abruptly sprang into focus —the unflattering implication about her age in his account of his erotic juvenile reminiscences.

Two

It was Doriana's final postoperative visit to Dr. Tamashiro's office. Now that the bruising and swelling had completely disappeared, even where the fine stitches had been, she knew that the operation was a success. But because she subconsciously associated it with the horrifying experience in her hospital room, she realized that she was frowning and smoothed her brow by forcing a kind of smile on herself. Dr. Orgood had once told her that it took seventy-two muscles to frown but only fourteen to smile. Besides, she no longer had any cause for worry, as before her operation, when she had suddenly noticed puffiness under her eyes at the TV studio makeup room. She had wondered if it amounted to real bags. Not like June Fleming's who, after all that help from the makeup people and the trick lighting on camera, had to dazzle the TV audience with a five-carat diamond pendant and a bosom-baring neckline, even though rumor had it that June had silicone-filled bags in her freaks.

But what right did she have to deride June? she thought, reflecting on the folly of her own impossible goal to stay young forever in a normally aging world. Perhaps if youthfulness and beauty were not her stock-in-trade and she were a wife and mother in her middle years content with her existence and its simple joys as people grew older, it would be different. Or did the carefree-looking aging women she saw everywhere hide behind their placid smiles the same anxiety she knew?

She suddenly pictured all those women who usually crowded Dr. Orgood's waiting room, all hoping for unlined, smoother faces, all those women who could afford plastic surgeons' fees, and who had no reason other than their

10

vanity to want the fingerprints left by time erased by cosmetic surgery. And despite the realization that, if only for strictly professional reasons, she needed her smooth face as much as anybody, maybe more so, she, too, was one of them. For, as all of them, she clung to her youth or the illusion of youth, a kind of hide-and-seek deception that went no deeper than her skin, a transparent skin that was as thin as it looked. And because of this awareness she had little self-respect, but all the same had to go through with it, for there was nothing else she could do. Not only because she was what she was and had to keep alive the Doriana Delor myth, but because following plastic surgery she would somehow forget the truth most of the time, and her smile familiar to anyone who owned a TV set or went to the movies, would suddenly come "from within" rather than be an empty gesture which required as much acting as in front of a camera, and for a short while she would be lighthearted again, the way she was now.

Dr. Orgood, who was a bit of a philosopher, had once told her: "The prescription for a young-looking face is a little cosmetic surgery and a lot of happiness." Cosmetic surgery would take care of the first part of his formula; Hugh and Arlen, the two guys in her life, were there to provide the other, the most important ingredient. She must not jeopardize the magic recipe.

And still smiling, she was already wondering if anybody had noticed her slight eye bags before they had been successfully removed. Maybe somebody had. Maybe that's why when she had said on "Chicken Coop" that she was brought to the U.S. as an eight-year-old just before the war, that bum Valerie Bing had wanted to know which war she was talking about. It was fortunate that she had come up with a clincher: "It was World War II, of course, darling, when you were already a big star and Mark Trent's leading lady in 'Abandon.' Remember? *Variety* had a piece on old stage hits not long ago." Naturally, this had made Val at least a dozen years older than her, and not the other way around, as Val had tried to imply with that bitchy question.

Of course, had her lids looked then as they did now after Dr. Tamashiro's retouching, Val would never have started a public skirmish that had ended in her losing the battle. And thinking about Dr. Tamashiro's mastery, Doriana couldn't help thinking about Carol, the perennially "temporarily at liberty" actress who had recommended him to her.

She had run into Carol at Bonwit Teller's Cosmetics only a couple days before her eyelid operation. Carol did not appear to have changed in years, and judging from the old girl's ironed out face with its fixed expression of someone whose repeatedly stretched skin had lost its elasticity, it was unmistakably more cosmetic surgery. It had been the slightly tipsy Carol leaning towards Doriana's chair at the circular bar of the now defunct Gold Pub restaurant, and whispering loudly enough to be overheard in the adjoining dining room, who had once made her realize more than ever that staying young was most everybody's obsession and not hers alone.

"When all those women's mags and TV commercials keep brainwashing you that youth is a cardinal virtue, you begin to believe that getting old is some kind of sin. If you're made to feel old at thirty, goddamit, what does it make you at fifty? All that crap's driving every single woman up the wall," had said Carol.

"Especially in our business," she had allowed. Youth and good looks, unless one was a truly great talent, mattered a lot in the entertainment field. How well she knew it. "In fact," she had amended herself, "it's true of any business. Older people, both men and women, who must work for a living, have a rough time competing for jobs with the young, and they need to have a few years stripped from their faces."

"If they are able to afford it," Carol had pointed out.

It was strange how vividly she now remembered what they talked about so long ago. Maybe it was because that evening Carol had initiated her into the wonders of cosmetic surgery with which no clever makeup or frequent Helena Rubinstein facials could compete.

"A woman I know, who had a facelift, told her husband

that all she was having was an abortion. A lift requires only twenty-four hours' hospitalization. And you're all set for the next ten years," Carol had said. . . .

Since that distant day, Doriana had learned how excessively rosy both contentions were. Even with such an outstanding specialist as Dr. Orgood, it took quite some time to get rid of the bruising and swelling, and the results were excellent only the first year, and only good the second, and at best fair after the third year.

And, all these years later, Carol was still full of useful information.

"A friend of mine has to have her eyelids done in a hurry. I suppose Dr. Orgood is still the best in town, isn't he?" she had asked Carol. Maybe she needed reassurance before an operation she had already decided on. Perhaps it was the same instinctive uneasiness before surgery that had suddenly made her remember the many instances of cosmetic surgery mishaps she had been told about, that happened time and again—facial paralyses, keloid scars, hemorrhages, and scar-stretching owing to excessive tightening of aged skin. Carol, who had probably been unable to afford plastic surgery for years, still had fairly youthful looking eyes. Somebody expert must have fixed her lids. Was it Dr. Orgood?

"Anyone who'd let Dr. Orgood mess around with their lids would have to be balmy. It would be almost as bad as going to that lousy quack on Fifth Avenue, in that flamboyant trap of his, who gets five grand in advance, and butchers the dupes. No, for a lift, Dr. Orgood's the best. But eyes—that's a job for an eye man—Dr. Tamashiro, the very tops. He's a Nisei. Ronald Tamashiro. He's a professor of ophthalmology at Cornell—or is it at N.Y.U.? Anyhow, tell your pal to be sure to tell him I sent her and maybe he'll do me a favor one of these days," Carol had said. . . .

And again, reminiscing about their conversation, Doriana felt grateful to Carol. Perhaps Dr. Tamashiro would remember who had recommended him to her.

She was so deep in thought that she barely paid attention

to anything as she walked the short distance from Dr. Tama-shiro's office at 69th and Madison to her Fifth Avenue triplex, which was even closer to her home than Dr. Orgood's office at 71st and Park. In all likelihood it was actually not a coin-cidence that most high-priced cosmetic surgeons had their youth factories in this neighborhood where the rich could uncomplainingly afford them.

As she entered the vast lobby of her co-op building, she saw the former screen and radio idol Robert Narvel coming out of one of the elevators. But the old man was so engrossed in himself, evidently reliving some unhappy moment, his face an accordion of deep wrinkles, that he apparently didn't notice her, and she was glad he didn't for he might have stopped her and thanked her for the umpteenth time for her attempt of talking a TV program producer into reviving his old radio show in a contemporary setting. Perhaps Narvel had learned about it because the project was so unrealistic it had caused talk at the studio. Maybe that's what the old man was brooding and frowning about—the collapse of an unexpected, fleeting hope. She felt guilty, although she knew that she had no reason for feeling guilty about her constant impulses to help others, and suddenly felt even sadder for the once proud man forgetting himself in public.

It was probably some minutes past four now, and while she was rummaging in her handbag for the latchkey, Louise, the French maid she had stolen from the Liberté years ago, opened the front door.

Louise's small, usually appraising eyes were now studiedly lowered. "Monsieur Botain called from Dallas," she whis-pered.

She pronounced the name French fashion, and managed to inject a hint of conspiracy into the simple phrase, as if she were mentally winking.

This whispering even when there was nobody about, just to tell Doriana that Hugh had called, was Louise's way of letting her know that she was perfectly aware that Doriana's marriage to Hugh had become a bit rocky. After serving an international cabin de luxe clientele of a large ocean liner, followed by years in New York, this stubby, red-cheeked middle-aged woman had remained as Gallic as she had ever been in her native Paris where she had begun specializing as personal maid to famous performers decades ago while still in her teens. Her devotion to Doriana Delor was sustained not so much by DD's also being a celebrated artiste, however, as by the idea of serving a compatriot. For wasn't Mademoiselle Delor born on the glorious Côte d'Azur? "Monsieur Botain said he wouldn't be back tonight as expected," Louise continued to whisper.

What did Louise tell her husband? Of course she didn't say that her mistress had "that kind" of surgery. It was odd how, without ever having been coached, Louise, who as a rule was slow on the uptake, had caught the subtle difference between the prevailing attitude toward cosmetic surgery, and Doriana's secretiveness about it. These days of breast and buttock lifting and remolding, people made no bones about trifles like nose jobs and facelifting, which had become a kind of status symbol. "It's a sort of like wearing a brassiere on your face," as Gypsy Rose Lee had once quipped. And many men and women even bragged in public about having had a helping hand from plastic surgery witch doctors. But to be so outspoken about having cosmetic surgery was to admit to needing it, and this Doriana could never bring herself to do. Perhaps it would be a lot easier to confess to the world that DD was an ordinary mortal, who, like any other human being, could not escape aging.

It was practically quitting time for Noelle Martin, her private secretary. There undoubtedly were several messages which Noelle would give her in her melodious voice that was at such odds with her appearance. Doriana hesitated briefly, then crossed the foyer and entered the study.

Three

Noelle's irregular hump nose with its abnormal width at the base, combined with a saddle depression near its tip, startled her as usual, although she should have become accustomed to it, since the girl had been her secretary for over a year.

She had hired Noelle after scarcely glancing at her credentials. There was something pathetic in the girl's beseeching eyes, in her tenseness betrayed by a twitching eyelid and her hands which appeared stiffly frozen to her sides. How many unsuccessful interviews did the girl have before getting into such a state of despair tinged with hope? Maybe she had gone hungry? It was possible that had Noelle tried to misrepresent her efficiency and experience, she would perhaps have compared Noelle's qualifications with those of some of the other applicants, and would possibly have chosen somebody else. There probably were many others who badly needed a job, and who could tell how badly? But Noelle had confessed that she knew so little, that she was not a very speedy typist, only a beginner who had never held a lasting job, but she would try, try so hard, please. . . . And the combination of her pitiful state and her uncommon honesty had proved decisive.

But one thing was to hire Noelle on impulse, and quite another to be subjected day-in-and-day-out to the unfortunate girl's sight. Besides, after a few months, when Noelle had apparently concluded that her position was securely established, she seemed to have also acquired a touch of artfully masked arrogance, and no longer inspired sympathy. Why then had she kept her on?

It had nothing to do with the conscientious work that Noelle ground out, replying to hundreds of Doriana's fan

16

letters a great deal better than Doriana could herself. Noelle put her heart and soul into keeping alive the image of sparkling wit and glamour that people the world over had of Doriana Delor. Yet even had Noelle proved to be an inefficient worker, she would never have the heart to fire her.

"Miss Delor, you have letters from two of your foster kids. The boy in India and the Peruvian girl. I've already started to reply—"

"You know that I always like to write to the kids myself," Doriana cut off Noelle.

This was one thing she would not delegate to anybody. The responsibility of helping to raise a few kids around the world went beyond just sending money. It meant an interest in their progress, the spiritual involvement of a volunteer mother anonymously sharing something of herself with youngsters selected at random and known to her only from snapshots. Why did this girl constantly try to meddle in this fragile relationship? Why couldn't she understand a simple thing like that?

"Let me have those letters," she added, already regretting her abruptness.

She had been edgy and getting unreasonably short with people lately. But it was one thing to lose her temper with an important producer or a fellow performer and quite another to be brusque with a well-intentioned secretary who could only protest with the hurt look on her young face.

Perhaps she was upset not by Noelle's insignificant intrusion into her relationship with "her" children, but by the growing realization of how superficial this involvement with them really was. There were many people, not even prosperous, who adopted, not just fostered, homeless children, and reared them, gave them a home and a future.

And without knowing how, she began to fantasize about what it would be like to bring two of her orphans, a girl and a boy, and legally adopt them. But the image of any two among them, who had only their poignant legacy of human misery in common, seemed too unrealistic in this sophisticated New York triplex. And when she began mentally to substitute her multilingual, multiracial dependents by the more familiar picture of a couple of blond kids, the projected adoption remained as hazy and illusory as before. What was wrong with her, what was it that kept her even from dreaming realistically about adoption? She had so much love to offer them, and she could afford all the help she needed, and she certainly could find time for her own two children who would fill her demoralizingly quiet place with laughter. And Hugh, who liked anything she liked, and who was not afraid of anything she feared, would have nothing against the idea, would probably be all for it. No, there was some other reason, a vague thought, that she did not allow to linger in her mind, that it might be too late for her to do anything of the sort. And miserable, she tried to keep her daydreams alive as much as possible, which was so little, just a few letters filled with words that no secretary could write for her. . . .

"Yes, Miss Delor," Noelle said, handing the letters to Doriana.

She had to turn away faster and faster of late, Noelle thought, or she might betray her true feelings toward this spoiled woman who did not deserve any of her fantastic good luck, her beauty, her international fame and popularity, her money and, least of all, Arlen Redfore. That Doriana was mad for Arlen, she didn't doubt. What woman in her right mind wouldn't be? But maybe if Arlen knew Doriana better, he wouldn't be so crazy about her himself. She realized that she was not being quite fair or even completely honest, since she knew that, like most famous show people, Doriana had to work long and hard to get where she was, and she really couldn't think of anything Doriana had ever done that she or any other woman wouldn't have done in similar circumstances, but she couldn't help it. She resented being treated as though she were a convenient robot. She knew that this was not reason enough to allow her dislike for Doriana Delor to slowly grow out of proportion, but did not care and did not try to understand and analyze her animosity.

"Any special messages? I mean, anything really important?" Doriana asked, unaware of interrupting her secretary's
brooding.

Why in the world should Noelle's mother have given her
such a melodious name? she wondered. Noelle. Would the
magic of this lovely name influence the course of a life that
otherwise appeared confined to uneventful drabness? And
she also thought that her own mother, fascinated by the story
of "The Picture of Dorian Gray," had probably no concep-
tion to what extent the name of "Doriana" would mold her
baby daughter's whole future. But, of course, her own fixa-
tion, her pathological fear of losing both youth and beauty,
went far deeper than just a jinxed-name superstition.

"No, there were no messages, nothing important," Noelle
said, intruding on Doriana's musing, without noticing the
strangely emotional look in Doriana's eyes.

Noelle did not mention the message from Arlen Redfore.
She had watched his TV newscast on a portable set, as she
did every day, putting aside the unanswered mail for a full
fifteen minutes. And while he spoke, she began daydreaming
as usual, lightly stroking her small but firm breasts, making
her nipples erect, and imagining that it was Arlen caressing
her with his long well-manicured fingers while holding the
script he was reading in his disengaged hand. "Arlen, stop it,
you goof, everybody's watching us," she had murmured,
squeezing her breast. And although she knew that it was all
in her mind, she wondered how Arlen managed to keep his
deep, beautiful voice with its stirring sexy huskiness so steady
while he was petting her.

Then she had sat quietly with her eyes shut, her hand
forgotten on her breast, gradually allowing her excitement
to ebb, waiting for Arlen to call Doriana, as he always did
after his afternoon broadcast when Doriana's husband was
out of town. And later on, listening to his familiar voice that
sounded so much more personal on the telephone, she had
tried to visualize close to hers his handsome young head with
unruly blond hair almost falling over his brown eyes. And

how she wished that it were she instead of Doriana in bed
with Arlen at least for a moment! She knew she would be
even better at that game than at answering Doriana's mail.
But she had no choice. "You bet, Mr. Redfore . . . I'll tell
Miss Delor you'll be waiting for her at ten at the '21 Club'
. . ."

"You'd better go now, Noelle, it's getting late," said Doriana, and could not suppress a weary sigh.

"Good night," said Noelle, and paused at the door.

She felt no guilt at keeping an important message from
DD, but caution made her sacrifice getting her little satisfaction that Doriana would not meet Arlen. "Oh, yes," she
finally said, "Mr. Redfore called to say that he would be
waiting at ten at '21'." This sounded a bit confusing, but
Doriana seemed to be far away, her unbelievable violet-blue
eyes fixed somewhere in space beyond the closed door, and
Noelle did not insist. After all she gave her the message,
didn't she?

Four

It was uncommonly mild for late November and the sudden breeze from Central Park, racing across Fifth Avenue and chasing some crinkled auburn leaves before it, enveloped Noelle in its warm, still autumnal fragrance of drying grasses. There was not a wisp of the smog that at midday had shrouded the treetops in the park and the downtown skyscrapers. And because two handsome Maltese terriers walked on long leashes by a solemn uniformed elevator man, probably out on their evening constitutional, barked at her joyously and jumped around, tangling their leashes; or maybe simply because she was out and finally through with her work, Noelle's spirits soared. But a young man talking to Tim, the doorman, who had turned away sharply after glancing at her, ruined her mood again.

This was the usual pattern. At times men followed her for quite a few blocks. She was not tall, but her long legs could outdistance many of her pursuers who, lured by her shapely figure and the swing she put into her narrow hips, ran after her. Then they would dash up and turn to face her, and sometimes she almost expected a loud gasp of disappointment as the abruptly disinterested men hurried away.

Noelle, who was painfully self-conscious about her appearance, did not realize how much she herself unwittingly contributed to such ego-bruising incidents. Most of these men, on the prowl for easy sex, would probably pay little or no attention at all to her features. But after a while she developed a violent dislike for all of them, a dislike which had gradually turned into loathing. It was her furious expression, even more than her deformed face, that scared them off.

She started across the avenue to the bus stop that was

21

diagonally across from Doriana's co-op, still thinking about the young guy talking to the doorman. What could they be talking about for such a long time? The young man didn't look like somebody who might own an apartment in the building. Not that he wasn't well dressed. Her observant eye caught in a single glance his expensive topcoat and well-polished black shoes. People who lived here simply didn't have long chats with their doorman. But neither did the young man appear like a domestic or even a secretary. There was a look of great confidence and independence in his strong face, and the cut of his dark, wavy hair did not belong to either a butler or a chauffeur.

But what the hell; she really didn't care. She turned around once again and suddenly realized that the natty dark-haired stranger was crossing the street after all, and because he was almost running she thought that he was trying to overtake her. Then the traffic light turned red and this of course explained it; he had merely tried to make the light.

There was no bus in sight, and following the low wall of the park, she determinedly started walking downtown. ɪne innumerable stars of the luxury buildings' lighted windows across the avenue danced a little in her rhythmic stride and seemed to call to her with their inviting blinking. She would keep on walking fast like this for maybe two or three bus stops, until the number 5 bus had caught up with her. Or she would walk all the twelve blocks to the Plaza and continue on to the fifties to Rockefeller Center, where an immense spruce would soon be trimmed for the yearly December lighting ceremony, and watch the tireless skaters in the rink below for a while. Then, crossing Fifth Avenue, she could have an always breathtaking look at the top of the already lighted Empire State Building farther downtown, emerging from above tall buildings like New York's own permanent giant Christmas tree. And she would mingle with the crowd that had already acquired the spirited holiday mood, flowing in and out from St. Patrick's Cathedral and the lavishly decorated department stores, a faceless crowd in which she could melt without fear of rejection.

She looked over her shoulder to see if a Washington Square bus was catching up with her and realized with consternation that the man who had been talking to Tim was actually following her. He must not have given her a close look, or maybe his eyes weren't too good. "And if your legs aren't any better than your eyes, you won't be trotting behind me for long, Mister," she whispered to herself and put an extra effort into her swift legs, already trying to forget about the stranger.

She had had precious little exercise since she had started working for Doriana Delor. She hadn't played tennis, her favorite sport, for such a long time. She used to play often two years ago, when she lived in the Bronx in a small frame house that looked so tiny in the shadow of the Fordham Hill apartment buildings, when she was so close to the tennis courts just across the Harlem River. But she had not played since moving to the East Village. Besides, with Doriana, she could scarcely count on her weekends. For the private secretary of *The* Miss Delor does not take her days off like just any secretary, but only when it's convenient to Miss Delor. She felt her face flush with anger. You would think that working for a star whose lover was a former tennis champ would give you an entry to Forest Hills or something.

"You sure can walk," she heard a man's voice behind her, then his laugh.

He laughed very loudly, without inhibition, the way some people do at theaters or the movies, but it sounded jarring in the street. And two teen-aged boys wearing jeans and turtlenecks who were slowly jogging uptown started grinning as if to participate in this outburst of hilarity.

Noelle, still disturbed by painful memories, transferred her resentment to the man who had been following her, whose laughing face, she had no doubt, would soon change to an expression of disappointment.

"You talking to me?" she asked crossly, knowing that what she was saying was stupid. Obviously he wasn't talking to the street light or the boys. She turned abruptly toward him.

He was not too tall, perhaps five-ten-or-eleven, but his stocky build, broad shoulders and rather thick neck implied power. His dark, smiling eyes were staring straight at her in that certain way she had always seen men look at other women but never at herself, and momentarily she stared back at him with puzzled incredulity.

"Don't look so uptight. I didn't mean to be fresh," he said.

He was still eyeing her admiringly, and she found herself blushing, but the unfamiliar feeling did not last. There, only slightly delayed, was coming the usual finale. His expression had already changed. He was not smiling and seemed annoyed. Then she realized that he was no longer peering at her but at the sky.

"It looks like it might rain any minute," he said.

Presently he was again gazing straight at her, that same caressing look in his eyes, even though she had lifted up her face to the street light right above them.

"You should never walk alone after dark on the Park side of the Avenue," he continued. "Some creep might drag you into the bushes before you know it."

"Over the wall?" She laughed.

They were walking slowly side by side now.

"What a musical laugh you have. You must be a singer. Are you in show business?"

She shot him a covert glance. No, he was not poking fun at her. And he was not drunk. They had reached the corner of 66th Street and waited for the green light. And the headlights of the oncoming cars turning into the cross-park road, illuminated their faces with passing waves of light, and his attentiveness momentarily made her forget the familiar sense of apprehension and she felt herself attractive and desirable.

"No, I'm not in show biz," she said, "but I'd sure like to be. I'm a private secretary. And what do you do?"

"I have many interests."

He was glad that she had put her question that way. He would have a hard time explaining what his occupation was. Come to think of it, he was so many things—almost but not quite. He was almost a lawyer, but not quite, for he was kicked out of the Columbia University Law School for cheating on exams. Actually, not for trying to pass his own after getting hold of the questions, since they had never caught him at it, but for selling the information to others. Just as he was not a real veteran, since he had ended his military career with a dishonorable discharge; and he was never a real prizefighter, for all the bouts he had ever won were thrown by his similarly "fixed" opponents, the only kind of fights that paid well for obscure club fighters like himself.

He omitted mentioning his true lifelong interest—horses. Not the betting on them, which he did as most other racetrack goers, but his love for horses and his secret dreams of perhaps someday breeding them on his own farm. He would most likely be hard put explaining to anybody and maybe even understanding himself this passion completely unrelated to any hopes of profit or wealth, since it was so unlike any of his other ambitions, planning and scheming. This vague craving to love something and take care of something for the simple joy and beauty of it, seemed at variance with the rough stance he exaggerated to survive in his environment. And he did his best to conceal emotions he considered effeminate rather than redeeming, a weakness certainly not to be confessed to a total stranger.

If she insisted, he could improvise a few yarns about himself, just the right kind of stuff to impress her, for while she knew nothing about him, he had learned quite a bit about her from his talkative army buddy, Tim. "What's with you man, you lose your touch? Can't make out with a better-looking chick?" Tim had concluded, chuckling. "Any old time, buddy. But these ugly broads are so appreciative when you try to screw'em," Ben had remarked. "Have you ever had an ugly kid like that in the sack? After the light is switched off?"

That wasn't really altogether fair to this little filly, he thought, shooting Noelle a glance. She had a lot going for her.

"I forgot to introduce myself, sorry. The name's Ben Strong," he said.

"I'm Noelle Martin."

"Tell you what, Noelle," he said, "if by some chance you're free tonight, why don't we have a snack someplace?"

"I really have a date for tonight," she said. "But I'll break it for you," she added after a brief pause.

He squeezed her arm. "Taxi," he shouted in his loud voice, and as if by magic a cab obediently pulled up to the curb.

The "snack someplace" turned out to be a continental restaurant on 56th, just west of Fifth. Perhaps they knew Ben, or maybe he had slipped a good tip to the captain, but comfortably ensconced behind the corner table she watched the narrow room as it filled to capacity, and it looked as if she and Ben had all the attention, with the waiter, the wine steward, and even the proprietor watching over them, helping to select their menu, carving their meat and filling their glasses.

After two very dry martinis the Château Rothschild hit her hard, and the room with its oil paintings and subdued lights turned into a gay carrousel, and it was only natural that in its crazy swirl she sought the security of his strong body and did not mind in the least when he moved very close to her on the semicircle of the red leather banquette.

"You really turn me on, babe."

She listened to the trite phrase with a mounting sense of fulfillment. It didn't have the corny ring of repetition, for it was the first time that anybody anywhere had ever said it to her. She looked at Ben, wondering if he would believe that she had never had sex? She had often masturbated and had pitiful self-induced little climaxes, but she had never had real intercourse with any man, and had never experienced the kind of orgasm she had read about or had heard discussed. Well, he would find out after they'd gone to bed together, she thought, anticipating both the pleasure of finally having real sex, and Ben's reaction to finding out that he had had himself a damn virgin.

Christ, the kooky broad is already stoned. Ben thought, glancing at her nose that seemed to be swelling even more and had acquired a darker hue. The table hid her nice legs, but she had promising-looking, firm boobs of a youngster, and maybe, just maybe, she had hidden talents worth discovering.

"I'd like to hear some more about you. Tell me everything. About your job, for openers."

"I'm Doriana Delor's secretary," she said, hating herself for dropping the name and for making it sound so important.

"Tim mentioned that she lives in the building. Sounds like an interesting job. I've never seen Doriana Delor in person. Is she really as gorgeous as she looks in pictures and on TV?"

"Mmm, she is, but I'd rather not talk about her any more, if you don't mind. I think she's egocentric and selfish." Why did she tell this lie? She, of all people, knew how untrue that was of Doriana, who was always a caring friend of the needy, generous with her time and her money. Was she even more envious of Doriana than she was willing to admit to herself?

The maître d' was in front of them with the flaming crepes suzette, and tonight, for once, she would get off her diet-wagon and eat everything, and do everything she did not allow herself to do, or was not offered to do or simply could not do. She finally had found a man—a handsome man whom she did not turn off.

Briefly she let herself be drawn into the self-pity of old memories. . . . A little girl sprinting across the street on an errand to the store, past the shouting little bunch of neighborhood boys playing stickball. Then a swing by Pinky, the oldest and the biggest, who put into it all the rage of a frustrated loser jeered by the smaller kids, the crash and the blackout, followed by so many other blackouts under the anesthesia while month after month, year after year, a young city hospital doctor was trying to reconstruct what had once been a nose. . . .

She closed her eyes, shaking her head to get rid of the memories of the past. When she looked up at Ben again a moment later, his face expressed nothing but the same warm attentiveness.

"Let's have brandy with our coffee," he said. "We'll talk some more at my place."

But she was no longer listening to him. "To hell with everything," she said, and laughed loudly, and thought that he again told her that hers was the most beautiful laugh in the world, and did not care that a fat woman at the next table who was devouring a chocolate pastry glared at her disapprovingly. She was old and alone, and although she had a lovely nose, she had nobody to whisper magnificent lies to her and nobody to laugh with or for.

Only a bit later when Ben helped her out of a taxi in front of the old theatrical hotel on 43rd, just west of Broadway, where he lived, did she briefly sober up at the sight of a blond young man who was coming down the hotel steps with a flashy woman in a mink coat and for a dizzying second she thought it was Arlen Redfore. But she knew she was mistaken as soon as the couple came closer to take the same cab. Besides, what would Arlen Redfore be doing with a be-minked whore in such a dump?

"Come on, let's hurry," she told Ben. "I have a lot of catching up to do."

And again she saw admiration on his face, but somehow it was a little different, and she did not know why it was different, but she knew that whatever she might have thought before this new expression was unmistakably genuine, and did not care any more that right this minute Arlen probably was at his pad on Central Park South, sleeping with Doriana.

Five

Doriana watched Arlen's profile. He always slept on his back, breathing deeply and soundlessly, his arms crossed over his practically hairless chest in the position reminiscent of the dead body of her first husband, the only dead body she had ever seen.

"Arlen," she called softly, "Len?" Was he asleep? If he was, she knew that her murmur wouldn't wake him. And although she also knew from long experience that such deep sleep was normal for a man after an intense orgasm, it made her uneasy in this impersonally cold bedroom with its mirrored walls.

"Len, wake up," she whispered again, and a touch of irritation slipped into her uneasiness, as if she resented that having gratified himself he no longer needed her. She realized that she was being unfair and that with the recuperative power of the young he would wake after a snooze greedy for more sex, as if he hadn't held her pinned down only a short time before.

His loud laughter startled her.

"Who do you take me for, an old guy like your husband?" She would leap like a jungle cat now, he thought, sitting up and bending over her, and noticing her furious expression, laughed again.

"Len, I asked you never, but never, bring Hugh into bed with us," she scolded him, getting angrier and angrier. First, because he clearly mentioned Hugh deliberately to annoy her. And also because he was obviously not jealous of her husband. If he wasn't, then how much was he really in love with her? Another reason was subtler. It was the nagging sense of wrongdoing, that perhaps went all the way to the days of her early upbringing when she was taught to respect different and more basic values, which constantly interfered with her acceptance without a struggle of living by more corrupt standards. Or why should she feel guilty about two men in this age of new morality, of triangle marriages, and wife swapping? In the beginning of her affair with Arlen, perhaps because it happened rather soon after her marriage to Hugh, she had resorted to the classical evasion of trying to shift the blame for the situation on her husband who was leaving her alone for days at a time. Hugh, whose tremendous wealth sprang from a two-hundred-thousand acre sheep stud in his native Asutralia's New South Wales and some oil wells he owned in Texas, was often away on business, or simply just as he was this time, visiting art exhibits he felt he shouldn't miss. And left alone, in spite of her own busy schedule and the crowds she was engulfed by most of the time, she felt lonely and lost, especially on sleepless nights. And when Arlen came along, he filled the vacuum created by Hugh's taking it for granted that no other man could take his place, even if his wife was perhaps the idol of millions.

But was she being promiscuous, rather than responsive to a younger man with whom she could not help being in love with the same abandon and the selfless joy of giving all and getting nothing she had experienced only once before a long time ago as an impractical and idealistic adolescent? Or was she being inconstant rather than disloyal to her neglectful husband? And was the new design for living, prevalent among the young, less or more moral than the hypocritical prototype of clandestine sexual excesses and feigned puritanism of the old? Still, there were moments when such rationalizing could not effectively silence the gnawing thought that her affair with Arlen had to be relegated to the secret depths of her mind.

She's always had a hideaway from indiscreet eyes. In her childhood, it was a real *mansarde* under the sloping roof of her parents' small house in the Cimiez hills in Nice where she hid such of her treasures as the lustrous sea-polished conch with the murmur of the Mediterranean waves locked within it forever, or somebody's discarded, battered old rag doll, mysterious and disquieting because it had no face or name. It was there that she dreamed her first adolescent daydreams, as vague and infinite as the shapeless feathery clouds that drifted by in the azure nothingness framed by the oval skylights of the eerie, secluded attic. It was also there that she brooded over her first bitter disappointments, and when she left her parents' home, she carried it in her mind, where in later years of her adulthood she'd been secreting frustrating regrets of the right things she should have done but didn't, and the futile shame of the wrong things she shouldn't have done but did. . . . But whatever her ideas about sleeping with both Hugh and Arlen, she avoided having them cross paths in either shadow or substance.

Arlen wasn't laughing any more, and glancing at him she tried to guess if he could imagine what she was thinking. But she obviously need not have worried. She knew this look that never failed to give her a tremendous kick. He was so boyishly handsome with his ultraviolet-tanned torso and slim waistline of an athlete and former tennis pro who, even after a few years in the more or less sedentary life of a newscaster, had kept his smooth long muscles in top condition. If her love affair with Arlen lacked the elements of her more serious and durable relationship with her husband, it was Arlen's youthful ardor that probably accounted for her wanting him more than she ever recalled wanting any other man. It was as if sharing his uninhibited eroticism she also shed for a while emotional restraints that had insidiously piled up with the years, and which Hugh unwittingly kept alive with his inquiring solicitously at the height of their intercourse, "I'm not crushing you, luv, am I?"

Abruptly she felt furious at herself. Now it was she who dragged Hugh back into Arlen's bed with them.

Arlen may have guessed this time what she was thinking, for he was suddenly grabbing her again.

"Oh, no, you don't," she said, rolling over to the other

side of the bed, if a round bed could be said to have any sides.

Arlen was a snob who would have gotten rid of this round motorized bed after it had become so commonplace in fiction and real life, if he hadn't bragged that it was his original invention; that he had some bunnies jumping in it long before Playboy's boss, Heffner, had popularized it. To hear Arlen tell it, maybe that's how Heffner got his idea—from his bunnies, Doriana thought. As she hopped out of bed, her feet sank into the thick green velvet carpet that felt as if she had stepped into fresh moss.

"I've got to go to the Plaza," she said. She could tell by his open mouth that she had thrown him off balance, although she also knew that he was in no mood to be denied so easily. "Darling, I simply must go," she repeated. "I have to see that agent of mine. Cy said he'd meet me at the Persian Room tonight. And I'm late now."

"Last week when you had an early TV taping session you thought that midnight was too late to start pub-crawling."

"Never mind," she said, taking her body stocking and dress and crossing to the bathroom door.

"Don't you have any rehearsal or taping scheduled for this morning? It's past twelve now, you know," he argued against hope.

Then he realized that he was talking to himself. He rested on the bed for awhile, still feeling himself swell with desire, imagining Doriana as she was lying in his bed a moment ago, her excitingly generous breasts, mottled with pink, with their rigid nipples, the translucent gorgeous skin of the natural blonde, the flat belly and the inviting honey-colored triangle nestling between her slightly spread legs. He could tell that her body had not yet completely relaxed from the spasmodic contractions that had made her moan rapturously a while ago and which as usual magnified his wild gratification. She certainly had amazingly trained vaginal muscles; like those of the only other woman he had ever heard about whose special internal sucking talents had reputedly netted her a royal husband.

I'll have to cool off under a cold shower, dammit, Arlen thought crossly. He knew from past experience that if she had made up her mind to meet her manager at this hour, she would not change it. Business came first with this beautiful dame. Anyway, once she was out of bed, trying to drag her back in would amount to a wrestling bout, and although they had more than once made real history on the carpet, it was a poor substitute for his ideally suited bed. One of these days this broad would force him to masturbate like a pimply kid. Or make him catch clap banging that little hooker who lately had been trying to pick him up in Times Square. In spite of the recent cleanup operation, there still were swarms of them of all sizes, ages, shapes and colors in midtown Manhattan, which Time had once said they had turned into a "bawdwalk." Not that he couldn't have his pick among the non-pros, if he were interested. Well, Doriana's old man was away, so he'd get another chance later.

Only a year or so ago, at the beginning of his affair with her, he might have probably resented any mention of Hugh Botain, but in those early days he briefly imagined himself serious about this dazzling, sexy woman. But he was back to normal now. Any permanent commitment, even to the right young thing, was a long way off. There were high places in the upper reaches to be climbed and big money to be made and many, many broads to sleep with before he was about to give up the chase. And for the time being, maybe for a long time to come, there was Doriana, who still was not only the most gorgeous and flattering woman to be seen with, but also the best lay he'd ever had, and that was quite a compliment, maybe even a kind of love in his book. . . .

As for the old Aussie, he mattered little so long as he was blissfully in the dark about the affair. With his most likely Victorian ideas about sex, love and marriage, a good thing it would be, too, if the old boy never found out. A guy with his dough and connections could easily break a fledgling newsman.

Six

Doriana was standing in Arlen's bathroom, wondering if he would follow her and try to coax her back into bed. He was probably still sexually hungry, since they had not been to bed together for several days, while Hugh had proven unusually insistent in the afternoons, before going out of town. She'd wait a little longer, taking refuge behind this closed door, giving her heartbeat a chance to slow down and Arlen to cool off, flushing the john a couple of times now and then to keep him from suspecting that she was simply hiding in here.

Arlen's bathroom was a conversation piece of sorts, ever since he had a pixieish artist pal paint a life-size face of one of his bosses on the pale green porcelain toilet-bowl bottom.

She already regretted her practical ice-water remark about having to meet her manager. Perhaps she had made it because she was afraid that she might be unable to participate the second time as spontaneously as she had the first. Anyhow, despite her often useful reputation of bordering on nymphomania, even years ago at times she had to pretend to live up to it with potent young lovers for whom coming once was only an appetizer. And recently, while Arlen enjoyed his encores and would later plunge into exhausted sleep, she lay there wondering with distress at her difficulty of keeping up with his lusty pace.

She should never go to bed with him when she was feeling her age. A mature woman who foolishly allowed herself to become emotionally involved with a mere boy was pathetic enough. She couldn't risk subjecting herself to the humiliation of his suddenly discovering this "young-man-older-woman-generation-gap" between them. She must never let

34

that happen, not so long as Arlen was important to her. And it looked as if he might be indispensable to her forever.

What the hell, they could always come back here after the Persian Room. By then, fortified by some vintage champagne, she might be in the mood for more games of love and maybe really enjoy them herself again.

When she returned to the bedroom, Arlen was already dressing. He made no other attempt to change her mind, and when she was ready to go resignedly followed her out.

Central Park South was surprisingly more alive at this hour than Doriana had expected. In the past few days, with Hugh out of town, she was never in bed before the middle of the night, but still up at the unthinkable prenoontime hours like some provincial housewife. She shivered, as if at the thought, and wrapped herself in her sable coat against the chilly November night.

There was a small crowd around the elderly doorman, waiting for taxis, or maybe for their own cars blocked by the double parkers. Arlen took her firmly by the arm and made her walk a few short steps in the direction of Fifth Avenue, then cut through the parked cars toward the oncoming traffic, and as if by magic a cab, bypassing the whistling doorman, stopped in front of them with a grating screech of its tires, and moments later, since it was such a ridiculously short drive from the Essex House to the Plaza, the Plaza doorman opened the taxi door.

While Doriana and Arlen were being seated at a small table that had been hastily added for them at the expanding ringside that devoured more and more dancing space, Doriana as usual blossomed in this atmosphere where she monopolized everybody's attention. She distributed her smile number three left and right—the one usually meant for her hairdresser, her director and other useful people. She switched it to number two, which she reserved for important producers, for David Chirrem who was at a table nearby, and for the passing Edward Dawnee whose plays she particularly admired. Then she froze.

Plowing her way toward them was Carol Nemm, who, heaven forbid, would bring up her eyelid operation in Arlen's presence. But of course Carol, who was always so uninhibited about confiding in everybody about herself, was amazingly discreet about the affairs of others. At least she had never involved anybody else in her confessions. This was an unfailing test of someone's discretion. If somebody betrays to you somebody else's confidence, you can bet somebody else will hear all about yours.

"Sweetie, look what a gorgeous fall I got myself," Carol cooed, pointing to her head, and kissed Doriana on the cheek. "Everybody thinks I got it from Vidal Sassoon and that it cost five hundred dollars. You wouldn't believe it, but all I paid was ten bucks."

"Lovely, really lovely," said Doriana, to make Carol feel good, although the cheap Dynel mane was unbecoming to Carol, "don't you think so, Arlen?"

But Arlen, who got up when Carol approached was plunging his eyes from his strategic position into the always low-cut neckline of June Fleming in a large party presided over by the sought-after columnist, King Wead, at the next table. June was helping Arlen obligingly by bending forward. So the trick still worked.

Intercepting his stare, Carol said a bit louder but without conviction. "Have you heard that the flat look may be back? Big bosoms may after all be on the way out."

She caught herself glancing at Doriana's and retreated just as Doriana began to wonder how much longer she could let Carol stand there without inviting her to join them.

Maybe it was the Mimosa heavy on champagne after the love-making at Arlen's, but Doriana felt suddenly exhausted. She perked up momentarily when an older man with familiar features whom she couldn't place came carrying a menu to ask for her autograph for his little daughter. Quite a few older men had little daughters, she thought, trying to make a nice signature. But despite the firm, excellent quality paper of the Persian Room menus and a gold Parker 75 the man handed her, her signature came out badly. She could never sign her name elegantly with anyone looking over her shoulder. That's why she had even stopped using her credit cards.

A great many big and not so big fish seemed to be packed in this room tonight, probably because it was the sexy-voiced and much-touted singer Kelly Dee's opening night. But where the hell was Cy? He had better appear or else. She and Arlen had missed the last show. It might be a good idea to send Kelly some flowers. The kid's father was an old and generous friend; it was the least she could do after completely forgetting about this opening. Burl Sonwil and his wife, seated ringside with the lovely and forever young songstress Zena Lorne, were waving to her across the room, and she waved back, dazzling them with her choicest smile, since it was a cinch she would be a lead item in Burl's next syndicated column. She gulped another Mimosa and thought that Arlen who had been studying June Fleming's not-so-secret weapon had now transferred his exploratory attention to her own neckline, as if he didn't know what was beyond it.

"Why don't we go back to my flat?" he suddenly said. "Cy is evidently not coming or has left already, and it's damn dull around here." He was an ass to have let her talk him into leaving his apartment in the first place, he thought.

She felt her whole body tingling and glowing under his undressing eyes as her erected nipples pushed against her tight body stocking, and let herself be swept in this wave of the promise of bedroom pyrotechnics. And June, who had turned her head to talk to somebody at her table, suddenly exposed her profile with its baggy eye wrinkled in a tired smile, and it reminded her that she no longer had such a problem.

Hugh was away, and from Dallas he'd jet to Chicago for a day or two. Hugh traveled easily to all those art shows. He had once jetted to Chicago and back the same day just to see the Manet exhibit, only because the *New York Times*' John Canaday had said that it wouldn't be seen in the "cultural backwater" of New York. And while Hugh was away, she could spend all the time she liked with Arlen, without being missed. They had all night to themselves.

"We'll go to your place a little later," she said, giving Arlen her most alluring smile, "I adore dancing with you, darling."

Seven

Hugh was back. Doriana knew it as soon as she stepped off the elevator on their private landing, because of the Hi-Fi in the library which was turned on full blast. He had had it installed some months before as a surprise gift to her while she was away making a movie and taping TV guest appearances on the West Coast, but was the only one who ever put it to use. Through the thick mahogany doors, supposedly designed to screen out all noise, she recognized Grieg's rousing Concerto for piano and orchestra, one of Hugh's favorites, and the knowledge that he was home gave her a sudden sense of security.

This is how it has always been. In the strain of her work as a performer, in the gloom of her sleepless nights, and in her fleeting gaiety, she often completely forgot about her husband, yet each time he returned home from his frequent trips, she would realize how much she had missed him, how very important he actually was to her.

As if by magic, Louise met her at the front door as usual, and ignoring her maid's warning signals as soon as she entered, and without thinking about the jewels she was still wearing, so out of place at noon, she rushed into the library. Hugh was in his favorite armchair which she tolerated in the library despite its somber bulk that clashed with the rest of the furnishings. The slacks which sheated his long legs, perhaps somewhat too snug for his age, did not detract from his air of reserved dignity. Maybe because she always pictured him on horseback on his Australian "station," although she knew that in reality he inspected his immense grazing land in his copter, his legs in these tight pants looked as if he might at any moment pull on his riding boots.

"Darling, what a lovely surprise!" she said.

He started to rise, but she rushed over and laid a restraining hand on his shoulder. He looked up at her and grinned, his strong regular teeth, whose whiteness she so liked against his deeply tanned face, gleaming. And as usual she couldn't help thinking how youthfully handsome he was for a man in his early sixties, with his smooth dark hair already liberally streaked with silver at the temples, but his high forehead without a trace of receding hairline, and his only slightly baggy, thoughtful blue eyes clear and alert.

His admiring look gave her the customary stimulus of happiness. Then he went back to examining something he was holding, without changing expression, and she realized that his admiration was directed not at her but at a small object he was fondling in his strong, protective hands, as if it were a fragile little bird.

"It's an early Chelsea scolopendrium teapot. It's a beauty. I found it at Parke-Bernet. It came from London's Sotheby's."

So he must have come back some time ago. The TV rehearsals had started rather early, that's probably what Louise must have told him. But what if he had returned during the night, while she was at Arlen's? And she knew that her fear was not for herself, not because of the possibility of her being caught, but for him—to subject him to the humiliation of being deceived and to cause him bitter disenchantment. She did not think she could bear either hurting him or his contempt. Hugh was not only a man from another continent, he was a man from another world, who perhaps might forgive, but never understand. She had no reason for concern, however.

"It's a beauty," he repeated.

"That teapot must have set you back plenty, I bet," she remarked, peeling off her gloves, and giving herself time to recover. Hugh could afford practically any amount on his hobbies. Besides, it was far better if he collected teapots or other such bric-a-brac rather than call girls.

He could be such a baby, this big Australian koala bear

who was years older than she, that is, than she really was.
Perhaps this was Hugh's special charm—his seemingly in-
compatible traits that didn't clash. The childlike delight of
an amateur collector who acquired at cutthroat prices anything that came along, whether a Chinese Chippendale mahogany chair, an old bottle of Château Pichon-Longueville,
or a painting by Vuillard, blended miraculously with the
solid wisdom of a man who grew up close to the rich soil of
a Tasmanian orchard. And his modest personal tastes and
lack of sophistication that made him want to order ham-
burger at Maxim's in Paris, did not seem ridiculous despite
his tremendous wealth.

He was still examining his latest acquisition, and Doriana's
remark about its price nettled him. He should have taken
it directly to his Waldorf Towers suite, he thought.

It had been his bachelor flat two years ago, before he and
Doriana were married. While they waited for a suitable co-op
at One United Nations Plaza, Doriana persuaded him that
it would be absurd to abandon the luxurious triplex she
owned on Fifth Avenue. It was so well located, so nice and
comfortable and large enough for them both. Perhaps it was
at that. But he had kept his apartment at the Towers, just
as he had kept one in the vicinity of the Étoile in Paris,
another in London's Park Lane, as well as his large mansion in Melbourne. He needed the Waldorf place for an
occasional business meeting, as he had explained to Doriana.
But it was mostly a temporary museum of constantly acquired antiques, that somehow did not belong either in the
contemporary living-room setting of their Fifth Avenue
home, or in any other conventional room. Perhaps he simply
needed a retreat for himself and his new acquisitions where
he could enjoy them without Doriana's benevolent, but
slightly mocking approval.

Presently he was already thinking that he really shouldn't
hold her lack of enthusiasm for antiques against her. Did she
notice his annoyance? But when he looked at her, she appeared completely relaxed. How beautiful she was.

"You look smashing in this outfit," he said.

His eyes were gazing straight at her, and she knew that the admiration in them was no longer a tribute to his antique. Setting his precious teapot down on the coffee table, with a slight bang that should have alarmed him but didn't, he got to his feet and hugged her.

He was considerably taller than she. All her men have always been. She couldn't recall having a short husband or lover, except for Juan, her Argentinian husband of some twenty years ago. But that marriage was rather the work of circumstances. She often wondered at her partiality to tall men. It had many drawbacks—like forcing a man to stoop when they were dancing, or when she wanted to tell him something without being overheard in a crowded theater lobby. Perhaps it was simply the law of contrasts, since she was only five foot five. Or maybe, because she disliked to be kissed on the mouth while in bed with a man at the moment when her habitually volcanic orgasms made her moan and gasp for air, and it was much more natural to avoid being kissed when she could snuggle down into the man's chest.

She raised her head and noticed his scrutiny. Thinking about all her husbands and lovers and love-making evidently somehow reflected on her face, because she suddenly saw that aroused look in Hugh's eyes, that certain gleam she had seen so often in the eyes of other men she had known. Or maybe he was simply sex-starved after his long absence from home.

He sat down in his large chair, pulling her toward him, and she knew that she had guessed right and that any second now he would suggest going up to their bedroom. But *she* hadn't been dieting while he was traveling, and she was scarcely out of Arlen's bed, and she tried to cool his desire before he had a chance to speak without his realizing that she was not in the mood.

"A friend of mine had nearly been raped in a hospital after eye surgery recently," she blurted out. She had to say something in a hurry, and the dreadful experience was constantly on her mind.

She still had no idea who the intruder was and obviously could do nothing about having him apprehended. She would keep waking in cold sweat at night for the rest of her life remembering—and afraid and wondering when the maniac might reappear. She had had to tell somebody about it.

In one sense she was right that telling her husband about it would somehow ease her mind, for in his strong arms the awful memory seemed already less terrifying. However, the topic had also defeated her purpose of putting off having sex with him.

"Did the rapist actually penetrate the woman?" he wanted to know. "You said he had *almost* raped her."

"No, he didn't, but he touched her and—"

"Like this?"

She glanced at the door through which Louise might enter at any second. "You're crazy," she said, thinking that this's what she had called the rapist, but did not stop Hugh.

The erotic interlude sparked by her story turned out to be far more exciting than their usual love-making in bed, because of his boyish outburst of passion, so unlike his customary matrimonial approach, as well as the added spice of the possible danger of being surprised by the household staff. But he ruined his impromptu wielding of his magic wand, by starting talking, practically without any transition, of the importance of the snow-fed waters of the Australian Alps to the irrigation of the dry inland plains of southern New South Wales.

This was the telling difference between Hugh and Arlen. While under such circumstances Arlen, an insatiable sexual athlete with inexhaustible erections, would have done his best to prolong the risky little game, Hugh cooled rather immediately after an orgasm, and his brain, as if unable to keep idle, would regain control over his lower sexual reflexes.

She cut short her unfair comparison. Arlen was only in his mid-twenties. Of course Hugh, though anything but impotent, was no match for him. And besides, just as she hated Arlen's mentioning Hugh while they were in bed, she felt sordid envisioning Arlen's handsome, naked young body during her intimacies with Hugh.

Eight

It was darkening in the large library. It was growing dark so early now. The mid-December days were still getting shorter.

Doriana smiled at suddenly remembering running into Valerie Bing at the Regency last week, when Val came meowing to her about somebody having to hide baggy eyes behind large sunglasses, and how she let Val have it by removing the wraparounds and making Val's own baggy eyes pop at the perfection of her eyelids. It was fortunate that Dr. Tamashiro had prescribed for her massive doses of enzymes that speeded up the disappearance of her bruises.

In his favorite armchair, Hugh, also deep in thought, was trying to resolve a problem.

Years ago, while flying over the valleys of Wyoming, he was so impressed by the endless open spaces ideal for ranching, which were so like his vast sheep stud in Australia, that on impulse he had acquired thousands of acres of the rolling grassland, for raising cattle someday. This plan had never materialized, but he still owned the immense acreage that now more than ever before seemed destined never to turn into grazing pastures. It was ironic that a land-loving man like he, who on the insistence of his financial advisers had once bought some oil wells in Texas, was again the owner of some as yet untapped sources of energy, mostly coal, more oil and perhaps uranium.

Now, not so much because of the possibility of another Arab oil embargo, as because of growing awareness of the shortages of oil created by the Iranian revolution, and exploding gasoline prices, increasing pressure was being exerted on him to agree to the exploitation of the Wyoming property.

45

But to extract the so valuable low-sulphur-containing coal lying only a few feet below the grassy surface meant considerable strip-mining that would in the end turn the unspoiled emerald prairies into another dustbowl. It would mean an additional fortune for him, perhaps as great as the one he already had. But besides being a good businessman, he appreciated money mostly because it could be converted into beauty. He was troubled by the idea of contributing to the bringing to this lovely land mobile-home shanty-towns, crowded by an influx of roughnecks, with the inevitable saloons, booze, brawls and hookers. But even if such a distasteful price had to be paid for new sources of badly needed energy, how could he do anything but cooperate in this country's drive for self-sufficiency? This was his problem. A decision to take. He had not been faced with such a dilemma at the time of his taking over ownership of the oil wells in Texas. They had already been producing for years when he had stepped in, and it was strictly business. And it was still good business to this day, with domestic oil consumption far ahead of last year's. . . .

Hugh abruptly realized that he was thinking out loud. "Am I boring you, luv?" he asked Doriana.

Maybe he expected her to show more enthusiasm. "Not at all, darling! I'm interested." That was a clumsy way of putting it. It sounded as if she were interested in Hugh's getting still a little richer.

Louise, who suddenly materialized seemingly out of nowhere, interrupted her thoughts.

"I wanted to tell Madame that I must go to Paris at the end of this week," Louise said. She had put off for two full days announcing her imminent departure, before getting up enough nerve to bring it up, although her dear mistress was really far too kind and generous to raise any objections. "I won't be gone long, no longer than a month," she added apologetically.

Doriana realized that her staff had their own lives and their own problems, but somehow she felt a little betrayed when the private affairs of those on whom she was accustomed to depend threatened to interfere with her comfort.

"Why didn't you let me know sooner?"

"I didn't wish to disturb Madame and Monsieur."

Was it Doriana's imagination that behind Louise's imperturbable face there was this mental wink, this subtle conspiracy of a worldly-wise soubrette? Besides, Louise was far too sharp not to understand that "sooner" meant a few days sooner, and not a couple of hours. So maybe Louise did see her and Hugh romping in his chair, and wanted her to know it. And obviously the maid's strategy worked, for taken by surprise she meekly nodded acceptance of the unavoidable.

Louise had been going through some sort of crisis and, between her domestic chores, sobbed over a crumpled ink-streaked letter soggy with her tears, although the news from her native France announced the happy birth of a baby boy to her married niece. There was nothing tragic in having become a kind of grandmother, but her strange mood had brought about a startling aftermath. Louise who had confessed to being fifty-two when her husband, Charles, and she had first joined Doriana's household eight years ago as butler and maid, and who had obstinately clung year after year to the same age, had now unexpectedly admitted to being sixty. And this idea of having aged eight years in twenty-four hours seemed to have shaken her so badly that even the red of her once frostbitten cheeks no longer appeared wholesome.

"I've made all the necessary arrangements," Louise went on to explain. "With your permission, Yvonne, Charles's niece, who has been working as upstairs maid for Mrs. Tassiter up in the penthouse, has given notice and will replace me while I'm away."

So everything was settled. Perhaps she should inquire why her butler's niece was leaving the Tassiters? Could be the girl had been fired.

Doriana had met Anne Tassiter, the wife of a successful retired Wall Street broker who had made his fortune before the stock market slump. She had once impulsively accepted in the elevator Mrs. Tassiter's invitation to an anniversary party, and had later regretted it. She actually had nothing against this somewhat overweight, good-looking dark-haired woman, who fancied herself a blues singer and entertained her guests with her husky, rather unusual voice, accompanied by the vocal "boom-booms" of her husband's tuba imitations, which under different circumstances and clever management could be a nightclub hit. But ever since then she had had trouble shaking off the fun-and-games-loving Anne Tassiter, and, after all, the girl was her respectable couple's niece, so that ought to be reference enough.

"This arrangement suits me fine," she told Louise. "Now please go tell Miss Martin that I'll be in to talk to her presently."

Noelle would have to get Carol Nemm's phone number for her. She was anxious to thank Carol for referring her to Dr. Tamashiro. Seeing Carol at the Plaza last night, where she could not possibly have thanked her with Arlen around, reminded her of how overdue her thanks were.

"I have something to take care of," she told Hugh, "I'll be back in a jiffy, be a dear, fix me a Mimosa. Go easy on the champagne, make it half-and-half." Not only did she like the taste of the golden-colored drink, but also its name, evocative of the fragrant shrub of her native French Riviera. And Hugh, a connoisseur of fine wines who liked his drinks straight, never teased her about her preference, because he felt that the Mimosa suited her personality. "And get yourself a drink . . . another drink," she suggested, glancing at an empty glass beside "his" chair, that perhaps she now should call "theirs."

Charles, who faithfully kept freshly squeezed orange juice and vintage champagne for her Mimosas in the bar refrigerator, knew quite a bit about a good bottle and could be depended on not to run out of Hugh's twenty-five-year-old Ambassador Scotch.

She left without giving Hugh a chance to answer her, and

remained standing behind the door for a moment. Perhaps she shouldn't have encouraged him to drink, he was drinking a lot lately even without any urging. Everybody she knew drank heavily, and Hugh could hold his liquor. Did he actually like the stuff, or was something troubling him? Or was it the dangerous combination of both the enjoyment of the liquor and the need to find escape? Maybe he was already an alcoholic? She tried to fight the idea. No, it couldn't be. He was too strong a man to succumb to any weakness. Moreover, with his latest antique acquisition, he would not miss her for a while, and might even forget about his bottle. His Hi-Fi started blaring the piano concerto again. Was it Arthur Rubinstein?

On her way across the foyer she heard another sound coming from behind the closed door. The old IBM typewriter without the moving carriage certainly made a racket. Noelle had probably not stopped for her lunch break. The girl had been acting very strangely for the last month or so, she reflected. She was often late in the morning, but some days worked without interruption all day long. Maybe she, too, was troubled. Some people found escape in hard work the way others did in gorging and getting drunk.

Nine

After a few minutes with Noelle, who immediately busied herself trying to get Carol's phone number, Doriana went upstairs to change. She was surprised when she returned to the study shortly afterwards to find Noelle still on the phone.

"It's no use," Noelle said, with the receiver held slightly away from her ear. "Miss Nemm must be living alone, without anybody around to answer her phone, and she evidently doesn't have an answering service, either."

It was a nuisance that to reach Carol proved to be such an undertaking, Doriana was thinking. She was also annoyed that while Noelle was on the phone, Arlen could not reach her. What time did he start for his TV studio, leaving her soundly asleep in his apartment? If he left early, he couldn't know that she had stayed in his bed till so late. But then why after all that nightlong love-making hadn't he phoned her as usual at her place? And if he left home late, why didn't he rouse her before going to make sure she was all right? The fact remained that he hadn't called. Why hadn't he? Maybe he couldn't, maybe he was tied up on some special assignment, as he often was. And perhaps it was just as well, since Hugh was back.

Noelle has beautiful legs, Doriana thought, watching her secretary, and glanced up at her, as if to ascertain that these gorgeous legs showing from under a very short skirt actually belonged to the same girl. Then she knew by Noelle's triumphant look that Carol must have picked up the receiver.

"This is Miss Doriana Delor's secretary," Noelle announced into the phone. Miss Delor would like to talk to Miss Carol Nemm." She listened for awhile and her face grew baffled.

50

The girl also has lovely eyes, tired but beautiful, thought Doriana.

Noelle covered the phone mouthpiece with her hand. "It's her. She said to hold for a minute. I think she's not alone."

Doriana took the receiver from Noelle and listened. Judging by the faces Noelle was making, she might have meant that Carol was having sex. That's what was probably on Noelle's mind all the time lately—sex. Besides, who would pick up the phone in the middle of an orgasm? And who the hell would want to lay the old girl? Then she froze. Maybe Carol wasn't much older than herself. But she did look so much older, in spite of cosmetic surgery, she looked almost old enough to be her mother. Presently Carol's voice came on clear and steady.

"Sorry to've kept you waiting," she said, "but—"

"Darling, it's I who should apologize for calling at a wrong time," Doriana said, trying not to look at Noelle who was chokingly doing her best to control her laughter. It was astounding how her usually proper and solemn secretary had changed overnight. Maybe she, too, had been to bed with a lover. Maybe that's why she was so relaxed and her eyes looked tired as if she hadn't slept all night.

"Forget it, glad you called. What's up?"

Then, obviously without bothering to cover the mouthpiece, she called loudly, "Don't go, you fink, or I'll find somebody else.

Maybe Carol had said that and let me listen on purpose, Doriana thought. It was just like Carol and her exhibitionistic turn of mind.

"I'm sorry I didn't get a chance to talk to you at the Plaza last night. I wanted to tell you that my friend is very grateful to you for recommending Dr. Tamashiro to her. He did a terrific job. But don't let me keep you any longer, I'll call you back later," Doriana said, feeling like a damn fool, and hung up.

My friend, my foot, thought Noelle, and shut her eyes in a kind of double wink.

Noelle's deformed nose made people overlook her extraordinary green eyes and beautiful auburn hair. The girl also possessed something infinitely precious for which she, Doriana, would probably gladly trade all of her fame, riches and even her celebrated good looks; something that no one could steal or buy—her age, which the nineteen-year-old Noelle took for granted as though she were going to stay nineteen forever.

"Miss Delor," Noelle's voice stopped Doriana when she was halfway out the door, "I'd like to speak to you about something urgent."

Doriana turned around and saw a different Noelle. The girl's now wrinkled forehead, squinting eyes and compressed lips gave her face a determined, rebellious look.

"It's personal," Noelle added.

Doriana had a sudden suspicion. This incessant clatter of the IBM typewriter, that was keeping Noel busy before the holidays when everybody else seemed to slow down, and her secretary's wanting to speak to her about a personal matter —was Noelle also contemplating leaving her? Was the girl trying to catch up with the mail backlog, if any? Now she would announce that she was quitting, and that would be a catastrophe.

"Noelle, you've been working very hard lately. I was just thinking that you deserve a raise as well as a Christmas bonus," she said, approaching. Perhaps Noelle might change her mind at the last moment.

Noelle was leaning far back in her typist's chair, her long legs straddling the seat. And showing through the sheer pantyhose on her left thigh just under her short tight skirt was a definite outline of a bite that had left a purple pattern of strong teeth. But what Noelle told her surprised her even more than this unmistakable evidence that the girl she had always considered chaste was an active participant in the sexual revolution.

"That's awfully sweet of you, Miss Delor. I sure appreciate it. But I really wanted to ask you to do me a great favor, something far more important to me than a raise," Noelle said, getting up. Cry, she mentally ordered herself, cry hard, move this heartless woman who has never done anything for anybody. And despite her nagging preoccupation with her own problem, she couldn't help thinking of how unfair she was being to Doriana, who was probably the most compassionate person anywhere. But she couldn't allow herself this inopportune pang of honesty, which would destroy her show of despair. Cry, cry hard, she repeated to herself. Think of Ben. . . .

She and Ben had their first fight after a month of wild fun —a month that still seemed like one of her fantasies. He did not care for her less, she thought. He was more attentive, more flattering and more passionate with their every meeting. But last night in his hotel room, waiting for him while he went to the bathroom before going out to dinner, she picked up a crumpled sheet of hotel stationery, a discarded letter that had missed the wastebasket. She was too much in the habit of handling other people's correspondence to hesitate about smoothing out the letter and reading it. She had the time to read only a couple of lines, but that was enough. ". . . she would be a bang-up babe if it weren't for her inhuman shnozola. . . . You've no idea. . . ."

"Stop crying," said Doriana. "What is it? What can I do to help?" Did Noelle want to ask her for time off? "Stop crying," she repeated.

"It's about my nose. I can't live with it any more. I must do something about it."

"Are you thinking about plastic surgery?"

Noelle nodded and started to cry harder.

"Have you ever consulted a plastic surgeon?"

"A plastic surgeon operated on me three times years ago, and I was told I'm lucky to have what I've got. But I wonder now if that doctor knew what he was doing." Noelle tried to stifle her sobbing. "You know all the best plastic surgeons in town. If you asked them they'd do it. And they would make me a special price . . . perhaps I could pay them in installments. And the raise you've just promised me would also help to pay the bill."

Perhaps there wouldn't be any bill, thought Doriana. She knew Dr. Orgood well enough to anticipate the likelihood of such a generosity. After all, this could easily fall into a hardship case category. But, on the other hand, what Noelle was asking for was actually a leave of absence. It would be such a nuisance to have to do without her regular secretary even for a short time during the approaching holiday season.

"Why is it so urgent all of a sudden? You've lived with your nose for quite a few years, haven't you? Now, stop crying," she said.

"I have to do something about it in a hurry or I'll lose my boyfriend," Noelle finally whispered.

Of course; the man who had branded Noelle's thigh with his teeth. Perhaps it was he who was pressing her to have plastic surgery, Doriana thought, and she could hardly blame him. Noelle's skirts were too short to be thrown over her head while he was biting her girlish thighs. Maybe the operation was a good idea. Why hadn't it occurred to her?

She felt a little ashamed. Of all people, she who could feel so unhappy herself because of a faint wrinkle, should have empathy and compassion for this teenager. Why, when she looked at Noelle, did she think of her disfigurement rather than of her suffering? And she had the distressing thought that perhaps this lack of compassion, this ebbing interest in people, that finally shrinks the whole world to one's self; the progressive insensitivity, that goes hand in hand with increasing mental dullness; and the inflexibility of opinions, that parallels the hardening of arteries—these were the insidious changes signaling the inroads of old age.

"I will do all I can to help you," she promised Noelle.

Ten

While Doriana was with her secretary, Hugh remained sitting quietly, thinking. He was accustomed to his wife's mercurial moods that could be brought on by practically anything. What had caused her tenseness this time, from the first moment after she had joined him in the library?

He got an inkling of what might be behind it when after turning off the Hi-Fi and picking up the phone extension to make a business call, he heard Doriana thanking somebody for referring a famous eye surgeon to a friend. She had told him earlier about a friend who had nearly been raped at a hospital. Was she talking about herself?

Learning about Doriana having had plastic surgery was nothing new or surprising. How many nights after she had fallen asleep, spent by love-making with the abandon so characteristic of all she did, he had felt with light fingers the hardly detectable scars lost in the sunny avalanche of her hair, a testimonial to the mastery of her plastic surgeon. There was neither malice nor pity in his uncovering of her guarded secret.

Like a veteran fighter for the same lost cause, he acknowledged the evidence of uneven combats with time. Once he, too, had this obsession and had tried all the reputedly authentic and phony treatments available to a rich man, from testosterone tablets to rejuvenation cures in Switzerland. He had given up on it only after becoming convinced that all he had ever gained from these remedies had been purely mental, and that if youth could be gauged by sexual prowess, his quest had become unnecessary from the moment he had responded to Doriana's magic touch.

It had never occurred to him to have a surgeon correct the already developing bags under his eyes or to pull out the barely slackening jowls—cosmetic help that more and more aging executives were seeking lately. His fretting about keeping young had nothing to do with appearance, which he considered an indulgence for women only. But he understood Doriana's striving to stay young the only way she knew how, since she never realized that with her childlike spontaneity and simplicity unspoiled by success and fortune, she would never grow old, even if time webbed wrinkles upon her now unlined face.

What irritated him about it was that she did it all for the sake of her bloody career and refused to abdicate as glamour queen of international show business and to trade the sickly atmosphere of the smoky Manhattan nightlife world for his tranquil Australian home, which he still maintained, filled with its accumulated art treasures and its elusive but most valuable asset—peace of mind. And it also saddened him that Doriana evidently did not think, or refused to recognize, that her struggle was bound ultimately to lick even an outstandingly beautiful and seemingly ageless creature like her.

And because he felt like a total stranger and an outsider in her world of continuous thrashing about for ephemeral success and adulation, and was drawn into it against his will, he was beginning to lose what was left of his serenity. He was also losing patience with her for constantly dwelling on her own generally imaginary and trivial problems, and for not participating a little more in his life. And he also thought that his flare-up was perhaps not against her, but the result of too much Scotch. He had his first shot rather early and had kept on drinking here at home, just to kill the taste of the lousy booze they had been serving him on the plane. And in spite of realizing that this was only an excuse not to have to admit to himself the incompatibility of their lives, and that drinking, if it was at all related to their failing relationship, was the cause rather than the effect of his revolt, he felt guilty about his resentment without any direct provocation on Doriana's part.

Perhaps the worst thing about his drinking was that he could not take his liquor as well as he used to, or maybe did not know when to quit any more. He vaguely remembered drinking heavily in a Dallas cocktail lounge one night, ordering new rounds for everybody in sight, and later bringing two soused women with him to his hotel suite, where the two apparent lesbians had promptly stripped, jumped into his large bed and stuck to each other like two hungry leeches, completely ignoring him. And he also recalled that fight he had nearly got into in Chicago at his hotel bar, because some smart aleck had insisted that Australian farmers screwed their pet kangaroos, not really certain whether he had taken offense for his fellow Australians or the marsupials.

And while he was mentally shaking his head at what kind of drunkard he was turning into, he was already mechanically pouring himself another drink.

He was prevented from just as automatically emptying his glass by the appearance of Doriana followed by the penthouse owner, Anne Tassiter. He caught a mixture of embarrassment and annoyance on Doriana's face. Did Mrs. Tassiter drop in to personally tell them off for purloining her maid as Louise's temporary replacement?

"Hi," Anne Tassiter greeted him cheerfully, sitting down. "I'm here to thank you people for taking Yvonne off my hands. No, no, no, no," she stopped Hugh from getting her a drink. "I'll have to 'fill 'er up' later," she explained, patting her stomach, "we're having a thirsty bunch coming tonight." She was already dressed for the evening in a flowing, flowery chiffon gown.

So the Tassiters were having one of their customary all-night bashes. Anne Tassiter, who apparently finally got the hint, did not ask them to come up to her party this time.

"What did Yvonne do?" Doriana inquired, suddenly wondering.

"Something damn inconvenient. First she became involved

with our butler, then with our chef, and you wouldn't believe the fighting among the staff! Like the explosion of an
atomic bomb."

She wants this bomb defused before her husband gets into
the chain reaction, thought Doriana, amused and reassured.

"This maid must be an enchantress," remarked Hugh.

"That's just it, she's anything but. Yvonne is a homely,
thick-waisted, dumb French peasant. I don't know what you
two are thinking, but the fact is I'm glad to rid myself of
her before Mr. Tassiter gets into the act. I don't want her
around Mr. Tassiter."

She gave away her own lower-middle-class background by
referring to her husband as "Mr. Tassiter," Doriana thought.

"I must confess," she remarked, "that I don't quite get it.
If Yvonne were very attractive—"

"Yvonne is a simple-minded, placid girl, but she is an
extremely obedient one, she lies down as easily as others sit
down when offered a chair," Anne Tassiter explained. "And
Mr. Tassiter is used to giving people orders." She paused,
and smiled pleasantly. "I enjoyed you as the mystery guest
on 'Guesswork' the other night," she turned to Doriana,
abruptly changing the subject.

Doriana wasn't so sure whether her appearance on that
television show was such a hit. At the last minute practically,
not only its regular moderator, Drew Johns, but one of the
celebrity panelists, June Fleming, came down with the flu,
and the guest replacements might have made it look as if she
was invited to appear on a less important show than a star
of her magnitude rated. In addition, she had decided to try
to fool the blindfolded panel by disguising her voice into a
horrible high-soprano squeak. And there was also one slightly
embarrassing moment when one of the guest panelists, a
British TV star, asked, "Are you June Fleming?" and the
studio audience had roared with laughter. In the first place,
June was supposed to be out sick. And, to make things worse,
Adam Orsen, the guest moderator, commented that "Although our mystery guest is not June Fleming, they have

something in common," which made the audience laugh even more uproariously.

It was nobody's secret that June had recently again had her breasts blown up with polyvinyl alcohol sponges at Johns Hopkins University Hospital to replace her old silicone-filled bags. She must have read about the Japanese movie actress who following an insertion of the silicone type bags had one of her breasts collapse during the filming of a violent love scene. So they might have laughed at what they thought was the similarity of their busts' stuffing.

It was lucky that Hugh had been away and had not watched "Guesswork" and listened to her coloratura that evening and perhaps gotten false ideas about her breasts.

"Aren't you nice," she thanked Anne Tassiter, who was not a catty pest and sounded sincere. "It was just another show, nothing very exciting. They guessed me in no time."

"Mr. Tassiter told me that he saw you with a woman at the new Village Opera Company performance a month or so ago. Was she your secretary?" Anne Tassiter asked Hugh, and jumped up before he could reply. "I must run, I've still a million things to take care of before my guests start trooping in. I always sample all the canapés to make sure they're okay, you know."

This certainly explains your big behind, thought Doriana, seeing the plumpish Mrs. Tassiter out to the front door.

Eleven

When Doriana rejoined Hugh in the library, he was still grinning probably thinking about the Tassiters' penthouse shenanigans.

"I didn't know you had a female secretary here in Manhattan," she remarked.

Maybe she, too, was thinking about Anne Tassiter and her generalizations about male promiscuity, he thought. "I don't," he said. "If you mean Bob Tassiter seeing me at that poor man's Met, I was there with Stephanie."

"Who's Stephanie?" she asked absently.

"I told you about her. Stephanie Franchetti is a gal I met at the Claude Monet display a couple of years ago."

"Yes, now I remember your mentioning her to me. I didn't know you'd seen her again."

"It seemed a shame to waste a ticket, even if it wasn't at Lincoln Center. But it wasn't worth the trip, anyway. That pseudo avant-garde production was not for me. Could be I'm a bit old-fashioned, but I don't think that a topless Carmen is an improvement. People are really going overboard with this indiscriminate nudity craze these days. But the conductor, who was fortunately fully clothed, was topnotch, almost as brilliant as Leonard Bernstein. Stephanie agreed with me on that."

Maybe he felt that she reproached him for not telling her more about this Stephanie, for there was an apology in his voice, Doriana thought.

"Besides, she's no competition," he added, grinning. "Stephanie is not the type you might think. She doesn't diet and doesn't dye her hair. Silvery-gray is her favorite color."

"Well, it's not mine. Silver and gray are the cold colors signifying human aging. Look at how beautifully and gracefully trees age. Their leaves turn to gold. Maybe it's

60

because nature is assured of eternal renewal and recapture of youth with each successive springtime."

She nearly forgot what had started this theme. Oh, yes, Stephanie. Some gray-haired creature who found fulfillment at art shows. She suddenly realized that her remark might have hurt her husband's feelings since his hair was silver. The silver in her own hair was always so expertly gilded that she seldom remembered it. But with his characteristic lack of egotism, Hugh reassured her before she could look up at him.

"I liked what you just said, luv. It beats me that someone with your sense of beauty can't find time for concerts and art shows. You'd enjoy it, and you'd keep me company."

"I know I should, and I'm sure I'd like it." Naturally she would. She should and would do so many things if only she could spare the time.

"If you could break your date tomorrow, perhaps you'd join Stephanie and me at the Guggenheim Museum."

She glanced at him sharply. "I wish I could, but I've told you that I have a business luncheon appointment at Le Chevalier, and I must keep it," she said. Why did he call it a date? And why did he look away and scowl? Had he learned about Arlen whom she was meeting tomorrow?

But presently Hugh was again smiling and telling her about the excellent documentary on Australia's great Barrier Reef he had sneaked in between his business meetings in Cheyenne, while he was in Wyoming, and she decided that she had only imagined his displeasure at her mention of her lunch date, and relaxed even more after a glassful of Mimosa that Hugh mixed for her just as she liked it—half-and-half.

"I wonder what I should do while Louise is away in Paris. From what Anne Tassiter said, Louise's niece doesn't strike me as being a satisfactory replacement for her," she remarked.

"She will do for a little while. Louise will be back before you can tell."

"You don't know the French. Once they start missing la

belle France they end up going home for good. In any case, they seldom immigrate permanently. They stay here just long enough to save what they need to retire on in France."

"You ought to know, luv, you're French yourself, even though you have no accent."

"Well, neither have you, Aussie," she teased. "But anyhow, why should I talk with an accent? You know that I arrived here as a small child, and that I've worked very hard on my diction."

Even with her husband, she deliberately omitted mentioning at what age she was brought to the States. Figures trap you before you know. She regretted already having told Val on "Chicken Coop" a couple of months ago that she was eight when she came here. It was fine for now, but in a few years the tape might be rerun somewhere, or somebody might simply remember. It would have been better had she said "an eight-month-old baby" instead.

"But you've never thought of going back to France to live, or you wouldn't have sold your beautiful home in Nice."

Her "beautiful home in Nice." According to her agents' press releases, she was born in a fashionable section of Nice's Cimiez hills. That part of it was practically true, although she strayed a bit in her descriptions of the villa in which she was supposedly born and had spent her early childhood. She could still picture the tiny old stucco cottage, clinging to a few fig trees in a small narrow plot on rue Salonina in Cimiez, so incongruous in the vicinity of the baronial winter residence of the Rothschilds. Her parents, with the deep-rooted obstinacy of the middle-class French landowners, would not consider selling this property, even though for the price of the choice land they could probably have established themselves quite comfortably farther down along the Mediterranean Coast in an unpretentious little village.

In these references to her birthplace, she actually described as she remembered it the luxurious neighborhood villa where she was allowed to play with her childhood friend, Georgette. It was a lovely home whose terraced garden her father had landscaped and was tending for a small wage while letting wild flowers and crabgrass smother his own yard. More than once she felt tempted to confide in Hugh, a rich man of simple tastes untainted by snobbery, and share with him the true remembrances of her childhood molded by relative poverty, unsophistication and extravagant dreams. Perhaps if she could tell this strong, kind man she had married, who was her only true friend, about the attic under a slanted roof where she so often hid her childish frustrations, she might learn better to cope with her adult anxieties, a maze of complexes that no psychiatrist had been able to analyze.

But admitting the truth to Hugh would also mean showing him the dark side of her mind, where a little girl's fears grew into a sensation of panic and the frustrations turned into hopeless despair of an adult who has never really matured.

And as with all deceptions, one lie led to another. In telling Hugh about her late father she had transformed him into a magnate with the habits and tastes of their wealthy neighbor, plus the appearance of the millionaire's butler who had then epitomized for her the ultimate in aristocratic demeanor and authority. And, behind the fantasy of a ravishing creature, she camouflaged her real prematurely aged, tragic young mother who told and retold her little daughter about endlessly looking at beautiful pictures while she was pregnant, superstitiously believing that her child would be born the most beautiful under the heavens.

Doriana noticed Hugh's curious glance and composed her face which the abrupt plunge into the past had stripped of its outward serenity. And she wondered if maybe Hugh was only trying to appear happy to mask his true feelings, for he kept on drinking, and afterwards, talking about current world events, mentioned Arlen's name, although that in itself meant nothing of course, since Arlen was already a popular young newscaster.

She forgot about it the next day, perhaps because so many pleasant things happened. She had run only into charming people at lunch at Le Chevalier, and later that night had enjoyed the admiring "Oh's" and "Ah's" of the sidewalk crowd when she and Arlen were making their way from a midnight champagne snack at "21," after a few well-spent hours in his bed. Hugh, who had a group of businessmen in from Texas, called earlier in the afternoon that he wouldn't be home till very late, and the realization that there was no need to hurry had contributed to her relaxation.

It was not until late at night, when she returned home, with Hugh still out somewhere with his businessmen, that she remembered his eyebrows shooting together in a fleeting expression of annoyance at her mention of her luncheon date yesterday, and again felt troubled at the idea that perhaps Hugh, the uncomplicated man who believed anything she told him about herself, was actually much too observant to be absolutely blind.

She tried to soothe her growing anxiety by thinking that maybe Hugh wasn't much of a saint himself. He did not confide in her each time he dated his Stephanie, did he? And the notion that he possibly was cheating on her with some frowzy female was perhaps not so absurd after all. Not long ago, when she was making a movie in Rome, the Italian press was full of reports about the incredible crime of passion involving a twenty-five-year-old Neapolitan fellow who in a jealous rage had strangled his seventy-year-old mistress, because she was unfaithful to him. And this Stephanie was probably a youngish woman still, younger than she, and Hugh wasn't a youngster, and if he went for Stephanie he didn't run the risk of being ridiculed like that young Italian fool. But even this farfetched speculation did not dispel her uneasiness, for she knew that nothing would save her were Hugh to learn about her not-so-imaginary love affair with Arlen.

Her doubts were soon silenced by deep sleep. And in her wildly erotic dream, she was with her two men, and they were all three joyously happy together, because Arlen and Hugh loved and desired her, and she needed and, in her own way, loved them both.

Twelve

Soaking in warm, liberally scented water that filled the bathtub up to her neck, feeling buoyantly light and relaxed, her pleasure heightened by the narcissistic watching of her pink nipples in their darker halos breaking through the milky foam with her every deep breath, Doriana was trying to recall her sensual dream that had seemed so vivid last night. But the more she tried to revive it, the more unreal it seemed, and the langorous mood brought by the hazy recollection was ruined by Louise who, instead of coming herself to announce that the masseuse was waiting, had sent in her niece, whom she had already started to train as her replacement.

Yvonne was a chubby brunette with heavy arms and legs, whom Anne Tassiter's unsparing description fitted to a T. After gingerly pouring more of Doriana's favorite Je Reviens bath oil into the tub, she had remained standing at the door, her awestruck dark eyes bulging. Perhaps people didn't bathe much in her native village near Marseilles, or perhaps neither did Anne Tassiter, thought Doriana. Or maybe it was just this huge, opulent bathroom with the adjoining sauna, thick wall-to-wall carpeting, gold fixtures and its sunken pink marble double tub, which Juan had had installed for her on their first anniversary, long before Britain's Godfrey Bonsack had conceived his first Sagittarius supertub. Or was it the Jaguar Juan had given her the first year and the bathroom the second that actually never came to a happy ending?

"You may go now, but hand me the phone first," she told Yvonne, "and tell the masseuse I'll be right out." She would really be curious to know what this French peasant girl was thinking.

"When you see Mademoiselle Delor without any clothes on," Yvonne remembered her aunt Louise admonishing her just before sending her into the bathroom, "don't stare and show surprise at her having the body of a young girl. That's how stars are, and that's why she is a *vedette* in the first place, just like Mistinguette was—ageless. You're too young to remember her, but she was the greatest entertainer of them all, known all over the world." She finally forced herself before leaving to look away from Doriana's fascinating breasts.

Maybe it was this young maid's covert attention to her breasts that made Doriana all at once conscious of the acute pain around her nipples that had been bothering her off and on for the past few days. Perhaps Dr. Somney, her trusted gynecologist, didn't know what he was doing when he had prescribed her the daily dose of 2.5 milligrams of estrogen, the female sex hormone. But whatever the drug's therapeutic effect, it had its pleasant side as well as a drawback. The pleasant part was that stimulated by estrogens, her even normally plump breasts had suddenly swelled in size and had acquired this youthful firmness that they had been lacking for some time. Possibly it was her sexy bosom that had made Hugh so impetuous in the library the other day.

The unpleasant side was actually manifold. First of all, her swollen breasts had started to ache like hell, with a stinging needle-like pain that came and went through her nipples before spreading all over. It was also alarming, because despite the brochure accompanying the drug, which flatly stated that estrogens are not contributory to cancer of the breast, Doriana had heard the opposite on so many occasions. This denial by the pharmaceutical company was disturbing in itself. Why would they bother denying something unless there were indications to the contrary? And why did Dr. Somney order mammography for her, if there were no suspicious lumps in her breasts, even though lately some medical authorities have warned that, as a routine precautionary procedure, mammography might not be as entirely safe as it had been regarded a few years ago?

There was also the disagreeable thought that Dr. Somney, despite the age she gave him and her looks, after glancing at her Pap test report and after taking a look at her vagina, while she was in that awkward position so humiliating unless it was intended for love-making, had ordered female sex hormones for her. Was it possible that from what he saw he knew the truth? Middle-aged she really was. How well she knew it, and how passionately she tried to forget it. Forget also that even the sessions on the plastic surgeon's table, with all the stretching of the skin, wouldn't delay her eventual horrible transformation into a shriveled, aged woman.

Perhaps it was all this that brought on the recollection of something disturbing while she and Hugh were having a wild go at it in the library. It was something other than the fear of being surprised by the help. And it wasn't Hugh's talking about irrigation in New South Wales immediately afterward, when every cell of his body should have been quivering, prolonging his enjoyment. Subconsciously she was concerned about her own reactions rather than his. The estrogens that had enlarged her breasts into voluptuous virginal organs had clearly not turned her into any kind of nympho, as she had playfully suggested to her gynecologist, at least not with her husband.

Still, her response to most men had once been automatic. Of late, however, unless she had gone without any sex for a while, love-making with Hugh did not arouse in her anything but a brief flicker. It soon died altogether and left her listening disappointedly to his labored breathing. And this shallowness and brevity of her orgasms was perhaps another tragic symptom of advancing age.

She was glad when the ringing of the phone at her elbow brought her out of her depressing musing. Perhaps because of it, she was more cordial than usual to Cy Winters, her Tom Thumb manager.

"What's up, Cy?" I'm still in my bath," she said.

"Wish we were talking over a Picturephone," he said.

She would certainly not be talking to him on one of these phones, even if they were already available for mass private use. Cy was a squatty, thin man, full of loose skin wrinkled like a premature infant's despite his passion for food. And his nickname, "Little Cow," was probably inspired by the seven biblical "leanfleshed kine" that had remained lean even after eating the seven fat cows. She wished she didn't have to see "Little Cow" so often and have to look at him, although she ought to have been conditioned by constantly seeing Noelle—which reminded her—she must not forget to talk to Dr. Orgood about her secretary.

"Why are you calling so early?" she asked, instantly realizing that mid-afternoon wasn't too early even for show folk. But probably he had also been carousing all night, for her remark failed to get the expected reaction.

"Sorry if I woke you in your bath, dollface, but I have a replacement spot for you on 'This Is Your Hobby' tomorrow night. June Fleming is sick again. and I know you like this show. And I also happen to know who two of the mystery guests will be. Lily Byron is one, and Ted Ketley the other."

So June was sick again. Maybe something had gone wrong with her breasts. Maybe her plastic sponges were too tight. Thinking about breasts again brought the stinging pain to her own, which, unlike plastic sponges, could be stimulated by estrogen.

"Who is this Ted Ketley?" She knew of course who Lily Byron was—the author of a few cookbooks, especially one on exotic dishes that had almost made the best seller list recently, even if her recipes smelled to heaven.

"Ketley is an Australian tennis player who in a year or two will probably be on the Davis Cup team."

"Oh." She knew very little about tennis. "There isn't

time to start doing research on tennis." She was griping, and she knew it.

"I figured you might be glad to be tipped off on who the two guests are going to be. This'll give you an edge over the other panelists, research or no."

Cy sounded even more reproachful than she, and it made her feel a bit remorseful. He was right of course, she thought. Knowing in advance about the hobbies of two guests, on a show whose blindfolded panelists were supposed to guess the hobbies of celebrities, gave her more than just an edge. It gave her a chance to prepare a few witty "ad libs" which the audience liked because of their "spontaneity.' This was a little game she had been playing for some time now. All she had to do was think in advance of clever cracks and steer the conversation to them.

"Don't be silly, Cy, of course I'm glad." Perhaps she should work out a few "extemporaneous" remarks with him for Lily Byron too. "Little Cow" was a glutton; he might be useful.

"Cy, how about giving me some ideas on what to ask Lily? Something clever."

He got an idea right away. Cy wasn't stupid, not if he could make an easy living doing nothing, spending his life stuffing himself.

"How about asking her if her hobby has anything to do with some part of her body? The audience will love it. She has a big belly and a behind to match."

"That's O.K. It will get a good laugh. What else? A punchline to lead to her identification."

"Ask her if it would help to identify her if you knew who her friends are."

He meant, of course, that Lily's culinary friends might be fat slobs like her. "Maybe I could ask her if it would help if I glanced at her teeth. You know, 'Show me your teeth and I'll tell you what you eat,'" she suggested in fun.

"You might also ask if it would help to glance at her choppers to tell her age."

Cy started to laugh, making the phone rattle, but it wasn't the least bit amusing, she thought. Of course, Lily Byron was a big Percheron of a woman, but the connection was too subtle for most of the audience. Besides, Doriana had a sudden suspicion that "Little Cow" might be laughing because he thought that it wouldn't be such a bad idea to have a peek at her own teeth.

"Yeah, you ask her that," Cy added, still laughing.

"My water's getting cold, and besides, my masseuse is waiting. I have to hang up," she cut him short.

He did not insist. Cy was not the persistent type. That's why he was such a lousy manager. Naturally, he didn't need to be persistent handling Doriana Delor. She actually suspected that Cy made his living by trading her to all the major TV shows. It probably went something like, "I'll arrange for Doriana Delor on your show if you give me a spot for another of my clients," this "other client" invariably being some unknown.

After hanging up, despite the waiting masseuse and the cooling water, Doriana remained sitting in the tub for a little while longer. Without giving herself away about knowing who would be on "This Is Your Hobby" tomorrow, she could pump Arlen who knew everything there was to know about tennis players. After last night's rendezvous with him, she didn't actually plan on meeting him so soon again, but he would be thrilled of course. This daily sex would murder her, one day with Hugh, even if he was a one-shot man, and the next with this machine gun of Arlen, and again with him the next day, since getting together with him would unquestionably end in a sleep-in in his kooky bed. Possibly she ought to forget about it and just get the laughs by asking this Ted Ketley, or whatever his name was, if seeing his hands might give her a clue to his "racket." The audience might lap it up.

Well, as it was only about 3 P.M. she would make up her mind later. She had all the time to think up other laugh-getting lines. Perhaps Hugh, who knew quite a num-

ber of things besides high finance, music and art, also knew
something about popular Australian sports figures. But she
would have to wait for him to come home. He wasn't at his
Waldorf Towers pied-à-terre, nor at the Century Club, and
she had just missed him when she phoned the Union
League, where he had left no message as to where he might
be reached.

It suddenly occurred to her that she actually knew next
to nothing about how Hugh spent his time when he was
not with her.

The water was really cold now. And the masseuse was
probably getting impatient. Had it not slipped her mind,
fifteen minutes in the sauna would have really been a better
idea than this soaking before a rubdown. But the massage
would do her good anyway. Preventive care of her buttocks
now while they were still apple-shaped and youthfully firm
was much wiser than to allow them to sag and have to get
them lifted by a "body sculptor." She got up, shivered, and
rang for her substitute maid.

Thirteen

"The Locker," on West 50th, was not the most elegant restaurant in town, but Hugh believed that it served excellent seafood. It was a small, busy place, crowded more than ever before, because of the general awareness of the benefits of unsaturated fats. But the long line in front of them consisted mostly of larger groups, and only minutes after Hugh and Stephanie got on line, the tall, dark-skinned maître d' showed them to a table against the middle of the left wall.

"What do you say to a martini?" Hugh suggested after they had settled in the small booth. He was teasing her, since she never touched the stuff.

"Fine," she agreed, and noticing his startled look, began to laugh.

It did marvels to her face, and his puzzlement deepened momentarily, for all at once she looked so much younger and more attractive.

"I know I shouldn't drink, but today everything seems to be out of hand," she said, serious again.

And without her pleasant smile, her face was once more plain and pale from lack of sunshine and fresh air.

"I also know that I should be preparing the list of new books for my hospital library instead of taking the afternoon off and—"

She was interrupted by the waitress who came to take their order, and tentatively sipped the martini the girl had brought her almost instantly, as if the martinis were standing there waiting to be served at tables. Maybe they were, she thought, or maybe the waitress was simply efficient. Quick

72

on her feet. Appraising eyes. A person created for just a job by a computerized world.

She felt extraordinarily relaxed. Hugh was so nice, although a bit eccentric perhaps and probably spending more than he could afford. Only now and then did she get the impression that he might actually be much richer than she imagined. When he studied the menu, for instance, without ever glancing at its right side. But if he wasn't pretending that prices mattered so little, the dear man shouldn't be wearing this old sports jacket and those narrow already out-of-date "mod" pants, most likely bought at Macy's or Gimbel's. She liked his air of quiet assurance and his authoritative manner that he must have picked up playing this innocent little game. Like now, for example, deciding on the menu, not even asking her what she preferred.

It crossed Hugh's mind that she might think that he chose the broiled scrod because it was one of the least expensive dishes on the menu. And it also occurred to him that she clearly had no idea of his wealth. He had not mentioned either his huge sheep stud in Australia, his oil holdings in Texas or the potential value of his land in Wyoming to her. And he had never bought any of his art treasures with Stephanie or even told her of any of his acquisitions, and when he had once referred to his collection, she had not insisted on asking questions, possibly because she thought that he was just bragging about some worthless junk.

"I'd like to show you an Apostle spoon I got," he said when the waitress had left with their order. "It's a rather unusual spoon, portraying Judas."

The poor man had been taken in, she thought. She hesitated. Perhaps he could still get his money back for this fake. "You realize of course that your spoon is an imitation?" she couldn't help remarking. Maybe it was the martini.

"Imitation?! How can you tell without ever seeing it?"

She moistened her lips in her drink. "I happen to know that the set of the thirteen Apostle spoons at the Williamstown, Mass. Art Institute cost thirty thousand," she explained apologetically.

He grinned. "Suppose I can afford a couple of thousand for one such spoon?"

"My dear friend, even if you had that kind of money to spend on a sixteenth-century spoon, none of the seven complete sets known bear the likeness of Judas."

"In that case my spoon is worth ten times what I've paid for it," he argued, and regretted it. It was nice to know that a woman was not after his money. It was true that Doriana didn't really care either, but then she made so much of it herself; money meant nothing to her.

"I hear that later this month there might be a set on sale at Parke-Bernet," he added. "We'll see if it has a Judas knop. After all, Judas was present at the Last Supper."

She smiled indulgently. He took it for granted that she would go with him to that sale, just as he didn't ask her if she could make it when he produced a couple of tickets to that Village opera production a month ago. This was the kind of authority that was Hugh's—a forcefulness that made her give up the idea of offering to share in the expenses, which, in spite of all he said, she was convinced he couldn't really afford.

"How about another martini?" he suggested.

She realized that he was already waiting for her to drain her glass. "No more martinis for me, thank you. You get one, if you like."

"And after dinner let's go up to a small place I have. You'll change your mind after seeing my spoon."

She didn't answer, and because he was looking over his shoulder trying to catch the waitress's eye, he did not immediately notice the look on her face. And when he did, he couldn't say anything, because the waitress was serving their broiled scrod.

It gave Stephanie a moment to recover somewhat, but the crimson that suffused her ordinarily pale face was receding very slowly, and he thought that it was not becoming. And it also made him feel ridiculous. What the hell did Stephanie imagine?

"Have many women admired your spoon?" she asked, when after a brief pause the waitress left with Hugh's wine order.

"No, not many. In fact, only one."

"Is she a very good friend? A special friend?"

"Very special," he said.

This was of course the right moment to tell Stephanie that he was married, married to Doriana Delor, who made all talk cease and all heads turn when she entered a room. It would be the natural thing to do, and it would also put an end to any false ideas Stephanie might have, even if she might think that his was an "open" marriage. But to tell Stephanie would almost amount to putting her down, to unavoidably making her feel hopelessly drab by comparison with one of the most celebrated beauties in the world. And it would also abruptly end the amusing game of allowing her to think that he was as poor as she. Possibly there was even a more subtle reason for his evasiveness. He had been told so often by friends and enemies alike how uncomplicated and predictable he was, that for once he got a kick out of this innocent deception. Perhaps it was this harmless fun of passing for somebody else that added a pinch of spice to his strictly intellectual rapport with Stephanie.

Stephanie glanced curiously at the bottle of wine the waitress had brought to the table. She knew next to nothing about wines, but by the way the girl was turning it around so that she might see the label, it probably was an expensive Chablis. French. She watched Hugh taste the wine and the waitress pour it after a sign from him. Then the waitress stuck the bottle in an ugly ice bucket and left.

"You shouldn't have let yourself be talked into such an expensive bottle. What does she do?"

"Who, the waitress? She waits on tables."

"Not her, your friend." She hesitated. "Do you mind my asking you all these personal questions?"

"Not at all, but you'd better concentrate on me."

He avoided answering her. Maybe his "friend" was a pretty young woman, she thought. And suddenly she became self-conscious about her eyebrows that she had again neglected to pluck, and the gray in her hair. She also thought that her old dress made her waistline seem even thicker than it had lately become because of that damn sedentary existence of hers and her yen for starches and sweets. What a frump she must be in Hugh's eyes. She would really have to work on her appearance. Diet, and tint her hair, to begin with, then do something about her dowdy clothes. And already she was thinking that this sudden idea wasn't altogether frivolous, and that there were valid reasons, other than just getting a man's approving nod, for trying to become more glamorous. Competition for good jobs was fierce, and there were so many fine looking younger people around. Youthful good looks counted far more than background, experience and a college degree. She simply had to streamline her looks, unless she was willing to resign herself to remaining stuck forever in the small hospital library. Yet these solid arguments were unconvincing, perhaps because she had always despised women who used their sexiness and prettiness to achieve their goals. . . .

"Your scrod will get cold," Hugh said, interrupting her musing.

She gulped the white wine. She drank it the way a thirsty person drinks water, and he immediately refilled her glass.

And while forcing herself to eat the fish, Stephanie was dispiritedly thinking about this girl friend of his.

And Hugh, too, was thinking about Doriana, so conscious of her beauty yet so totally unaware of her inner splendor, and how marvelous it would be if with all her attributes she could also possess the wisdom to accept life as it came, to compromise, like this plain woman sitting across from him now.

He was so wrapped up in his thoughts that he shuddered when Stephanie touched his hand. She bent a little closer to him and pointed with her eyes toward somebody a few tables away from theirs.

"Don't look now, but a bit behind you and to the right, there's a girl staring at you all the time."

Hugh turned casually to glance in the direction Stephanie was indicating, and met the amused stare of Noelle who smiled at him as if at an old acquaintance.

Fourteen

"Are you sure it's him?" asked Ben, turning to glance at Hugh again.

"Sure I'm sure. I see him practically all the time," Noelle lied. She tossed her head as high as she could without looking ridiculous. In this position her nose seemed somewhat shorter and less crooked.

"Then why don't you go over and say hello."

"I can't. I'm in no position to do something like that." She suddenly realized that she was talking very loud and attracting the attention of the people at the next table. "It might make Miss Delor mad, and I can't afford it—especially now when she's supposed to get Dr. Orgood to operate on my nose," she finished in a hushed tone.

"There probably won't be any operation anyway."

She stared at him with such horror that he felt a little guilty.

"What are you talking about?!"

"Do you honestly believe that Doriana Delor will pay for your operation?"

She was still staring at him. "She said she'd do all she could to help."

"When? A month ago?"

It had been about that long. No, longer. "Well, you told me *you'd help*."

Her nose was already turning a darker shade, signaling the tears she was trying to hold back.

Oddly enough, before talking to Doriana about that plastic operation she had become almost resigned to her fate; she even sometimes derived a pathological pleasure from her ugly nose, like startling the men who chased behind her

78

in the streets. But since she had suddenly imagined herself rid of her deformity, she no longer could bear it, like a re-signed lifer unexpectedly given a hope of parole is unable to bear the sight of prison bars.

"You know that if I could help you out I would, kid. But I've found out that this Dr. Orgood who you say is the only guy who might do you some good asks maybe several grand per throw. You know I'd gladly pay it too, except that I've had lousy luck lately. I told you I was busted." He lit a cigarette, watching Noelle through a cloud of smoke, won-dering if she believed in his sincerity.

He was really sincere. He wished he could help her. With-out knowing why or how it came about, a kind of attach-ment had slipped into his relationship with Noelle. He would be hard put to define this feeling, a feeling he had never known before in his casual affairs with any of his other pickups. Perhaps it was Noelle's puppy-like devotion that had somehow affected him. Or maybe it was simply a sudden urge to give after a lifetime of taking all he could from others. And the odd thing was that he was not ashamed of this unfamiliar mood as he ordinarily would be of any sentimental weaknesses.

There was also some truth in what he was saying about bad luck. His financial deals were quite simple. Playing the races wasn't part of these transactions, although he gener-ally bet on horses half of what he happened to have. But that had very little to do with the actual winnings. He did it mostly out of his love for horses and the sense of pride he derived from occasionally picking winners. The other half he invested in stocks, on margin, through an old army buddy who had connections with Wall Street brokers. But despite the slump on The Street, the latter financial venture Ben considered a solid investment as compared with his dealings with bookies. He had faith in his friend's financial genius, in spite of the fact that all his qualifications were limited to owning a hole-in-the-wall luncheonette in the Wall Street district, from which he was catering coffee and sandwiches to the brokerage firms. However, Ben's enterprising friend apparently had some connections, after all, and Ben's confidence in him seemed justified for a long stretch of time. And the easy money he was getting from buying and selling stocks he had never heard about before while Dow Jones were steadily slipping down, money that he recklessly pumped into horse races, made him feel like a rich man with a steady income who need not worry about the future.

This had been true until last week, when he ended up with a pile of worthless racetrack tickets and, because of his financial adviser's unexpected miscalculation, a debt to settle with a Broadway loan shark. And while he was talking to Noelle, the little scheme of his own, which he had conceived some time ago while listening to Noelle's chatter about her secretarial work for Doriana Delor, slowly crystallized as he watched Noelle.

He had not intended to discuss it with her in public. From past experience he knew that while a restaurant was the best place for talking over business with men, a bed was far more conducive for a persuasive talk with a woman. However, there was a certain similarity between a woman's frenzy before a delayed orgasm, when she was ready to promise you anything, and Noelle's present state of mind. Tense, excited, impatient, she was desperately longing for plastic surgery, and would promise and do anything now to get it. There was no sense putting off his plan. He glared away the curious glances of the people at the next table, and moving closer to Noelle started to whisper.

"I've lost all I had, and I'm in a few grand to a loan shark. Not only am I unable to help you out, but if I don't skip town or don't pay off soon . . . You know what happens to those who cross those bums," he said melodramatically, playing on her gullibility. "Unless—"

She grabbed the straw he held out. "Unless what?"

There was so much passionate hope in her whisper that momentarily he was touched. He put his hand over hers resting on the table and felt his own pulse pounding.

"Unless we make Miss Delor pay for both of us—my debt and your operation."

She stared at him uncomprehendingly, but by the expression on her face he knew that his plan was going to work. She wasn't shocked or indignant, she only looked doubtful, as if wondering how they could get all that money from Doriana Delor.

"Didn't you tell me that you open all of Miss Delor's mail?"

She nodded, still puzzled. "What has this got to do with my operation?"

"You also told me that uncashed checks lie around before she sends them to the bank."

She was beginning to understand. "Miss Delor has to endorse her checks, you know." Now she was skeptical.

"She will, she will," he mumbled, "just as she signs all her replies to fan letters," he said, winking.

The waitress approached their table to remove the dishes —his cleanly polished plate and her barely touched lobster tail.

"You haven't finished your lobster," the waitress said solicitously, glancing at Noelle's still red nose and tearful eyes. "You got a bad cold or something?"

"Yes, she has a real bad cold," Ben confirmed. "Check please," He turned to Noelle. "Let's discuss details at home."

Noelle felt suddenly relieved. She didn't give any thought to the risk she and Ben would be taking or that what he suggested was a felony. Without going through with his plan she faced far more dreadful things than a problematical jail and even more problematical remorse. To go on living the way she was. To lose the only guy of her own she had ever had, the only guy who was genuinely interested in her, who was prepared to risk anything for her.

She did not know that Dr. Orgood was attending an international congress of plastic surgery abroad, combined with a few weeks' vacation, making it impossible for Doriana to get in touch with him. And in addition to the exhilaration that within minutes had replaced the darkest despair, there was the cunning little sense of satisfaction that, after all, it would be Doriana, the unfeeling Doriana, who would pay for her long-overdue transformation. She dabbed her face with the powder puff, and for once did not mind the reflection of her nose that filled the small mirror of the fancy compact Ben had bought for her. Only briefly did the sobering thought that she still had to ask Doriana to introduce her to Dr. Orgood to get him to reduce his fee cross her mind, for the less she and Ben had to steal, the easier it would be. She had a sudden chill thinking that Dr. Orgood hadn't even examined her yet. What if any significant corrective surgery was impossible?

"Let's go," Ben said, getting up.

"Real January thaw outside," said the man behind the cash register while Ben was paying his check. "Well, another two or three months and we'll have spring."

"It can't miss," said Ben, answering his own secret thoughts more than the man's remark.

Ben started to laugh loudly as usual, and some people still waiting in line for a table turned their heads in his direction and one or two grinned, as if his contagious laughter were an invitation. A tall woman in a drab gray coat who was walking past him toward the exit also smiled, and he suddenly realized that she was with Hugh Botain. Botain himself was waiting behind him to pay his check. Ben mentally cursed himself for attracting attention with his stupid exuberance. Now that he and Noelle considered forgery, he must be connected with her as little as possible, just in case there should be a slipup later on. He glanced sharply at Botain, who was removing some bills from his money clip. So this was the husband of the fabulous Doriana Delor. Some lucky bastard, this old guy, just because his pockets bulged with dough, he had it all made. He forced himself to look around casually, his eyes searching for Noelle and finding her.

She had edged nearer to him and was also staring at Botain. Did Botain notice her? Apparently he didn't. Then Noelle cleared her throat, as if to call for attention, and Botain looked up and recognized her, and made a friendly gesture with his hand full of bills, and Noelle smiled her best smile, and Ben moved away as nonchalantly as he could, as if he were not together with her, and cursing her for being so dumb.

He walked over to the checkroom, carefully turning his back to Botain, his mood rapidly souring again. But the hope of suddenly coming into some cash, which embezzling of Doriana Delor's checks would soon turn into reality, never deserted him.

It can't miss, he again murmured to himself, and handed the girl attendant a dollar bill, one of the three he had left.

Fifteen

"Well? Is my Apostle spoon a fake?" Hugh said, his eyes smiling teasingly, putting his arm playfully around Stephanie's shoulders.

She was still looking at the exquisite antique she was turning over in her hands and said nothing. Since entering Hugh's apartment at the Waldorf Towers, she seemed to have lost all notion of what was real and what was not.

Perhaps in finding herself in this unusual place Stephanie had also lost all notion of what was right and what was wrong. Somehow what normally would have troubled her—that a man could spend a fortune on a little spoon, no matter how rare or beautiful, didn't seem to disturb her now. And it wasn't wrong that Hugh forgot his large, heavy hand on her shoulder. Maybe it was the unaccustomed martini and the wine at the restaurant, and now the dark, clear liquid that appeared so harmless in the large brandy glass. Hugh's valet, before disappearing from the apartment, had poured it as sparingly and respectfully as if it were a hundred years old. It could very well be. Anything was possible in this unreal world.

She looked up at Hugh and smiled, and was not surprised when he sat down beside her on the soft brown-velvet sofa and, drawing her close, kissed her. And all that followed seemed natural, and was not inhibited by any doubts, fears or hesitations.

He lay motionless, gradually recovering his senses and feeling guiltier with each passing second. He thought that a moment ago he heard Stephanie moaning and tossing under him, but he had been too absorbed in his own pleas-

ure to be quite sure. He glanced at her just as she opened
her eyes.

"Let me up," she said.

He released her from under the weight of his body and
watched her getting up and walking toward the bathroom
door.

Possibly she noticed the tense expression on his face, for
she smiled at him reassuringly before leaving the room. And
unaccountably he suddenly felt as light-bodied and carefree
as he used to long, long ago as an adolescent in rural Tas-
mania where he spent many of his vacations with his mater-
nal grandparents when spring turned the grasses in their
orchard into fragrant blankets and making love with willing
country girls was unrelated to any qualms, responsibilities or
obligations.

While Stephanie was in the bathroom, he picked up the
Apostle spoon instrumental in this impromptu development
in their relationship and imagined Judas winking at him
ironically, as if reminding him that there were other angles
to be considered. Stephanie was not the type of woman
one dumped. But he had Doriana and was anything but
starved sexually. Why did he let himself have intercourse
with Stephanie? He had to figure out how to let her down
gently. It wouldn't make any sense to allow this little epi-
sode to develop into anything even remotely serious.

Stephanie appeared far less self-assured when she came
back. Her eyes did not seek his, and she did not seem to
know what to do with her hands—like a bad actress in a
poorly rehearsed scene. She was not smiling any more and
looked cold sober.

He surveyed her face that had turned pale again, despite
the reflection of his Tiffany lamp shade, the face of a working woman in need of a vacation.

"I don't know what to say—" he started lamely, as if her
obvious embarrassment was contagious.

"It was as much my doing as yours," she said evenly, and
looked up at him.

And watching her sit down in the same corner of the sofa

where she was sitting a while ago examining the Judas
spoon, her hands, which had been so excitingly bold during
their intercourse, carefully covering a dark wet spot on her
dress, somehow put him at ease. Or maybe it was what she
just said.

"You're much too pale for your own good, Stephanie.
How long has it been since your last vacation?"

"I haven't had one in a long while. I've been saving for
a trip to Paris," she confessed, and abruptly felt awkward
again, thinking that Hugh might interpret it as a hint to
offer her to pay for the vacation. He did not.

"Are there any windows in the hospital library where you
work?" he asked.

"Of course there are windows, but they do face an inner
courtyard, so —"

"You see!" he interrupted. "Well, I just had a brainstorm!
I've been thinking of getting someone to take care of my
art collection at my old country place in Australia . . ." He
stopped, unable to guess by the look on her face what she
thought of this idea. "And I think that this job would suit
you perfectly. And you would get plenty of fresh air and a
healthy tan in no time!" he concluded enthusiastically. He
really did need somebody he could trust to take care of his
collections, and of course Stephanie was just the person he
had in mind.

There must be plenty of sun "down under," all right,
she thought. And a marvelous houseful of art treasures.
Maybe rare books, too, that would be so rewarding to
classify and catalogue without being constantly interrupted
by patients and residents as in her hospital library. By now
she realized that Hugh's way of life was worlds removed from
what she had imagined. With the great fortune he obviously
commanded, and the beautiful women he most likely knew,
Hugh could hardly be interested in a plain bookworm on
the wrong side of forty. He had taken her simply because
she chanced conveniently to be there to satisfy his whim of
the moment, and nothing else. He was probably already
sorry for what had happened and was just trying to pay her

off with a good out-of-the-way job at his distant Australian home that he most likely seldom visited.

"I've been planning this trip to Paris for a long time and I already have my ticket," she said. "Besides, once I'm in Australia, when shall I have another crack at visiting France? But I accept your offer of course and will go to Australia as soon as I get back in a couple of months and tie up some loose ends here," she added quickly, as if afraid that he might think that she was turning him down.

Things were working out fine, he thought, and felt like a damn heel. Stephanie would go to Paris while he flew to Australia. He should have visited his stud long ago. And she would go there after he had returned to New York. There was plenty of time to cool off their relationship back to normal. He would have gladly offered her to pay for her trip to Paris, but thought that it might look almost as if he were offering to pay her for tonight. He could not do that, naturally. Just as he couldn't offer to buy her a new dress to replace the one she had on, probably her best dress she wore on their date, which was in all likelihood ruined by this wet spot. Not Stephanie. Fortunes in gifts were given and as easily accepted and taken for granted in Doriana's world of show business where way-out-of-proportion incomes made everybody on top feel so rich, and his own more substantial world of big-time landowners, breeders and oil men.

"That's all right with me. In two months then," he finally said.

Stephanie had already begun fretting because of the time it took him to answer.

"I'll be jetting to Australia myself very shortly, with a stopover in Texas," he went on. "And I'll have everything ready for your arrival. We'll discuss details after we both return here to Manhattan."

So perhaps she had blundered by not chucking her trip to Paris. If she had only known, they might have gone to Australia together, and perhaps. . . .

He didn't understand why she suddenly appeared so dejected, but did not ask her why.

Sixteen

Doriana still needed the dope on that Australian tennis player, Ted Ketley, for "This Is Your Hobby" tomorrow night. The simplest thing of course would be to have Arlen give it to her over the phone. But, on the other hand, one never knew who might be listening—maybe the switchboard operator, or maybe even somebody fooling around with one of those new sophisticated electronic devices. It would be compromising if somebody were to leak to the press that the sparkling witty and always-on-her-toes Doriana Delor was actually a fraud who did her "extemporaneous" pearling beforehand.

But when she had made up her mind that after all she had to see Arlen so soon again, something she had never expected happened.

"Arlen, I'm so glad I reached you before you got involved in a poker session," she said, when she finally got him on the busy line.

"I wouldn't play poker this afternoon even if I were guaranteed a royal flush to the ace of spades," he said.

"Good, 'cause I must see you."

There was a few seconds' pause before he answered, but it stretched uncomfortably.

"Would like nothing better m'self, but no can do, have something very important to take care of," he finally said with genuine regret.

So he had another special assignment. What was it this time? A Gracie Mansion Press conference? A VIP arrival at Kennedy Airport? Something at the United Nations?

"I must keep an appointment with my tailor," he added candidly.

"You mean you can't see me because of your tailor?"

"Angel, you don't understand! My London tailor is in town, and I've only just learned that he's about to fly back, and if I miss him. . . ."

She could swear that there was a note of near panic in his voice. Arlen could not survive without a suit from Saville Row. She was beginning to lose her temper. "I understand. I suppose you've nothing to wear. I only wonder how they let you in your studio without your pants on."

"Angel, you've practically described the actual situation. By the time I get my order, I'll have to stay in bed around the clock."

"But it won't be with me!" she snapped, forgetting about bugging devices and the eavesdropping switchboard operator. Hugh, who could probably buy all of Saville Row, wore pants that looked as though he had grown since getting them, but Arlen, who most likely had nothing besides his newsman's income, could not force himself into a Brooks Brothers suit.

Evidently the reference to his bed exercised its magic.

"Why don't we get together later tonight at my place? Please? My tailor has to retake a polaroid of me and it will take at least an hour for the measurements."

Obviously Arlen had already learned that Hugh had unexpectedly jetted to Australia. Sometimes she wondered if Arlen kept tabs on Hugh's comings and goings.

Arlen sounded as if he were pleading for his life, swaying her somewhat in spite of herself. Of course he needed the four buttons that unbutton on his sleeves to pass the inspection commitee at "21".

"Well . . ." she began, and all of a sudden remembered that going to bed with Arlen was precisely what she did not want tonight. That's all she needed—to appear on "This Is Your Hobby" with tired eyes and perhaps a lined face from sleeping too deeply after orgasmic exhaustion. "Well, you'd better spend your night with Henry Poole and Company," she suggested, and hung up.

So she was where she had been before, with one measly

pun about that racket for this Australian tennis player for the show. How did it go already? Would seeing your hands help me guess what your racket is? Perhaps she could invent something else. After all, she had come pretty far using her own wits. How could she tie in something about a kangaroo? Perhaps. . . .

A knock on her dressing room door killed the germ of an idea. It was Noelle, and she still had the apologetic expression that had not worn off since her reporting for work. She was getting in later and later it seemed.

"Arlen Redfore's on the phone. He said it was urgent," Noelle told her.

Noelle looked even guiltier now. Maybe it was she, and not the switchboard operator at Arlen's TV station who listened in on her phone conversations with him on the study extension?

"Tell him I can't take the call now," she said, visualizing with pleasure a very unhappy Arlen. Let him suffer a little. Did she imagine that Noelle smiled? "Oh, yes, I will be seeing Dr. Orgood today. If you come along, we'll ask him to have a look at you."

"Thanks a lot, Miss Delor," Noelle said.

Dr. Orgood should be back from his European trip. Besides, it was not entirely for Noelle's sake that she suddenly decided to see Dr. Orgood. Her breasts were hurting more and more, and when she called her gynecologist, he didn't hesitate. That's how Dr. Somney was—quite positive, as though he never made a mistake, which naturally gave one confidence, even if it appeared that he might have been wrong. "Stop taking the estrogen tablets immediately. I'll mail you a prescription for hormonal vaginal cream instead, but keep up your monthly breast self-examination," he said. "And the mammogram we've done on you doesn't show anything to worry about."

But more than the sharp pain that came and went and sometimes stayed for long stretches, the alarming thought that struck her during the night was that perhaps these estrogens might already have done some harm unrelated to cancer, and the fact that Dr. Somney cut off the drug so abruptly added to her preoccupation. It would be all right if her breasts, which had swelled somewhat, stayed that way, although they were large enough for her slender frame. What bothered her was that they seemed to shrink with the disappearance of the pain. But how infinitely more horrifying cancer would be, she thought with a sudden involuntary shudder. . . . Still, it would be a problem if her bust became flabby and collapsed like June Fleming's did before June's plastic inserts. Maybe something could be done to prevent it before it was too late. That's where Dr. Orgood could be useful. Even if his specialty was facial wrinkles, he was a topnotch surgeon, he should be able to help her.

"Call Dr. Orgood's office and make an appointment for six o'clock," she instructed Noelle before her secretary left the room.

She never doubted that she would get an appointment with Dr. Orgood at her convenience and didn't think it necessary to check with Noelle about it. Six o'clock was convenient for her, and this was Dr. Orgood's office day, wasn't it?

Contrary to the usual routine there were only three people in the waiting room when accompanied by Noelle Doriana arrived at Dr. Orgood's. One woman, already on her way out, was obviously crying, for she was dabbing her eyes, nervously taking off and putting back on her sunglasses and occasionally blowing her nose into a dainty handkerchief, with a startlingly loud hornlike sound. Doriana was not given a chance to speculate about the weeping creature, because almost immediately Hilda, Dr. Orgood's secretary, approached them.

Hilda had just the right kind of features for a plastic surgeon's office. It made sense that neither a beautiful nor an ugly secretary would do. An ugly receptionist would be a poor advertisement which might discourage those who came to consult the surgeon for the first time. And a beauty would be a disturbing reminder to women patients after surgery of how unrealistic their dreams had been. No, Hilda's plain face, an honest, unpretentious face, made rather pleasing by a winning smile, was just right.

It came to Doriana as somewhat of a shock to learn that Dr. Orgood was out of town.

"Out of town? Still in Europe?"

"Dr. Orgood came back from Europe last Sunday, but he had to jet to the West Coast to see . . . I really shouldn't be mentioning names," Hilda started to whisper, "but the story's been on all the front pages and all the TV newscasts, anyway. It's the real estate tycoon Ralph Walden's son who was kidnapped in April. They've just found him, left for dead, with one of his ears cut clean off. Now the father wants the young man to have a new ear rebuilt, and naturally they wanted Dr. Orgood to do the job."

Naturally. Dr. Orgood was one of the best reconstructive surgeons in the country. He had done some reputed surgery, and he had restored hope for countless men, women and children disfigured during endless processions of big and small wars. Then suddenly, still vigorous in his early sixties, he began devoting more of his time to making some long overdue money by lifting the sagging faces of aging people, while continuing to help out at the University Clinic free of charge a few victims of congenital defects that made them monsters in their own eyes, or accident cases with horrible scars that marred the mind as well as the skin.

So now he had another of these cases that helped enhance his public image of a dedicated surgeon. And Mr. Ralph Walden Sr.'s money wouldn't hurt.

"Why didn't you tell my secretary that Dr. Orgood was out of town?" she reproved Hilda, and thought she caught in Hilda's eyes the contemptuous expression which always belied her almost fawning manner.

"Your secretary made the appointment with Dr. Jerginian," Hilda explained, looking at Noelle who was blushing guiltily.

"You should have told me about this! We could have made

it some other time," Doriana said, turning impatiently on Noelle, but instantly cooled down. The girl was understandably anxious, and who could blame her?

Oh, no, you don't! Noelle thought. "I figured it wouldn't make any difference, since it was for me, for a preliminary examination, that is."

"Dr. Jerginian is the oldest of Dr. Orgood's associates. You know him well, Miss Delor," Hilda came to Noelle's rescue.

Yes, indeed, she knew him well. The prominent nose of the stereotype Armenian; the bushy dark eyebrows that could not conceal the lecherous gleam of his small, deep-set dark eyes; the grinning mouth baring strong teeth that would look yellowish were it not for the background of a perpetually congested face; and the big, heavy body, that for some reason she always imagined sweating.

It was not that she lacked confidence in Dr. Orgood's senior associate who had assisted Dr. Orgood in a couple of her operations. After all these years he was probably as good as the old boy himself. But Noelle's was major surgery and not a simple eyelid operation which required very little work, as Dr. Orgood had once described it to her—just to remove some fat that starts to bulge from underneath the weakened fascia, the membrane that lies under the skin, and to cut out a sliver of skin no longer elastic enough to stretch back into place after the eye bags have been corrected—something like taking in a distended girdle.

Noelle would probably have to have surgery under general anesthesia. It had its advantages and disadvantages. Of course, nervous creatures like June Fleming, who couldn't stand the slightest pain or the unsettling awareness of their precious flesh being cut, were put to sleep. But Dr. Orgood had hinted once at the dangers of having cosmetic surgery under general anesthesia, because the possible scratching at the bandages on coming out of it, and perhaps postoperative nausea, could have disastrous consequences. She wasn't quite sure that this sales talk for a local was necessarily sincere. Perhaps, when he spoke to June Fleming, he stressed the advantages of a general, to avoid June's tantrums during the intervention.

And Noelle would also be spared the punishment of Dr. Jerginian's endless chattering that pierced the serenity induced by the bedtime Nembutal sedation reinforced by a preoperative shot of Demerol; his historical, but under the circumstances nerve-shattering, account of Gersuny demonstrating for the first time in 1899 the spectacular result of the use of paraffin in plastic surgery, its harmful effects upon the trusting, guinea pig patients, and the kaleidoscopic run of names of other pioneers of early operations . . . Lexer, Hollander, Joseph, Passot . . . 1906, 1912, 1919. . . .

Hilda's voice startled her. "There will be a room free in just a minute. You're a little early," said Hilda, and sneaked out without waiting for an angry explosion.

It was the first time ever that an examining room was not waiting for Doriana and she stood near the inside door, as if Hilda had nailed her down with her unexpected remark. "Of all things—" she began, but caught herself, realizing that there was no reason for her to take it out on Hilda, who was no longer around anyway. She wavered a second. Perhaps she ought to storm out. Get herself another good specialist for facelifts, just as she got an eyelid specialist. Perhaps Dr. Orgood and his associates were not so great after all. She had heard of a plastic surgeon in Los Angeles, who employed a new technique, "the muscle-flap facelift," using the platysma muscle, lying just beneath the skin of the neck and serving no useful function, to create a sling effect under the jawline, which improved the contours of the chin and neck. And that L.A. surgeon was achieving this hitherto impossible, remarkable result, by combining the facelift with chemical peeling of the face, and doing it all at his well-equipped office, saving his patients the extra expense and nuisance of hospitalization.

"Why don't you sit down for a moment, Noelle?" she said, suddenly remembering that she was at the office not for herself but for her secretary.

"Yes, Miss Delor," said Noelle.

How can a girl be quite intelligent about certain matters and so stupid about others, Doriana thought. Was Noelle calling her loudly by name intentionally? But naturally, the two remaining women in the waiting room had probably never heard of Doriana Delor, unless of course TV sets were not taboo in all convents.

Mechanically, she pulled off her left glove, uncertain whether she should go back and sit down beside Noelle, or stand waiting near the door. It was rather awkward to stand there right in front of the two nuns.

"Oh!" the younger nun, with a bandage on her nose, whispered, staring at Doriana's hand.

And Doriana only now realized that before leaving home she had forgotten to remove the thirty-carat emerald-cut diamond ring, she had tried on for effect with her new white Halston gown.

"It's so lovely. . . . It looks very expensive," commented the older nun, also in a whisper.

Doriana wanted to repay the nun's compliment, but how does one compliment a nun? She raised her eyes at the nun with the bandaged nose, and suddenly found what to say. The crucifix on a chain around the nun's neck was resting against a red Star of David embroidered on the chest front of the light brown habit. It was a rarity nowadays to see a nun in traditional clothing.

"How beautiful," Doriana said sincerely. "They go together."

The nuns nodded understandingly. "Thank you," said the younger nun.

"They represent the Old and New Testaments," explained the older.

"Please come in," called Hilda appearing in the doorway, and Doriana, smiling at the nuns, followed her to one of the examination rooms.

"What order do they belong to?" asked Doriana, still under the spell of the symbolically harmonious combination that many people probably never noticed. Hugh would most certainly notice and admire it. And Arlen most likely wouldn't give it any thought at all.

"They are Franciscan Sisters of The Atonement. The younger one fell and broke her nose," Hilda said, adding indifferently, "Dr. Jerginian will be with you in a second."

The idea of facing Dr. Jerginian did not becloud her mood, all at once brightened by the encounter with the nuns.

Restlessly pacing the small office, Doriana listened to the strange crackling noises from the intercom on the desk, and unintentionally approached it.

"The old man carries a good liability insurance coverage," Dr. Jerginian's voice suddenly rumbled. Somebody had apparently neglected to switch off the intercom connection in another office.

"What you should have said is that we have a good insurance," corrected another, unusually high-pitched, almost feminine voice which Doriana instantly recognized as belonging to Dr. Clayton, another of Dr. Orgood's associates. "You were assisting Dr. Orgood that day."

"So what of it?" retorted Dr. Jerginian. "It was the old man who made all the incisions. Besides, the eversion is not very pronounced. With time it may—"

"Like hell it will. Once the lid is turned out, it's turned out for good." The screechy voice became almost a falsetto.

He is gloating, thought Doriana. Was the tearful woman in the waiting room involved in this? And she also thought how fortunate it was that she had followed Carol's advice and did not let Dr. Orgood correct her eyelids, with who could tell what dreadful results.

"Accidents will happen," Dr. Jerginian continued spilling the beans. "That's why we have liability insurance. And we'll continue carrying it even if the already exorbitant premium is tripled."

The voices were cut off with a click, and in what seemed to be just one or two seconds, Dr. Jerginian filled the small room with his bulk. For once he rather appeared deflated and limp.

"What a pleasant surprise," he said, and, with amazing agility, moved to meet her, towering over her. "Why, you look more and more ravishing each time I see you."

Down boy, he was thinking, you must be out of your mind to go for this violet-eyed celebrated beauty and the wife of a multimillionaire.

"What can I do for you?" he regretfully switched to a more businesslike manner, without giving her a chance to acknowledge his compliment.

He must be terribly upset by that eyelid accident, Doriana thought, or he would have continued flattering me for a while longer. "I really dropped in to arrange a nose operation for my secretary," she said, "but I'd like to ask you what you think about estrogens while one's breasts hurt and are swollen. Could that lead to eventual loss of firmness?"

He misunderstood. "Why does your secretary take estrogens?"

"No, no, it's me," she blurted out, sorry to have started it all.

"I'd have to examine your breasts first."

She thought that he had begun to stiffen, and all at once remembered his inquisitive hands, his tendency to linger on her skin, and his elbow that dug into her breast when he was steadying his hand at the operating table.

"Perhaps some other time, Doctor," she said. "I was merely curious in principle—"

"In principle, I don't see why a young woman like you should be taking estrogen in the first place," he interrupted her.

And although he sounded quite unprofessional and rather insincere—for how could he tell without lab tests and an examination on that dreadful gynecological table like Dr. Somney's—she forgave him everything.

Seventeen

"Today is a day of anachronisms," continued Dr. Jerginian. "A beautiful young woman like you talks about taking female sex hormones, and a young girl like your secretary wants a cosmetic operation."

What he was actually saying, Doriana thought, was an indirect admission that he was lying to her about his considering her young. Since when is it an anachronism to have cosmetic surgery when one is young? The damned fool.

"When you see the poor girl, you will understand why she's so anxious to have this operation," she said. You won't have to use Dr. Somney's speculum to diagnose *her* needs, she thought.

"Yes, from what Hilda said, I understand that your secretary would require a major job," he confessed. "Hilda tells me it's rather urgent. Poor kid, three plastic operations on a nose are two too many."

So Noelle did not just make an appointment. The little vixen must have spent some time softening Hilda's heart. It was then better to get it over with. "Yes, it is rather urgent," she said.

When some minutes later Doriana watched Dr. Jerginian examining Noelle, she was amazed by the abrupt change in him. Outside the operating room she was always attended to by Dr. Orgood himself, including the changing of dressings and taking out of stitches, and the only time she could mentally relate Dr. Jerginian to his specialty was when she lay drugged on the operating table. She saw him now appraising Noelle's nose with clinically attentive eyes, touching it lightly with his big paws and taking some measurements that were probably as meticulous and time-consuming as those taken

98

of his clients by Arlen's London tailor. And Dr. Jerginian's concentration-lined face all at once looked older and nearly as tense as that of Noelle who sat there in the white examination chair gripping the seat under her with both hands as if trying to prevent the tension coiled within from projecting her to the ceiling.

"Miss Delor, perhaps we might talk it over while Hilda takes Miss Martin to another room to prepare her for picture-taking," he finally said.

Hilda appeared as if she had been listening behind the door.

Doriana looked at him warily. From experience she knew that there were no preparations involved in the doctor's customary "just-in-case-insurance" photographing of patients before surgery. But of course Noelle's was a special case.

"It's a problem, all right," he announced when he and Doriana were alone.

She did not need him to tell her that, she thought. So Noelle would have to go on living as she was. Briefly, she felt sorry for her secretary.

Everybody called himself a plastic surgeon nowadays and made a fortune producing such horrors, Dr. Jerginian was thinking, working himself up more and more against the unknown quack who had operated on this nose several times. Then he suddenly thought that some years ago, when he was only an intern or resident himself, he might have done this job with the identical result, and softened his attitude.

"Perhaps whoever operated on her didn't have an easy task."

"You mean somebody loused her up?" She was too indignant to choose the right words.

The instinctive professional solidarity instantly made him come to his incompetent fellow surgeon's defense. "Well now, she must have had quite a blow on her nose. A simple operative technique couldn't have caused the development of all this connective tissue growth."

"It's awful that it's impossible to correct it," she said.

"Who said it was impossible?"

"Maybe Dr. Orgood —"

This was of course another slip of the tongue. Dr. Jerginian turned purple.

"Perhaps I can handle it just as well," he retorted.

"I'm sure you can, Doctor, of course you can," she hastened to repair the damage, putting her hand on his arm.

"I've already told Hilda to make a hospital reservation for tomorrow, just in case," he said, mollified.

Noelle must have sold Hilda quite a convincing story, Doriana thought.

"Frankly," Dr. Jerginian continued, "I would prefer to have a little more time for a preoperative psychological assessment of your secretary. She seems very high-strung and troubled. Naturally, in her case, she may simply be anxious at the prospect of another operation on her nose. However, one never can tell."

"What do you mean?" Doriana surveyed him suspiciously. Was he trying to back out of the operation?

"Well, a patient with an inadequate personality may not be satisfied even with excellent results."

Actually, he thought, this little secretary will probably be happy with any kind of improvement, and after all the operation was not really that difficult. Long and tedious, but not difficult.

"But of course an emergency is an emergency," he added quickly, noticing her expression.

Doriana forced herself to keep quiet. It was such a particularly bad time to lose Noelle even for a week or two. Louise was still in Paris, and Charles's niece who was filling in for her was still bewildered to a point of flooding the bathroom every time she washed the *bidet*. And Charles, who silently missed Louise, was not the impeccable butler as usual, and he had had liquor on his breath when she came home early enough to find him waiting up for her. But on the other hand, since things had been set in motion. . . .

"By all means, Doctor, let's do it as soon as possible," she said. "We haven't yet discussed your fee," she reminded him.

"I hope you will charge her less than your usual, but whatever it is, I'd like to take care of it."

He did not hesitate. That little secretary had told Hilda she could pay whatever it took. Of course his regular fee for a nose job that he could charge a young working girl would seem like a substantial reduction to Doriana Delor, whose plastic surgeons' bills paid for quite a few charity cases from Dr. Orgood's University Clinic. But it was nice to be able to impress her with a grand gesture. And anyhow, he would like to show her what he could do without Dr. Orgood's pedantic routine. Perhaps he might take Doriana out to lunch in some famous restuarant to be seen with her in public and be able to brag about it.

"How about having lunch with me some time soon? We would consider it my fee for this operation," he said. "All your secretary would have to pay would be hospital expenses. She has Blue Cross, I suppose?"

This man is full of surprises, she thought. She was accustomed to trading her beauty and fascination for so many things. A luncheon date at a swanky place he would probably take her to was actually a small price to pay for the prompt return of her secretary. Besides, it would do no harm to get to know him a bit better and see what he really could do on his own. Dr. Orgood was getting on. One of these days. . . .

"It's a deal," she agreed. "As soon as my secretary is back on the job with the prettiest nose in the world."

"It's a deal," he said, and seizing her hand planted a loud smack on her thirty-carat diamond. "You will be amazed at how fast she will be back at work."

He evidently meant business, for Noelle was operated on the next morning. And Doriana, who paid her a visit, remembering how difficult it proved to get a private room for herself on short notice, was surprised to find Noelle in a beautiful large corner room filled with fresh flowers. She suspected that in addition to skipping Noelle's psychological assessment, Dr. Jerginian had also neglected some other preoperative details—such as giving Noelle Demerol, subjecting the girl to needless pain, for Noelle appeared like someone after major surgery. Maybe it was a major operation, Doriana thought, and it looked as if Dr. Jerginian would have to wait for that luncheon date for a while.

It also looked as though she was going to be without a secretary for some time to come, unless she admitted a stranger into her home without Noelle there to brief the replacement. No, she would have to wait and just skim through the mail and fish out the really important items. The other disturbing thought was that Noelle's nose still looked abnormally large under the bandages, and it would really be a disaster if after all this trouble Noelle's nose was not improved. Perhaps it was only a mass of gauze that hid the new nose Dr. Jerginian had promised, or maybe just some edema. She had kept a few enzyme tablets that helped to reduce the edema and resorb the bruises after her eyelid operation, and had now smuggled them in to Noelle, but the girl was still too dazed to take the drug.

When Doriana was leaving, a young black nurse approached her near the elevators.

"Miss Delor, how nice to see you again."

The voice was strangely familiar, but not the pretty, smiling face under a coquettishly tilted nurse's cap.

"I was on duty the night that insurance man sneaked into your room, remember?"

And how she remembered. The "insurance man," the maniac who had nearly raped her while she lay helpless, blinded by her bandages, not daring to move or even scream after a lid operation.

This was another opportunity to find out from this young nurse what her molester looked like. It would be so much safer to be able to recognize him before he had another chance with her. Or was the farfetched story of his lifelong passion for her just a trick of a clever and articulate lecher who tried to talk his way into the bed of a woman dazed by sedatives and postoperative shock?

"I must go now Miss Delor. I hope you will be back soon and I hope they assign me to you."

"I hope so, too," she said, smiling appreciatively.

No, she could not question the nurse. It suddenly dawned on her that the girl was calling her by her real name. That's what her incognito registrations were worth. All she needed was a hospital rumor that sooner or later would spill out into the streets. Imagine that! While Doriana Delor lay here with her eyes bandaged after cosmetic surgery, she became interested in an insurance man and subsequently came back asking nurses what he looked like. It must be true what they say about her being a nympho. . . .

Doriana nearly bumped into a burly man, who had stepped off the down elevator she had waited to take. But looking straight into her face, he showed no sign of recognition, and she stopped brooding about the unknown sex maniac and thought again about the amiable nurse who had enjoyed taking care of her and would like to serve her again.

"People like you, Doriana," she murmured, and repeated it two or three times while a taxi was taking her home, as though trying to convince herself that among the millions who watched her and admired her only as an entertainer, there were some who liked her for what she really was—a lonely, vulnerable human being in need of friendship and understanding just as anybody else.

Eighteen

The disruptions created by Noelle's operation that Doriana foresaw proved minor by comparison with what she found on returning home. At first things appeared rather reassuring. For helping her out of the cab, Tim, the doorman, had informed her cheerily: "Mrs. Russard is back!"

It took her some seconds to connect the unfamiliar name with her maid. Of course, Charles and Louise Russard. Off duty her couple had their own private life and their own surnames. To this uniformed man, who also must have a last name, Charles and Louise were substantial citizens with a solid income and a good standing in their own "upper crust" hierarchy.

So Louise was back. At least that much was a relief. But why hadn't she cabled to let them know?

As usual, as if she had been stationed behind it, it was Louise who opened the front door. Ordinarily it puzzled Doriana, since the kitchen and pantry adjacent to the dining room were at the far end of the hall downstairs and the servants' quarters on the upper level of the triplex. Naturally, today Louise was waiting behind the door to greet her after her absence. But it was a distressed Louise, pressing a slice of stiff raw steak from the pantry freezer against her left eye, with tears streaking her eternally red cheeks.

"Oh, Madame," she wailed, and started to cry as if Doriana's appearance had reopened the dam she had briefly held in check.

Doriana took her by the shoulders and walked the shaking Louise up the stairs into her pink boudoir on the second level. There the maid slumped on the edge of the large round silk-upholstered pouf on which Doriana did her belly exercising.

"The bastard, the bastard," Louise whimpered.

Momentarily Doriana thought that perhaps Louise meant her niece's newborn son whom she went to see in Paris. But between tears and sighs, for the first time exposing her shiner from behind the thawing steak, Louise finally told her the tragedy.

It was about two hours ago that bursting with happy expectations, Louise had unlocked the front door with the latchkey she had taken with her on her flight to Paris a month ago. It was quiet in the large triplex, except for some strange noises in the library. It was there that Louise had caught Charles banging Yvonne.

"So what did you do?" Doriana couldn't help smiling. It was hard to imagine her respectable butler in that sort of situation.

"Oh, that! I dragged the little *putain* out by her hair!"

"Then you and Charles had a fight? How about the neighbors? Anybody say anything?"

"*Mais, non*, Madame, we wouldn't compromise Madame by creating a scandal. I didn't even make a sound when Charles slapped me."

"I trust you took the door key from Yvonne before she left."

"She didn't have the key, she lent it to Miss Noelle yesterday. Miss Noelle was here quite late before reporting to the hospital for that operation, Charles said. He told me she had run out on an errand earlier and had borrowed Yvonne's key. She must still have it. I'd better go ask Charles about it," Louise said getting up.

Louise probably wanted to find Charles to make up with him, thought Doriana. She watched her maid leave the room. Her skirt was somewhat too tight for a uniform but maybe she hadn't had a chance to change yet.

Doriana followed her into the hall and slowly walked to the study to face the chaos of the unopened mail.

The room was surprisingly tidy, considering Noelle's haste

to check into the hospital, and Yvonne's love affair with the butler. The pile of unanswered mail on the small table near the desk did not seem too high. Noelle must have taken care of the backlog of fan letters forwarded by the networks and from Hollywood that, owing to her coming to work at impossible hours, had been slowly accumulating. She glanced at a few letters at random. There were none from her fosterlings. The others were always the same, mostly insipid fan letters, with an occasional obscene note. There was another stack of mixed mail on the desk; today's yet unattended mail and, on top of it, a cable from Hugh.

"Important business will detain me in Melbourne longer than expected. Will call you at four. Love."

It was after four now, but there was no note from Charles about the call. Maybe the phone had been ringing longingly while Charles and Yvonne were in the library. In any case, she had no more time to lose; she had to dress for the evening show and refresh her memory about the clever "off-the-cuff" remarks she had ready for "This Is Your Hobby." It was rather easy with Lily Byron, that phony food expert. "Now I'm in a stew." "You make met feel as if I were in a frying pan." "Mystery always sharpens my appetite for knowledge." But she still hadn't thought of anything better than that "racket" bit for the Australian tennis player.

She got mad at Arlen all over again. She glanced through the small pile on the desk. Yes, he had called twice. She could still get in touch with him in a hurry, but changed her mind. He left a message that he would call in sick at his TV station to be able to watch her on TV later. Now that he would be watching her rather than doing his own program in the same time slot, she couldn't even ask him for any dope on that tennis player without having him realize that she had prepared her questions in advance.

Well, she would come up with something, wing it, if need be. The audiences usually liked whatever she said. Like the day when she said, "I couldn't even say then, as GriGri Sandor does, my 'middle husband,' since at that time I had just ended my fourth marriage and there was nobody in the middle," and she had said that quite spontaneously. And she actually honestly meant that when you've had three husbands, the second was the middle one, and if you've had five, the third, but you can't talk of a "middle husband" in that amusing fractured English when you've had four. Unfortunately the studio audience misunderstood her entirely that time and the producer, a damn prig, nearly swallowed his fat cigar.

But nonetheless, even if the show went well, she'd punish Arlen for his giving his London tailor preference yesterday by not sleeping with him for at least a week. Then she remembered that Hugh was away for she didn't know how long, and about Arlen's sex carousel that was unaccustomed to remaining unoccupied and motionless, and of her own bed that made her feel so lonely and afraid without Hugh in it with her, and mentally cut Arlen's punishment to forty-eight hours.

Dressing wouldn't require too much time, she was thinking, but it would take a while to "put on" a new face, even though it would be retouched by the fussy make-up girl for the cameras at the studio anyway. And she could definitely use a short beauty nap.

Why was she lingering in the study which actually was Noelle's domain? Sitting down in the typist's chair Noelle used for long hours answering her mail, she absently pulled out the top drawer on the right. There was a pile of papers in it and at first she was baffled by several sheets covered with her own signature. Doriana Delor, Doriana Delor, Doriana Delor. Then she realized that this was Noelle practicing her autograph, to make it look authentic on the photos and on the replies to fans Noelle composed and signed for her. What a conscientious girl this Noelle is, she thought, glad that she had arranged for Noelle to get that operation. Perhaps she would call the night nurse after the show and inquire about her secretary. And she would order an "autopen," a robot writer that can realistically reproduce an autograph, to help Noelle.

Her puzzlement deepened when she opened the second drawer. There, all by itself, occupying the whole space, was resting an expensively framed photograph of Arlen autographed across his well-tailored athletic chest. It was the photo Arlen swore he had sent her, she swore she had never received, and Noelle swore she knew nothing about. Why was it stashed away and forgotten in this drawer?

The idea that Arlen might have any kind of affair with Noelle was too absurd even to consider. He was a wencher, but only of the very beautiful. What was more likely was that her secretary had a secret crush on Arlen and had appropriated the picture Arlen had sent her. A young girl would do a silly thing like that. Then she remembered the marks of strong teeth on Noelle's thigh and frowned, and sat there for a while, frowning, as if each passing second did not stamp a tiny imprint on her brow.

She wondered about the hour. It was probably half-past four. Or five. She rose and crossed toward the fireplace with its pink mirror over the mantel—the only dependable and truthful recorder of time, the only device that really counted. And the glass gazed back at her with wide-set violet-blue eyes that even Elizabeth Taylor might have envied when she was younger, a beautiful creamy-complexioned face, a high, smooth forehead that did not reveal the hell brewing in the tormented brain beneath its lovely fine covering, the natural blond hair, which took so well to the gold-plating of the insidious silver in it. And her reflection suddenly dispelled her gloom. In another few hours she would be taping the show before an admiring studio audience and she would later be seen by millions of television viewers from coast to coast, and all of them would appreciate her beauty just as much as Arlen's photo did now in this quiet study.

She left the picture standing on the desk as a subtle rebuke to Noelle when the girl reported back to work, and mentally cut Arlen's punishment to one day only.

Nineteen

It was the seventh day after Noelle's nose operation, and she was again sitting under the glaring light in front of Dr. Jerginian in the same chair where she sat only eight days earlier while he examined her for the first time. And she was again clutching the cold metal seat with both hands, listening to his scolding.

"You're not a child to behave like this. First you embarrass me by vanishing from the hospital the day after your operation without a discharge. Then you don't call or come in for a checkup, and you give your employer's address instead of your own, making it impossible for us to reach you!"

"I'm sorry, Doctor, but —"

"Do you realize that even a routine nose intervention is fraught with serious consequences should an infection set in? And your nose reconstruction was far from simple."

"Yes, Doctor, I'm awfully sorry."

"Do you want to compromise the final results?" He glanced at her and noticing her sudden pallor added quickly: "Well, it doesn't look as if you've done it any real harm anyway."

He picked up another sterile swab from a tray and wiped off a droplet tinged with blood that protruded from her nostril. Perhaps it had not hurt to have removed the stitches one day later, he thought, and lifting her chin scrutinized her face again. It was amazing how little edema this girl had after all the manipulations. And how relatively little bruising. She was a healthy young specimen. Young. That was the answer.

And observing his expression, she suddenly felt her heart thumping wildly.

"May I see it now?" she asked in a very low voice.

She did not think that she would ever have the nerve. It was this dread of the first glance, and not Dr. Jerginian's stern warning before the operation, that had made her hole up in her small Village apartment and had kept her from stripping the bandage to peek at her nose. It was this same trepidation that had kept her from coming in on the scheduled day, and not the complicated lies she had told him to explain her sudden flight and disappearance. It was actually more than fear; it was a bone-chilling, overwhelming panic that had replaced her earlier dreams in which she saw herself with a nose like Doriana's, a sculptured little nose that would transform her into a desirable young woman. For long desperate years she had faced the picture of herself. But now, with hopes reborn, her former resigned adaptation, if not humble acceptance, had abruptly vaporized as if it had never been. She could not and would not face her old image. She had had it. . . .

"You may look now," Dr. Jerginian's voice brought her back.

Her hands trembled visibly when she let go of the chair and accepted the large hand mirror he was offering her. She held it in both her hands in front of her face as if its light white plastic frame were made of iron, not daring to open her eyes, not knowing if she was holding a cruel piece of glass whose cold reflection would shatter her hopes, or a magic mirror, like the one Doriana faced each time she glanced at herself.

"Open your eyes and look."

And obeying Dr. Jerginian's impatient command, she opened her eyes widely, as one might to face something difficult to see, for it was easier than starting slowly, just as it is easier to jump into cold water than to wade into it gradually. From the oval frame of the magic mirror two scared eyes, so surprisingly strangely wideset on both sides of a small, unfamiliar nose, glanced back at her.

She did not hear him, or rather, she heard him, but it penetrated her mind as if through a **thick mist.**

"You're not very bruised, amazingly little. Now let's put a light bandage on."

"Oh, please."

She sounded so anguished that at first he misunderstood.

"You're not satisfied?" Perhaps she was after all one of those high-strung, neurotic types whom nothing would satisfy. Well, they had her unretouched photograph on file. Maybe she already forgot what she was like before. As far as he was concerned, he had done quite a job on her, a great job of reconstruction, an almost impossible task.

She was still looking at herself. No, at somebody else's beautiful reflection that was staring at her. At first she did not even see the swelling and bruises. All she saw was the absence of her old nose that had once filled the space between her eyes. And then suddenly she realized what had taken its place.

"You gave me her nose, Doctor," she murmured ecstatically, and started to cry.

He held her slender, shaking body in his powerful arms, touched by this unusual tribute to his ability. Yes indeed, that's what he had instinctively tried to do. For when he was sawing off her hump with a bayonet saw, and cutting away the cartilaginous portions with a button-end knife and scissors, and chiseling with chisels, and smoothing with Fomon rasps, he had Doriana in mind, as if she were modeling for Noelle all along. Of course the new swollen nose of this girl who was crying happy tears was far from Doriana's perfection, but in time. . . .

"Now stop this," he ordered her severely. "You don't want to get a hemorrhage and ruin everything?"

Her sobs stopped as if cut off by an abruptly shut, sound-proof door. He released her from his bear hug, but could not see her nose, which was again obstructed by the mirror she was holding in front of it.

Her nose had swelled a little more now and was rather red, and some pinkish liquid oozed from her nostrils. But she was not worried any more. Of course, she was only seven days after surgery. Not a simple cosmetic operation like Doriana had time and again to pull out an invisible wrinkle here and there, but an important major operation that had reshaped her whole body, that had moved her eyes apart, that had brought out this lovely mouth with its delicately etched upper lip and had already straightened her shoulders even more and had thrown up her head with its mane of lustrous chestnut hair.

She extended her hand and, understanding her, he put a square of gauze into it. She gingerly wiped off the pink tears that had run through her nose, and finally handed him the mirror.

"You're the greatest surgeon in the whole world, Doctor," she told him gratefully, and getting up threw her arms around his neck to kiss him, but didn't quite reach his face.

For at this unexpected compliment he had instinctively straightened up. He was again holding her in his arms, pity gone from his feelings toward this lovely girl, his penis starting to swell as it usually always did in Doriana's stimulating presence.

"There, there," he said, visibly pleased.

Her arms still around him, she was standing with her body against his, her face raised up.

"You are also the best-informed man and a fascinating story teller," she said. "I forgot all about being scared and the pain, listening to you while on the operating table."

"You were half asleep, you little liar," he said, grinning indulgently.

Only yesterday that punk Clayton had remarked to him in his irritating falsetto that he disturbed patients on the operating table by his continuous chatter. So how about that, Dr. Clayton?

"Well, although I was dazed, I still remember a lot of what you said, Doctor. Even names, and maybe dates. Like Trendelnburg being the first to attempt the correction of noses in 1889, and also that the chisel has a tendency to cut too deeply on the upward thrust, whatever that means. And I also remember your saying that last Sunday you took a spill from a snowmobile in Lancaster."

"You have a remarkable memory," he said, more and more flattered. "Now I understand why Miss Delor praises you so highly. Incidentally, you can go back to work tomorrow." It was high time to have that lunch date with Doriana Delor, he thought, and tried to step back, away from Noelle.

She did not let him go. "I'd like to stay under cover for a bit longer, Doctor, till the swelling goes down. My nose still bleeds."

"Not really. It's because I took out the stitches. You won't need any heavy bandaging any more. And the swelling, I told you . . ." Over Noelle's head he watched the door open slightly and Hilda's eyes staring at him disapprovingly.

"Sorry, Doctor," she said, pushing her head inside, just to make sure that he realized she had caught him with a patient hanging from his neck. "Dr. Orgood is waiting for you," she added sourly, shaking her head from side to side before withdrawing it.

If Hilda expected an embarrassed Dr. Jerginian to push Noelle away, she was mistaken. The slight contact with Noelle's body had already aroused him, and Hilda's priggishness had only made him conscious of it.

"Doctor, would you do something for me, please?" Noelle begged him.

"Yes?" he asked, and did not push her away.

"Will you please tell Miss Delor that I should stay home for awhile? Two weeks maybe? No? Another week, then? I'd be so grateful. . . ."

He felt her clinging to him more and more. Perhaps he had unconsciously moved closer to her slim young body arching toward his, a body that felt amazingly warm through his white coat. The way this girl acted he could most likely be compensated for the successful operation by more than a lunch date with Doriana Delor. But even as he was contemplating a double reward, he already knew that he should not allow himself to get involved with a patient.

"I couldn't do that," he said somewhat regretfully, and taking her by the shoulders to pin her down where she stood, took a determined step back, making her arms slip away from his neck and stabbing his back against the desk corner. Goddam, he silently swore. "Will you please sit down so that I can put a light dressing on your nose," he said impatiently.

Hilda showed her face again. "Dr. Orgood —"

"The young lady will give you her address and phone number," he interrupted her.

He pretended not to notice Noelle's pleading eyes while he took care of her dressing. Hilda's head was still stuck in the door.

"I'd like to have a look at your nose next Wednesday," he said, stressing the word "nose" for Hilda's benefit. "And do be careful of it. No skiing and no wrestling until I examine it next week," he joked before leaving the room.

"Yes, Doctor," she said meekly.

A certain plan was already taking shape in her mind. The dressing would stay on till tonight. She wouldn't lose a minute longer showing off her new face to the world, even if her nose was still swollen and her face discolored. She would sweet-talk Ben into taking her out to a disco tonight. One could do the boogie or even rock a little without too much shaking, couldn't one? And even if she had to sit it out most of the time, she could parade her beautiful nose and explain to the curious how she got bruised in that snowmobile spill in New Hampshire repeating word for word Dr. Jergianian's account of last week's snowmobile races at Lancaster.

This would be the birth of a scintillating new life, and nobody would make her delay its beginning. Not Dr. Jerginian, nor Doriana Delor, heaven nor hell.

Twenty

An urgent call for a retake of a beach love scene with a talented young newcomer in her latest movie originally shot on location in Spain and Israel, sent Doriana jetting off to Hollywood. It was an important sequence in the nude. With the filming dependent on the lifting of the smog, it was a week before they could start shooting, and she used the time to tape several TV game shows. And she also went to a lot of parties, at some of which the guests were entertained by unclad young people who did the sexiest dancing this side of any bed. She was also recruited as one of the "presenters" of the forthcoming annual telecast of the Oscar Awards ritual.

As on each of her trips she realized, even though the old movie-making Hollywood was practically gone, how wise it really would be to reopen her shuttered Beverly Hills home and make her headquarters on the West Coast where most of the TV industry had moved a long time ago. But she knew that, no matter how practical for her and perhaps geographically more convenient for Hugh such a move might be, she could never bring herself to leave New York.

It was not until she came back to Manhattan that she fully understood how indispensable her secretary had become in her life.

To begin with, there was not only the forwarded fan mail, but also her personal correspondence at home. It had all accumulated on the desk, spilling over the typewriter on its stand nearby, and had finally slipped to the floor in a growing landslide, probably burying bills and important letters under it. Then there were the telephone messages. With Noelle off, the only two who could answer the phone were Louise and Charles, but according to the answering service they evidently didn't. There had been dozens of calls while Doriana was away, including frantic messages from Hugh in Australia, and from Arlen. If only she hadn't procrastinated about having the message-recording device installed, she thought.

It turned out that her couple's breach had something to do with this annoying situation. After a second fight, they had stopped talking to each other. One day, when the phone rang, they happened to pick up etxensions on different floors, and and told each other, "The Botain residence," and hearing each other's voices, had both hung up, with neither having apparently picked up the phone since.

The worst of it was that she had no way of getting hold of Noelle, the indispensable Noelle she did not appreciate enough. The day after Noelle's operation she was surprised to learn that the girl had left the hospital. Although she knew how soon after cosmetic surgery one could get a discharge, in Noelle's case it was a major operation. It was then that she suddenly realized that she had no idea where Noelle lived, except that it was somewhere in the Village, and of course there was no phone listed in her secretary's name. She had jotted down Noelle's address and phone number somewhere, but God alone knew where it was.

She spent the afternoon at a TV studio, taping two talk shows, and allowed herself to be coaxed into joining a small group for dinner. Perhaps she didn't try to leave early, despite her fatigue that at this late hour might already be showing in her face, because a young producer and a starlet from Rome in her party, who were in love, held hands all evening. Or because the violinists remembered two of her favorite tunes they had played for her and Hugh a year ago. Or simply because the romantic atmosphere of this small East Side bistro was so much pleasanter than her large ivory tower with her fueding servants. When she finally left, the gaiety of the place accompanied her and her multiple escorts up to her Fifth Avenue entrance. And another explosion of laughter and gaiety materialized in the lobby around Bob and

Anne Tassiter and their guests who had just returned from somewhere and were going up to their penthouse for a nightcap, although it was rather time for breakfast.

"Darling," Anne Tassiter called to Doriana, "all alone? What happened? What about a nightcap?"

It was hard to shake her off after having once accepted her invitation. "Love to, darling, but I have to make a long distance call," Doriana lied.

"Why darling, you can make it from our place."

It would serve her right, Doriana thought, if I went up and called somebody in Hong Kong and talked for an hour. But of course the Tassiters could afford that, too. She need not have worried about finding another good excuse. The Tassiters had apparently had quite a number of "nightcaps" already and had instantly forgotten all about their invitation.

"Darling, how about coming to us tomorrow night? We're celebrating an anniversary. We don't remember what of, but it is an anniversary of something," said Anne Tassiter.

Not on your life, Doriana thought, not again. "I wish I could, darling," she said, "but I have a late TV taping session."

Why didn't she just say no? It was certainly not because she imagined she might be missing something at their penthouse. Probably it was rather because she was still tired after her trip to Los Angeles and all the work and partying there. Where did she get all that vitality for all those nightlong parties in the past? Parties before jetting to Europe to attend some other parties there, and parties to celebrate her return? Even "Little Cow" had started scolding her for turning down some "must" invitations lately.

"Why don't you join us at Rexine's disco then?" Bob Tassiter suggested. "We'll have a table at midnight."

Then the Tassiters took their high spirits up to their penthouse, and the elevator man deposited Doriana on her private landing and as usual waited for her to get in. Charles opened the door before she had put the key in the keyhole. It was almost sunup, she thought, so maybe he was trying to compensate for the inconvenience his foolishness was causing her.

Presently he, too, was gone to his quarters, and she was all alone.

She called the answering service again before going upstairs. Yes, there were two more messages. One from a worried Hugh who pleaded with her to cable him or he would fly back tomorrow, despite some important unfinished business, a modernization of the irrigation of his sheep-grazing land, she didn't quite get that part of it straight. The message from the equally anxious Arlen was briefer, characteristically uninhibited and as usual a bit childish. Arlen had left word he would burn all his English suits already hanging in his custom-built closets and those on the way to him from London, if he should not hear from her by noon tomorrow.

She felt really tired now. How long had she been sitting in the study? A minute? An hour? She knew that it must be about six, because the sky over Central Park had taken on the pinkish hue that in the east must already be scarlet. More often than not she no longer needed clocks to tell time. She heard somebody stirring at the upper level. Perhaps Louise was getting set to go marketing as soon as the Madison Avenue stores opened, or maybe Charles was already coming down again to inspect the neglected apartment.

She mustn't put off making up with Arlen, a reconciliation that was now long overdue. She dialed Arlen's number and started to laugh when the receiver, taken off the hook and apparently dropped by his clumsy, sleepy hands, softly relayed the cursing of a man lost in his round bed without the customary bearings of either head or foot, left or right, like an astronaut in a capsule lost in space.

"That you, Doriana?" she finally heard his hopeful whisper.

"Don't you dare burn your pants," she said, and laughed again. "They might catch fire spontaneously by tonight anyway."

She enjoyed his bewildered "What you talking about?" and made certain he was completely awake before giving him any details.

"I'll be at your place by five. We'll ride your carousel. Then we'll have dinner and come back for another spin. And later we'll go to a disco. Call your precious studio and tell them you're sick today. And tomorrow you probably really will be, luv. Now go back to sleep."

She hung up. She was no longer amused by her conversation with Arlen in the affected style she had evolved to keep her true feelings from him for fear of appearing ridiculous in his eyes. And because she had to pretend, and sound as flippant as she knew he felt about their affair, she was always frustrated afterwards, perhaps not unlike a consummate humorist forced to mouth crude jokes for an unsophisticated audience. She had given up attempting to analyze why she was so in love with Arlen. Her emotions did not fall anywhere between Christina Rossetti's sentimental definition of love as a lovely rose, and Oliver Goldsmith's cynical comparison of love to an intercourse between tyrants and slaves. There was something more involved than the unquestionable element of simple erotic fulfillment, and other than her frantic desire to associate herself with the young, and in spite her knowing him so well and actually respecting him very little. He was intelligent, but he did many foolish things. He was self-centered and vain, and probably because of this spent a great deal of money to create the impression of wealth and largesse although he was actually stingy with others, not only with his money, but also with giving of himself, not ever sharing any of his inmost thoughts, always skimming the surface. Yet she could not help being in love with this boy.

She started for her bedroom to finally get some rest herself. She could cable or phone Hugh from upstairs. Then perhaps she would turn on the large electronically controlled color Magnavox recessed into her bedroom ceiling, which she could lower and manipulate to any desired angle from their double bed, and watch one of the early morning shows for awhile to lull herself to sleep. It was just as well that there were no old movies on TV this early in the morning. These old flicks were mostly graveyards populated by two-dimensional ghosts of men and women she once knew or had made movies with herself; nothing but dead people who reminded her of the flight of time as surely as if she were gazing at the faces of clocks.

She paused absently at the open door of the large living room. As always lately, it appeared cold and empty in its elegant vastness, and very, very quiet. This room used so seldom since her marriage to Hugh, did not echo with the gaiety and glitter of the parties she used to give so often before. The only sign of life seemed to be her life-size portrait, smiling out of an elaborate Florentine frame, hanging against the whole clear expanse of one wall.

She entered the room, drawn by the beauty of this oil masterpiece by the late René Bouché, depicting her as a semi-reclining modern Venus emerging from the blue-green waves of a diaphanous Dior evening gown, her honey-blonde hair swept into a beguiling crown of soft curls, her violet eyes set off by the priceless sapphire, emerald and jade necklace and earrings, so artistically created for her by Tiffany's. How breathtakingly lovely this picture was! It easily overshadowed the Manet and the "blue" Picasso in the room.

Suddenly she thought that one of these days she would probably be wise to exile her portrait to her private sitting room. For despite all the Dr. Orgoods and all the Elizabeth Arden beauty farms, she could not eternally sustain the unfair competition with her own immobilized image. But of course the subtle difference would not become noticeable for a long time to come. Even her old movies had so far never betrayed her.

Happily she returned her portrait's carefree smile on equal terms, feeling still as beautiful and seductive as it was, and lingered for a few more seconds near it.

She was still smiling when she started up for her bedroom, but when she passed the pink mirror at the foot of the stairs, for the first time in her life it unexpectedly reflected an alarmingly tired-looking face, so different from the serene young beauty on the canvas.

Twenty-One

It looked as though everybody had made a date with everybody else at Rexine's disco. Doriana felt a bit dizzy from the heat radiated by the lank-haired cuties, and lank-haired young men in tight pants they seemed to have grown rather than to be wearing which left nothing to the imagination. They twisted, rocked and bumped in a compact mass of tirelessly energetic young legs and arms, to a deafening din of stereophonic sound mixed with loud conversation and laughter.

Perhaps she was simply exhausted after Arlen had kept her on the floor during several different versions of the hustle and the boogie. And while she was hardly able to hold back her labored and unbecoming panting, nearly collapsing in her chair, Arlen had remained standing at the table, his muscular young body coiling and uncoiling gracefully with the disco beat. He obviously could not understand why their whole group chose to sit it out most of the time, watching the young people.

Doriana found it convenient to be able to pretend that she could not hear over the loud noise and just smile and gesture instead of having to answer Brian Uxworthy, the producer of "This Is Your Hobby," sitting next to her, allowing her wild heartbeats to slow down somewhat. Then there was a sudden pause, an explosion of hand-clapping, and the hurricane of noise momentarily subsided.

"I was saying that you stole the show last week, Doriana," Brian Uxworthy repeated, taking the cigar out of his mouth this time. "You were so mobbed after the telecast I never got a chance to ask you if you'd consider doing 'Hobby' again next week." Then, before she could answer, he went on

121

hurriedly, "I actually want to ask you to do another show for me, a new—"

"Talk to him," Doriana said, indicating Cy Winters, and downed her Mimosa.

Theirs was an odd group. As mixed as it could only be at a disco. It was the Tassiters' party, the penthouse owners, who later would somehow perform a duet, with her singing and him boom-booming. They had brought along another of their neighbors, Robert Narvel, who would talk all evening about the glorious old times when his was the number one radio show, and who might embarrass her by asking "Remember?" as if she were of the same generation.

And around two joined tables sat a few TV industry characters like Brian Uxworthy, and that British star, Adam Orsen, who was the guest moderator on "Guesswork" the night he alluded to a certain similarity between her and June Fleming. Her own manager, Cy Winters, who looked more than ever like a small boy in long pants, was as usual munching something, and some assorted table-crashers who had drifted in around them, sat on empty chairs while the legitimate occupants were dancing. It was not a crowd Doriana would really normally enjoy. But it was late and the place was jammed, and she and Arlen were glad to take advantage of the invitation the Tassiters had practically forced on Doriana yesterday and join their party. One could not expect an extra table added here, when there was hardly room for a pin on the floor.

"Can I tell him it's all right with you? I mean, doing 'Hobby' next week?" insisted Brian. "I could bet my life you guessed who Lily Byron was from the word go. That frying pan bit and 'Now I'm really in a stew.' You had the studio audience roaring with laughter as usual," he recalled, and started to laugh himself.

So maybe she had overdone the bit; she must be more subtle, more careful. A loud record interrupted the conversation.

"How about it?" said Arlen, resplendent in a plum velvet suit and pink ruffled shirt, looking at her invitingly.

"Why don't you ask Brian's daughter to dance?" she suggested.

While he appeared to be weighing the idea, a tall, very young man with an Afghan hound's haircut approached their table, and Arlen, pulling the girl by the arm from her chair, beat him to it. She was the proverbial ugly duckling, smiling guilelessly, exposing her braces. Her thin, long and sweaty face was framed by dark hair that looked like chicken feathers, thought Doriana. But the girl had a beautiful trim body compensated with plump falsies that did not bounce when she gyrated and twirled, and a pair of good legs. Arlen and the girl remained near the table, showing off, and momentarily Brian proudly watched his offspring.

"About that other show," he turned back to Doriana, "it's a new game show I've been whipping into shape for some time. A quotation show with a permanent all-girl panel. I have June Fleming and Val Bing all sewed up for it, and I was hoping to get you, but I'd read in one of the trades that you'd be away on location in Rome, so I regretfully couldn't plan on you. But now that you're here—"

"Who can't make it?" she asked, ignoring his clumsy explanation.

"Grace Turner and Lucia Fontaine," he said lamely. "But I'd be delighted if you agreed to step in. Not only because you'd be saving my life, but because I honestly believe that you'd be perfect for it. I recall that you seemed familiar with most of the quotes on that old 'Quips and Quotes' show."

Although she didn't relish the reference to the "old" "Quips and Quotes" weekly telecast, too old to her liking to be remembered with her in it, she was interested, and, forgetting that she was not supposed to be able to hear in this din, bent a little closer to Brian. "Tell me more." She was no longer breathless.

"It's something like 'Code Cue' but instead of a word the two competing contestants are handed the same quotations whose source they must try to get their respective celebrity partner-panelist to identify. It's network, natch, and I've got a sponsor lined up, but I'm still taking the kinks out of the format."

She liked the idea. She was good on quotes. It was a radio show, much older than "Quips and Quotes" some years before the advent of television, which Brian Uxworthy, a relatively young producer, had probably forgotten or maybe even never heard about, also dealing with quotes, that had her try to memorize *Bartlett's Familiar Quotations* from Abercrombie to Zola. Even then, as a young beginner she had the same determination and the same instinctive skill, later honed to perfection, to simulate total recall and a wealth of knowledge by cramming the answers. Except that then, instead of getting the questions in advance from a manager like "Little Cow," she had to buy the information from a freckled young jerk, an assistant to somebody's assistant, who was in charge of selecting the quotes used on the air. She did not recall his name but she vividly remembered his dingy little room with an always unmade bed in which she paid the price of the break, one of the early slimy stepping stones to her fame and success. It was too many years ago to want to remember; too many lean years of hard work and failure before her eventual motion picture stardom, the time of Jaguars and unlimited bank accounts, of luxurious triplexes and golden bathroom fixtures, and finally her marriage to Hugh. . . . She shook off her reminiscences.

"It sounds like a marvelous idea," she said, taking a sip of her Mimosa. "Who'd be the fourth?"

Brian Uxworthy's face became even longer when he puckered his lips, putting a long finger against them. "Shhh or some Madison Avenue creep will try to shove his playmate of the moment down my throat," he said, looking worried.

The music stopped for a while, but the hot beat seemed to keep hammering against her eardrums. She was developing a splitting headache. Then, almost immediately, the guitars as if restored by a brief rest, sounded off with renewed vigor.

At that long-ago time, when the radio quotation show provided her with her first big break, she had the same drive and looks, so indispensable in the arduous climb up the slippery flagpole of success. But there was also something else. The robust vitality of youth that never had her end up with a headache after a sleepless night. And the boundless energy that never deserted her, even after nightlong exhilarating rhumbas, sambas and mambos, compared with which the gyrations that Arlen and that Uxworthy girl were at again, looked like a passionless exhibition of children imitating sensuality.

There were also the powerful orgasms, unhampered by either moral reservations, fear of pregnancy or of catching clap. Nor were her responses affected by a total lack of attraction, as with that colorless young man who bought her with quotation answers. She had contempt for him, and yet he had given her a taste of joyous orgasms and the realization of her sexuality. Now and then she could still recapture moments of sexual ecstasy with Arlen, all male without yet being a man, the handsome stag who didn't know the meaning of love but whom she loved and whose mad passions rejuvenated her own, the kind of excitement she had never felt with Hugh; dear Hugh whose urge to make love with her lasted longer than his erections.

If only she could have Hugh's wisdom, and instead of perching on this uncomfortable chair, go home and relax in an old-fashioned chair ilke Hugh's and doze away her headache. But that would be like resigning from life itself. To get up now and leave would be leaving behind not just a noisy, smoke-filled place and people she really did not like, but another kind of Shangri-la, a world of the young she must cling to, belong to, to stay young herself. . . .

Abruptly Doriana realized that the whole table was staring at her. She came back to reality when the disco beat stopped, like someone falling into an exhausted sleep in front of a blaring TV set brusquely awakened by a sudden silence.

"It's for you," said Cy, pointing to a waiter patiently stand-ing with a folded note in his extended hand.

"Thank you," Doriana said accepting the note. So one more autograph request. "Where are you going? Wait," she called after the young waiter who had already disappeared in the crowd. Well, somebody was out of luck. Unless the autograph hound would come by later to claim it personally. She unfolded the sheet of paper. The message was written in elaborate italics, obviously to disguise somebody's hand-writing. She read the note easily, despite the disco's dim lighting.

"Something wrong?" Brian asked her.

"They haven't served you with a subpoena?" quipped Cy, approaching her, and sat down, carefully pulling up his baggy pants at the knees.

"No, everything's fine."

"This reminds me that you never said a word about the last two checks I sent you," Cy added.

"I don't recall getting any checks from you lately."

"You got them all right. You endorsed and cashed them."

Doriana had no time to think about that now. Perhaps it was the new wave of molten sounds that sweeping the room bounced the bodies back onto the dance floor; or maybe it was just her fatigue combined with all those Mimosas; or simply the content of the note that she stared at uncompre-hendingly for a moment before it suddenly became clear in its brutality, but momentarily she lost control.

> *It was an old, old, old, old lady*
> *And a boy that was about twenty-three;*
> *And the way that they played together*
> *Was beautiful to see.*

So she was playing the quotation game even before Brian Uxworthy had premiered his television show.

She crumpled the note in her suddenly clammy hand. It was of course a paraphrase of Henry Cuyler Bunner's "One,

Two, Three." How the sense of this charming 19th-century stanza about an old woman and a three-and-a-half-year-old boy changed in the wicked twisting of words aimed at her and the boyish-looking Arlen. She had trouble keeping tears out of her eyes. How cruel, spiteful and mean.

She drained her once again refilled glass, and the Mimosa tasted strangely bitter. Who wrote this nasty note? Was it Valerie Bing whom she ran into at the entrance? Valerie might still resent her for the repartee of hers on "Chicken Coop" when she had made a fool of Val. Who else hated her so savagely?

If instead of concentrating on people close to her table Doriana had scrutinized the other end of the room, the even more overcrowded side where she would not expect to recognize a soul, just as she wouldn't expect to know anyone in the roped-off curious crowds at a gala premiere, if she could only see the small table pinned against the opposite wall, now securely screened from her by the forest of swaying and gyrating humanity on the dance floor, and recognize a pair of eyes constantly staring in her direction, how easily she might have solved not only the riddle of the cruel message, but so many future problems that were spawning somewhere to invade her life.

Twenty-Two

Perhaps it was risky, but Noelle couldn't resist the compulsion to watch Doriana read the note and see the anguish that she anticipated her stinging paraphrase was bound to provoke. She had sent the note while Ben was in the men's room, and had tipped the waiter well to forget who the note came from. It was so nice suddenly not to need to count money. There was plenty left where this five-dollar bill came from.

She regretted her impulse only briefly when she panicked meeting Arlen's eyes as he was dancing by with a surprisingly ugly teenager, but relaxed instantly, remembering that while she knew every minute detail of Arlen's handsome features, he had really never laid eyes on her. And even if he had. . . .

For the hundredth time on this eventful day, she allowed the feeling of intoxicating happiness to take over. Nobody could possibly ever recognize the monster that she had been in the radiant creature she felt she had become. Even Ben, whom she knew intimately, who knew her inside out, literally, remained speechless. After removing her dressing, she had triumphantly turned toward him to show what was supposed to be a bruised and swollen face after complicated plastic surgery. Vaguely she realized that it was not only this new nose that even swollen as it was, was so beautiful and made her so different. Neither was it the remarkable space between her now unobstructed dark-green eyes that she no longer hesitated dressing up with false eyelashes. And not even her other facial features that had all at once emerged as if at the touch of a miraculous wand.

It was her happiness, which continually made her bare her small even teeth in an unaccustomed warm smile and

128

that had torn from her eyes the veil of secret resentment, distrust and frustrations, that had really brought about the truly significant change in her appearance. It made nearly everybody turn to look at her admiringly. Perhaps it was the excitement of holding in his arms this new and strangely alluring girl whom he knew and yet did not know, and not fond solicitude, that accounted for Ben's trying to talk her out of going to the disco so soon following surgery.

Possibly if Noelle could see Doriana's expression at that very moment, she would exult even more, although Doriana's thoughts were not on her secretary but on the sex maniac about whom the nasty note she had crushed in her hand had somehow reminded her again. Not that this deliberately cruel insinuation could be from him. He lusted for her, he admired her, he certainly didn't hate her. But she couldn't shake off the idea that nothing was to prevent him from maybe coming near her and rubbing himself against her in this tightly packed sardine can of a room on the dance floor, on her way to the john or on her way out. Maybe he brushed against her in the crowded public elevators, in the streets or in TV studios. Was he here now, watching her every move?

She peered at the crowd around her. Which one was he? This thin bespectacled young man in a white turtleneck, his hands in the pockets of his pants? Or that fat redhead in a psychedelic jacket topped by an elaborate necklace? Or the man at the next table rocking himself on the back legs of his chair and sticking out his long legs, his feet in soft-soled shoes like those of her molester at the hospital impersonating a doctor? If only she could hear their voices, she would instantly recognize the one belonging to the man to whom she had listened so tensely with her eyes covered by heavy bandages. But what would that change? Would she take drastic action as any normal person might these days when rape was a real threat? . . .

"Okay, I know when I'm not wanted," Cy Winters said, rising and leaving her with an offended pout on his face, with all that loose skin participating in a forced scowl.

Doriana suddenly realized that her manager must have

been talking to her, but it was too late to stop him. Besides, his seat next to her was already taken by a very tipsy Carol Nemm who had flopped into it with an amazingly sonorous sound for her thin derriere. Carol looked older than usual, and Doriana thought that Carol was like a plot of grazed-out land, with nothing to expect from or show for.

"I'm drunk," said Carol, "but mostly I'm pooped."

"Why don't you go home?" Doriana asked. She herself longed to escape from this mod madhouse where everything looked like a parody of normal life, with the artificial sounds and movements, and the synthetic look of gaiety that she was forcing on her own face.

Carol was not given a chance to answer. Arlen and a group of young men pushed their way to the table.

"Doriana, we're getting up a skiing party in the morning. Sensational, eh? You're with us, aren't you, little girl?"

"Don't call her 'little girl,' don't encourage her follies," tossed June Fleming who sideswiped Doriana on the move, and who really should have kept quiet, for she was rather ludicrous herself in three-inch platform shoes and a short dress that looked like a long blouse, and wearing the most preposterously huge chandelier earrings. And Cy, who had reappeared from behind the crowd, apparently forgetting that condoning such digs was not in his client's interest, took his revenge by laughing.

"George has a lodge in the Adirondacks. You remember George?" Arlen went on excitedly. "How about a spin now? George would like to dance with you, too."

Doriana felt too tired to lift her head high enough to look up at George's face. She noticed four buttons on the rather short sleeves of his jacket, buttons that unbuttoned—another fellow patron of Savile Row. She wanted to dance. She really should be seen on the floor, she thought. And she would have liked to go skiing in the morning. She could take something to boost her energy. No. She would consider joining them if they were heading for some luxury winter sports resort where she could make her entrance to the lounge or bar in her stunning new Valentino ski suit, carrying her monogrammed light plastic skis not intended for skiing. But she could picture the probably isolated lodge where she would be cooped up most of the time recovering her breath after climbing up some wild slope without a ski lift.

"I've got something urgent to talk over with my manager, we'll dance a little later," she told Arlen, not noticing that Cy was gone again. The boisterous young men walked away before she could identify George who owned the lodge she would never go to, and she was startled feeling Carol's hand on her knee.

"I'm bushed," Carol repeated.

"Why don't you go home?" she suggested again.

Carol heaved a loud sigh, as if letting off steam under pressure. "I can't."

"You need help to get a cab?"

"Nope, it's not that. I'm scared. It's so lonely there. I have an heirloom grandfather clock in my room. I remember back home in Ohio, when I was a teenager waiting for my date to show up, I used to listen to its ticktacks and they were always so clear and cheerful. The passage of time then meant only the expected approach of something new, exciting and lovely. Now I'm afraid to listen to the ticking of my clock when I get back to my room late at night. It's like the noise of a hammer already nailing down the lid of my coffin."

"Carol, you *are* drunk."

"I can understand why Pascin threw his grandfather clock out the window. One of these days I'll do the same with mine."

And mixed with the pity she felt for Carol there was surprise that without having an art buff husband like Hugh who constantly talked about artists and art, Carol knew about Pascin, the insatiable painter of women. Maybe she did some reading during the long stretches between jobs and remembered the frightened man who felt old in his mid-forties and finally took his own life after attempting to stop time by stopping the hands of his grandfather clock.

And Doriana thought uneasily that she, too, shared the

crazed artist's phobia, for there were no timepieces in her house. It was another easy subterfuge to escape as much as possible any reminders of passing seconds that grew into years before one could count the minutes and hours. This quirk had immense drawbacks of course, for if she could afford the reputation of being incorrigibly late privately, it would prove deadly professionally. It fell to her entourage to keep an eye on the timetables and schedules, freeing her from the hateful enslavement to the clock.

She looked around. At the other end of the table, oblivious to the infernal noise, Anne Tassiter was already singing her blues, or maybe following the monotonous wailing of the electric guitars, with her husband probably boom-booming on the imaginary bass, for he was plucking at the invisible chords in the air. And two men, whose faces Doriana knew but could not label with names, were listening raptly, clapping their hands in tempo. Cy was back and wolfing a thick sandwich. And Brian Uxworthy was listening with a bored look to Robert Narvel who was whispering in his ear, probably tales of his past cinematic glory that had evaporated like a mirage long ago, together with the radio waves of his equally long-forgotten show. And Arlen and his young friends were still doing the double bump, the hustle and any other disco invention that caught the group's fancy.

There were two long-haired youthful couples, all four looking alike in their unisex clothes, with slips of paper in their hands, making their way to the table, maybe some autograph seekers, or maybe bringing her more disturbing quotations, and she determinedly sprang to her feet.

"Cy," she called loudly to her manager, "please tell Arlen Redfore that I went home. I have a terrible headache."

"Will do," Cy called back, and waved his hand without rising.

"Come on," Doriana told Carol, "get up, pal. You're gonna spend the night at my place. My husband is away, and there's plenty of room. And there isn't a single damn clock for you to be afraid of there."

Twenty-Three

Doriana watched Carol drop wearily into Hugh's chair, and was nearly impelled to stop her, as if it were improper for someone other than Hugh to occupy it, but said nothing. She wasn't a fetishist like Hugh, who attached such importance to inanimate things, as if objects had their own conscious life. Perhaps that's why he collected antiques, which according to him held the spell and emotional experiences of past lives.

Carol, slowly turning her head from side to side, lingeringly surveyed the Renoir, a Manet, two ultra-contemporary Chagalls and a Pollock on the walls. And by the look in her attentive eyes, Doriana knew that Carol was aware of the true value of the accumulating collection with which Hugh was filling their house. This assortment of artistic treasures reflected Hugh's taste in art and the understanding of a wealthy and thoughtful husband who knew that in present days these gifts were as much appreciated by a woman as diamonds used to be.

"After that thundering herd at the disco your place is sheer heaven," said Carol.

She had on one of Doriana peignoirs, the new Pucci, the one Doriana would have preferred to wear herself, but which she could not prevent Carol from slipping on after sliding open the doors of her huge dressing-room closet and inviting Carol to help herself.

"Yes, wasn't it noisy?" Doriana agreed, listening to the tranquillity of the apartment. It must be after four, since Charles had gone up to his quarters without waiting for her to come home. This was her standing order to him—not to

133

stay up after three A.M. It was really not necessary to wait up for her at all. There was something indecent in keeping a tired man up just for the purpose of opening the front door one could so easily open with one's key. Besides, the more time Charles and Louise spent in their double bed upstairs, the sooner they would forget their differences.

"My couple's feuding. I wonder how long they can go on sleeping in the same bed without talking to each other," she voiced her thoughts to Carol.

"It all depends . . ." Carol began, then started to laugh.

Carol did not seem sad or afraid any more and she did not look intoxicated either. But the flattering indirect lighting of the library did nothing for her, for the network of small, shallow wrinkles spread its betraying webs around her eyes.

"How about that drinkie we came to the library for?" said Carol.

Doriana, who smiled politely, was already beginning to regret her impulse to bring the frightened and lonely woman to her house. Perhaps it was because Carol no longer looked like someone in need of help, and certainly not like someone who might do something desperate if left alone with her loud grandfather clock nailing the seconds into her coffin.

"Well, how about it?" Carol repeated.

"Sure, sorry, darling," Doriana said, and crossed to the bar. Charles must have waited up for her quite late. The ice in the bucket had not even begun to melt, and a fresh bottle of Hugh's brandy she told Charles to open, just in case Hugh returned to New York while she was out, was half full. So her couple had not yet reconciled.

"Actually, being on speaking terms or not has nothing to do with making love," Carol returned to the old topic. "I remember how once my father gave my mother a terrible beating, I don't know why, but afterwards he didn't talk to her for months, which didn't interfere with his having sex with her. I was only six or seven then, and I thought it was another kind of corporal punishment. We lived in a tiny flat back in Cleveland, and I slept on a couch in the dining room, with the door to their bedroom always wide open."

"And they never caught you spying on them?" Doriana asked absently, bringing Carol a Scotch on the rocks and mixing herself a Mimosa on second thought.

"They didn't have to catch me, I gave myself away. One day after I'd broken a half-full bottle of my father's booze, he grabbed me and roared, 'What do you think I'll do to you now, you brat?!' And terrified I asked if he'd spank me or get on top of me and jump up and down like when he punished my mother. You understand that I got my bottom paddled. That other kind of 'punishment' I got some years later, when I was twelve or thirteen, from a vacuum-cleaner door-to-door salesman."

"You mean, he raped you?"

"Not exactly. You might say it was 'an assault with a friendly weapon.' I don't think I fought him off too hard. I was terribly flattered."

"Flattered?"

"Yes, because when I was young I believed that when a man wanted to sleep with a woman it was a tribute to her beauty and charm. Today I know better, of course. I know that all any man needs is a hole, a socket. But naturally you, Doriana, couldn't understand that."

"Why couldn't I? I hear and read all the time about all sorts of women being raped."

"Sure, sure, but things that happen to others are quite different from what they are when they happen to us."

"I was practically raped myself a few months ago," Doriana blurted out before she could check herself.

"But then it was somebody who was crazy about you. Right?"

"That's what he said."

"He must have been. All men are crazy about you. How do you do it?"

"Do what?"

"Keep so young. Young on the outside. We're all the same

age inside. We all come to that conclusion as we get older, but it was Gertrude Stein who's on record to have said it."

"You know all about cosmetic surgery, you were the one who gave me Dr. Orgood's name, remember?"

"It's got nothing to do with plastic surgery, lover. I've had plenty of it myself, as you know. Naturally, they've pulled out your chin and smoothed out the crow's feet around your eyes. But it's not that. There's some magic about the kind of youth that emanates from you that can't be faked. Doriana, for the love of God, tell me how you do it, what's your secret?!"

Carol jumped up from the comfortable chair and saw her own reflection in the mirror over the fireplace. She looked almost haggard. But she was finally so close to the miraculous formula that her hostess somehow possessed. Would she share it with her?

"I wish I had the answer. If I had one, perhaps I wouldn't feel so empty," Doriana said.

"Empty? You? Beautiful and successful, you got what you wanted out of life."

"Successful, yes. But one can be successful without having achieved anything worthwhile, just as one can be an achiever without knowing popular success," she said.

But even if she had achieved anything, a whole lifetime had passed attaining it and it could not make up for the sadness of aging. . . . "No memory of having starred atones for later disregard, nor keeps the end from being hard," as Robert Frost had so mournfully summed it up.

She got up, approached the window and glanced outside. The slushy, dark Central Park was asleep, but the moon was out, wearing a narrow white blindfold, as if refusing to look at the Park's stripped trees. But somehow since the astronaut's walking on the moon, it had lost some of its mystique.

"Pour me another drink," said Carol, sitting down again. "Maybe you could use another of your vitamin shots yourself."

Perhaps she did need another Mimosa. She refilled both glasses, and while passing the mirror glanced at herself, but it reflected a serene face which did not reveal the contradictory emotions that were tearing her apart.

She had a sudden compulsion to tell Carol about her weariness and frustration, with which all the sure characteristics of youth—youthful wonder, self-confidence and hope for the future—could not survive. Why did she feel like confiding in this pathetic woman? Maybe because Carol who always talked so freely about herself never betrayed anybody else's confidences? Or possibly because she needed a friend herself. A friend to whom she could talk without any reservations, to admit her weakness and all the doubts and anxieties that year after year, compounding regret upon regret, mistake upon mistake, were the price she had to pay for her synthetic youthfulness.

"I don't see how you could improve on your life even if you could start over again," Carol said, interrupting Doriana's melancholy thoughts.

"Maybe if I had a child of my own I wouldn't feel so frustrated," she said. "A child in whom I would remain young forever. The other day I read or heard somewhere somebody saying or quoting someone that the only true link to one's lost youth was through one's children."

Doriana sighed, and the depth of her sigh made Carol gaze at her inquisitively before answering.

"Oh, I wonder. A couple of weeks ago I met a young doctor at a party and we got to talking about famous show biz people and whether fame brought them some kind of immortality, which of course it really doesn't. Look at Robert Narvel. Why, with all his past fame he's already deader than any mummy. Anyway, the conversation shifted to survival in one's kids, something I didn't even understand then, but figured out later at home; something to the effect that if you had a child you would be diluted in it with each new generation. There would be only half of you in your kid, the other half would derive from the father. And only half of the half in your grandchild. What would your survival become a few generations later, provided the chain isn't broken? You'd be cheated worse than you feel cheated now."

Perhaps what Carol was telling her about children gave her unconscious comfort, as if arguments against having them could really console her for not having any, like Gore Vidal's remark that marriage with its procreative purpose was becoming obsolete because of overpopulation. And she thought without the usual sense of her own inadequacy about being a "non-parent" and didn't need to seek solace in thinking of her fosterlings who would be diluting somebody else's genes.

And all at once it took her back many, many years, when she was determined not to have pregnancies interfere with her budding career, long before the boon of the Pill. How panicky she got on a few occasions that she might be pregnant. And she also remembered how shocked she was and how passionately she began yearning for a child of her own when she was told after that emergency operation, following a bungled abortion, that she would never become pregnant again.

Carol no longer appeared agitated, but her face was still screwed up in a multitude of fine lines. Was Carol going through the same hell she was going through herself?

"Anyway, the question of survival is only incidental in our case, I think," Carol continued. "What we fear mostly is not the finality of death but the state of aging leading up to it."

Before the meaning of what Carol was saying had sunk in, it struck Doriana that Carol unhesitatingly put both of them into the same category. Two aging women. And this feeling of revolt grew irrationally stronger from second to second even though what Carol said was basically true. But there must be a difference between them! Not only because, after all, they were so dissimilar; not only because her own beautiful smooth skin was so unlike Carol's—an aged skin that was waterlogged despite its apparent dryness, a skin without elasticity that once stretched could never again spring back, that no cosmetic operation could help, even if Carol could afford one—but simply because Carol was chronologically much older than she. The only similarity, the only bond between her, Carol and millions of other aging people, who were frantically trying to shake the dust off the accumulating years, was that they all felt and agonized the same way.

Twenty-Four

Carol kept staring at her, and Doriana abruptly became aware that exhaustion and all that nipping had put her in an almost hallucinatory state of mind in which reality and fantasy had merged, and she made an effort to concentrate.

"I disagree with the philosophy that time brings beauty of transformation to everything. Aside from my personal fear of aging, I find the changes it makes in all living things unaesthetic. It's a lie that aging can be beautiful. How could anyone believe that?" she said.

"Walt Whitman did. 'Women sit or move to and fro—some old, some young; the young are beautiful—but the old ones are more beautiful than the young!' "

Doriana gazed at Carol with naked admiration now. She herself could have quoted a few more tributes to old women. But she was an expert, and, God knows, she had paid for this knowledge during all those hard times when she fought her way through the thick volumes of quotations to the unlimited horizons of future triumphs. But Carol?

"Doriana, darling, you're so surprised by my quoting Walt Whitman that your mouth's hanging open," Carol said, laughing.

"You're imagining things."

Doriana was really embarrassed that Carol saw through her, but her protests did not fool Carol.

"It's quite simple, though. Not that I'm anything near being an intellectual. But many years ago I crammed for months trying to prepare for that old Jerry show, the same show that you finally landed. I was no competition for you. But I've got total recall, and all those quotes stuck in my stupid head for good. Don't you remember another of Walt

140

Whitman's reflections on aging, 'Youth, large, lusty, loving—
Youth, full of grace, force, fascination. Do you know that
Old Age may come after you, with equal grace, force, fasci-
nation?' "

"I wonder how old Walt Whitman was himself when he
wrote his Leaves of Grass?" Doriana said pensively.

"What's the dif? That's how he felt about maturity, and
he's not alone."

"Yes, of course," Doriana agreed, brightening. "How about
'A good and true woman is said to resemble a Cremona fiddle
—age but increases its worth and sweetens its tone.' "

And while she recited, she knew that her voice lacked conviction, just as Carol's voice perhaps did not ring true, either,
as if there were an uncertainty, a hidden question in an
affirmative answer of a TV show contestant not absolutely
sure of himself.

"That's beautiful," said Carol. "It's wonderful how gifted
people like Oliver Wendell Holmes can put their ideas into
such simple lines, and how well you speak them. But despite
these comforting words, I'm so enraged by the thought of
getting old that, to borrow from Nabokov, I feel like 'picket-
ing nature.' "

Again Doriana marveled at Carol's unexpected erudition.

"You do remember quite a few quotations," she compli-
mented her guest. "You'd be a cinch on that new quotation
show—" She nearly bit her tongue, but it was too late.

"What show?" Carol asked very quickly, and her wrinkles
seemed more deeply etched.

Doriana thought only a few seconds. True, she promised
Brian Uxworthy not to breathe a word about his projected
new show. And, of course, his idea was to get such celebrity
panelists as June Fleming or herself, and not an obscure
unknown like Carol Nemm. But Carol was desperate. And
with her knack for quotations she would fit in perfectly. It
would only be fair for her to help Carol now to repay her
for that show she had unwittingly taken away from Carol
many years ago. How bewildering and unpredictable human

life was. If by some chance it were Carol and not she who had gotten the job on that old quotation show, who knows, perhaps it would have been Carol who would now be a celebrity and she, Doriana Delor, a struggling nobody. And anyway, it would probably be Carol's last and only opportunity if she succeeded to help her. Should she give it a try? Yes, of course she must.

"It actually doesn't matter. I'm considering taking a little vacation," Carol added.

It was no use, she thought wearily. It had been over a year since she got a bit part on a TV soap, and it had been six months now since she had stopped trying altogether. Luck came easier when you didn't try hard for it. Just as that last TV bit fell from the sky when she was surviving by baby-sitting in her neighborhood for Peter Cooper Village friends, when she had given up completely looking for TV work and didn't even try to find a new agent in New York after her old one had dropped her. Maybe if she asked Doriana she could help a little that capricious bitch luck they they had misnamed Lady, who had turned her back on her lately. Doriana was such a kind, generous soul. Maybe that's what gave Doriana's beautiful face the reflection of an inner warmth, the glowing warmth of compassion that made her beauty so strikingly different, so unlike the superficial attractiveness of so many others.

Doriana was watching Carol's changing expression. Why did Carol's face again freeze into its usual vacant mask of hyper-stretched skin? Alone her eyes, after losing their haunted look, suddenly were brimming with warmth. Had Carol started insisting on knowing what new show she was talking about and had started begging her to use her influence to get her on the panel, she might possibly have turned her down. But the obvious resignation, the lassitude and the disenchantment with it all that Carol could hardly conceal behind her proud lie about a vacation, had made up her mind for her. And to hell with her promise to Brian.

"Brian Uxworthy is planning a new panel show built

around famous quotes. Something like the old Jerry format you mentioned a moment ago."

"You were really great on that one. A real quiz kid."

The memory of the freckled slob with whom she slept to get in advance the quotations picked for that old radio show didn't interfere with Doriana's sense of sudden lightheartedness. Quiz kid. That's what Carol called her. A child. Carol must be even older than she thought if she remembered her as a mere "kid." Presently a little suspicion slipped into her mind. Did Carol say it deliberately to butter her up? . . . But Carol's hand was trembling slightly while she was finishing her second straight Scotch. Maybe she was hungry. Maybe that's why she drank. Alcohol was food, even if, like sugar, it was loaded with empty calories, which gave energy without nutrition.

"I'll do my best to get you on the panel with me, if the show materializes," she promised, and, watching Carol's instantly revived face, did not regret committing herself.

"How could you? A bit in a soap, yes. But a panelist alongside you? You've got to be kidding."

"If Brian wants me badly enough, he'll take both of us."

"I know that you have a lot of pull with the producers. But don't stretch it too far."

Again she glanced warily at Carol. Was she daring her? But of course not. It was this stinking business with its constant suspicions and intrigue that had poisoned her mind and made her doubt the sincerity of every friendly word.

"Don't worry about me, darling," she said. "Let's think about you."

"I don't even have an agent."

"You don't need one. Cy Winters, who I'm told is always bragging how well he uses his horse-trading talents, will take care of it. It will give him a chance to prove his boasts. You want Doriana Delor? Okay. You can get her, but in a package with my other client, Carol Nemm."

Momentarily Doriana felt somewhat uncomfortable about her own bit of boasting. But Carol had apparently failed to notice it. For the first time in all the years Doriana had known her, Carol smiled happily and her misty eyes, that seemed to be looking far beyond the windows, had a dreamy expression.

"I'll drink another one to that," Carol said.

Then, while Doriana went to the bar to refill her glass, Carol said in a low voice, apparently unsure of herself, "If you'd like me to spend the night with you, I wouldn't mind . . . I mean, to sleep with you in your bed."

Startled, Doriana dropped the ice tongs and turned around. Carol also got up from the low chair and was standing, the beige negligee open, and exposing a surprisingly lovely, trim body. A starvation diet had its points, Doriana reflected. Why did Carol make this suggestion? Was she still feeling scared and lonely? Or was she afraid that the sudden vision of possible rebirth on TV would fade as soon as she let Doriana out of her sight? No, she must be imagining things; she was too much of a man's woman for Carol to suppose that she might consider lesbianism, even if Carol were a young and appetizing morsel like Vardi's former child-bride whom she had met in Barcelona while making a movie in Spain.

"All I'm aspiring to is a good night's rest. I really need it," she said, and thought she read disappointment in Carol's eyes, and because of it decided to make sure that Carol got it straight.

"We have a guest room always ready. You won't be disturbed even if you sleep till dinnertime. But do ring for Louise, the maid, when you wake up and want your coffee."

This ought to do it, she thought. She was practically dismissing Carol, if indeed Carol had sex in mind. But Carol, despite the open negligee slipping from her shoulders, looked quite innocent. And her smile was only warm and friendly, and her eyes were looking straight at her, as if trying to read in hers.

Perhaps she's not all that old, Doriana mused. She felt herself blushing once again under Carol's scrutinizing eyes that had lost their customary dullness. Carol was telling her something, and she tried to focus on what she was saying.

". . . but content myself with wishing that I may be one of those whose follies may cease with their youth. . . ."

So maybe Carol did hint at an affair between them even though she did not seem embarrassed by Doriana's rejection, and stretched as if she, too, were only tired and longing for rest.

"William Pitt, Earl of Chatham," Doriana echoed mechanically, forgetting her inhibition, and they both broke into laughter.

Twenty-Five

Brian Uxworthy's brainchild premiered in TV's midseason doldrums and all concerned were unhappy with both the way the show was going and the ratings.

"It's this lousy weather," Cy Winters opined. "It's crazy. It just doesn't act like it's February. One week it's 70 above, the next it's a blizzard and 10 below."

Cy had unexpectedly put on a few pounds and it gave him a certain self-assurance he often lacked before. Or maybe it was the fact that he had talked Uxworthy into taking on Carol Nemm as a panelist that made him feel like a giant that somehow, despite his managing one of the biggest stars, he had never seemed to be in the eyes of the trade. It actually was quite a feat, and now "Little Cow" sounded off on a variety of subjects.

Perhaps one of the reasons why the new quotation show was lame was that Brian Uxworthy, instead of limiting himself to producing it, wanted to run the whole shebang. He interfered with everything and everybody. Not only did he bother the graphic arts director and the lighting crew, but he also ruffled the feathers of the show's English moderator, Adam Orsen. Adam, following his successful guest shots on American TV last year, had stayed on in New York to try a brand new career in the States on Uxworthy's "The Bright Belles." But still worse was Uxworthy's interference with the selection of the quotation material itself. It was an open secret that Brian had suddenly become preoccupied with death after a mild heart attack just before the first telecast. And this obsession invariably influenced his choice of quotes.

As far as Doriana was concerned it seemed a downright conspiracy against her. Possibly it was only self-consciousness,

146

but she had trouble smiling and being witty when she was handed a card with quotations such as Robert Herrick's "New things succeed as former things grow old," as if everybody in the audience stared at her and related the quote to her. She knew it was absurd, especially since she was as usual telegenic in full color, but she couldn't help fretting and hating Brian Uxworthy.

The show was in its third week when Doriana was handed a note marked "urgent" just as the quotation card was passed on to her by Adam Orsen. And since the involved format of the show Uxworthy had originally planned finally ended up in the panelists' accumulating points by simply naming the authors of the quotes on the cards, she read the card just before she read the urgent note. The Alexander Pope quotation was of course another of Brian Uxworthy's gems. Aware of Brian's recent absorption with aging, she memorized anything on the subject in bed every night, that is, when she slept alone.

"For gold we love the impotent and old, And heave, and pant, and kiss, and cling, for gold," Doriana read on the card. In a moment the quote would be flashed on the special board.

Yes, of course, it was Alexander Pope's from the prologue of "The Wife of Bath." She thought she heard some laughter in the audience, and hated both Brian Uxworthy and Adam Orsen a little more. People remembered her mansion in Beverly Hills and her much-publicized luxurious Manhattan triplex, her showy cars, diamonds and furs. Everything she had, most of which she bought with her own hard-earned money, was attributed to the generosity of her husbands and lovers. For gold we love. . . . Could it be that Uxworthy used this particular excerpt and Orsen handed it to her on purpose? To get some laughs? It was she who got practically all the quotes on aging and venal love. Why she and not Carol Nemm who was many years her senior? And why not Valerie Bing who was no youngster either and was known for her avarice?

Adam Orsen became involved in a joke with June Fleming —something about her emerald heart locket and, as usual, whenever they mentioned her trademark, June wouldn't allow the topic to die for a while, even if Uxworthy pointed to the second hand on the big studio clock and frantically waved his arms.

Suddenly Doriana remembered the note the usher had slipped her just as she walked out in front of the cameras. She was ready for the moderator, but now she had a second or two to glance at the note. The sheet of paper was folded in four and she quickly opened it. It might be an urgent telephone message from Hugh.

But it was not. It was unmistakably written by the hand of the same person who had sent her that abrasive quotation at Rexine's some weeks before. "Old women should not seek to be perfumed," said the note in her slightly trembling fingers, and it was not only the meaning of Plutarch's words that threw her off balance, but it was also the fact that Arlen had just given her a giant bottle of Femme perfume. Unless it was one of those uncanny coincidences, for who could know about it?

"Your answer, please," said Adam Orsen's Oxonian voice, and by the now completed quotation on the electronic blackboard Doriana realized that she must have been lost in thought for at least ten seconds.

She forced herself to concentrate. She knew the answer only seconds ago. She knew it. She knew it. The studio audience was more audible now. Did she again hear amused giggling?

"Five seconds, please."

Doriana was still holding the note in front of her card, and glanced at it, and it stared back at her.

"Plutarch," she said.

"Wrong, sorry. It's not Plutarch's. Miss Nemm, please?"

"Alexander Pope," said Carol and enjoyed the blinking of the green light on her nameplate and the applause of the audience.

"You were jolly close, though," the moderator turned to Doriana. "Both Plutarch's and Pope's names begin with the same initial."

The audience, evidently getting Orsen's implication that she memorized the encyclopedia, loved this, too, and laughed uproariously.

Obviously her antipathy for their moderator was mutual. Valerie, who was notoriously bigoted, had once remarked derisively that "Even though gays supposedly have larger-than-average size pricks, it sure doesn't seem like it in pretty boy Orsen's case who would probably look terrific in drag." He might be a homosexual, Doriana thought, but that of course was his own business and had nothing to do with her dislike for him.

"It must be a coincidence, since I haven't reached the letter 'P' yet," she met the provocation head on as usual, smiling brightly.

And the audience appreciated her retort as much as it did the moderator's sly insinuation.

This was the telling difference between her own showmanship and Carol's performance. Although her protégée rarely missed a quote, she just sat there woodenly, passing up every opportunity for stirring the audience. Carol was definitely small time among such veteran hams as June Fleming, Val Bing and herself whose competitive skirmishes and studied cattiness delighted the crowds. Carol never seemed able to think of an appropriate retort to Val Bing's withering digs, and this of course only encouraged Val to stress as often as possible that the fading newcomer to the star-studded show was as flat mentally as she was in the bosom department. Doriana actually suspected that Val wasn't wearing a bra to call attention to the difference between the liveliness of her opulent breasts and the stiff immobility of poor Carol's falsies. And naturally, surrounded by her three bosomy fellow panelists, Carol looked deflated, even without Valerie's mean antics.

"Why should that lousy whore pick on Carol and not

June Fleming?" Cy commented, when he heard about it. "The only dif between Carol's and June's celebrated boobs is that Carol wears the plastic foam on the outside and June Baby on the inside."

Unavoidably, all of this talk coupled with Valerie's skillfully aimed darts, made Carol not only miserable but so self-conscious that she grew progressively more tense and looked more and more unattractive in contrast with her dazzling teammates on the show, even if she was as well informed as a Rhodes scholar.

It was only when the show was over that Carol crawled out of her deep freeze. After giving autographs to a group of fans in the studio, Doriana found Carol all alone in the dressing room. Carol was slumped dejectedly in front of one of the mirrors, her TV makeup already creamed off, staring at herself, or maybe just thinking about something.

"Tired?" Doriana asked with a twinge of pity.

Carol nodded her head very slowly up and down, up and down. "Hmm, I'm dead beat," she finally said.

"You'll have plenty of time to rest up till the next show. You were really great tonight."

"Come on, you know I bombed," Carol said, continuing to stare at herself in the mirror.

"But you hardly missed a quote."

"So what. Who gives a damn?"

"I do. I thought you cared. Or why the hell are you knocking yourself out cramming those quotations? In fact, you're right. Nothing would happen if you missed a few. You're not working toward a degree, you know."

They were silent for a moment, and Valerie Bing's loud guffaws intruded through the door, and Carol shivered as if from cold.

"Is that stinker Val getting to you with her needling?"

"No, not really. I'm just bone weary of everything. You wouldn't understand, Doriana."

"You bet I don't! You were so anxious to get on this show, even if you didn't say so in so many words. And I practically stuck my neck out to help you get on it. And already, when you're doing so well, you're suddenly fed up with it!" As she spoke, Doriana felt her irritation mounting, replacing the pity and concern for Carol. It all made little sense.

Carol slowly turned to Doriana and gazed at her for a moment, and her face abruptly lit up with a smile that deepened the lines around her mouth.

What a lovely person Doriana was, Carol thought again. Smart and beautiful and so tenderly compassionate. "Don't be mad at me, Doriana. You've been very good to me. Forgive me if I'm letting you down. But I can't go on with this."

"What's the matter with you? Don't you like the show?"

"Sure I do. I haven't forgotten how I daydreamed about a comeback while baby-sitting. No, the term 'comeback' is wrong. I've really never been anything but a failure."

"Then what are you trying to prove?"

"Doriana, you probably aren't aware of it, but I simply can't hack it any more. To worry about a thousand things all the time. To worry that no matter what I might do I could never look glamorous enough to sit alongside any of you. Just to be presentable is a full-time job, and to fret constantly about saying the right things, to remember, when my memory is practically shot. And to be alert, to be quick and easygoing, when all I really long for is to relax and instead of learning quotations watch an old movie on TV or maybe simply sleep. It takes too much out of me. I didn't realize it before, when I was dreaming about living it up, but now I know. You, Doriana, with your pact with whomever it is—God or the devil—wouldn't understand it, but it's really quite simple. It's too late. I'm too old, too old, too old. . . ."

"Oh, be quiet!" Doriana snapped, and rushing to Carol grabbed her by the shoulders and joggled her as if Carol were a recording machine jammed on the same desperate complaint.

"Don't shake her too hard or all her bones will drop out," said a mocking voice from the door.

Startled, Doriana let go of Carol and turned around to face a sarcastic Valerie Bing, who, with arms akimbo, managed to look even more vulgar than usual.

"You kiddies should wait till you get home to settle your differences in your playpen," Valerie continued, and burst into laughter that swayed her heavy breasts.

It was easy to imagine the vicious gossip this bitch Val would start circulating now. Doriana had to do something, say something fast, but her usual knack for instant riposte failed her momentarily.

It was Carol who struck back at Valerie, perhaps because she did not take time to choose the right words, or simply because for once she and her tormentor did not have any camera staring at them with its prying eye. Carol had leaped up from her chair with surprising agility for somebody who felt so old and so tired, and placed herself between Doriana and Valerie. And although Doriana could not see Carol's face, its expression was mirrored in Valerie's whose smile melted into visible apprehension.

"So all my bones would drop out if somebody shook me, eh?! And what about you, you filthy bitch! What if somebody shook *you*? Not bones, because there isn't a decent bone in your whole rotten carcass, but an avalanche of pricks would drop out of you, that's what, you whore!"

"Carol, shut up!" Doriana said with mixed feelings—with fear of this scene getting out of hand, but relishing Val's unmistakable terror.

"I'll overlook this because you're obviously smashed," Valerie finally said, evidently reassured by Doriana's intervention. "But I'm not so sure that any producer, even a charitable guy like Brian Uxworthy, would stand for one panelist calling another names." She stuck her hand in her lowcut dress and corrected the position of her breasts.

"That goes both ways. It would be in everybody's best interest to forget the whole thing," said Doriana, thinking that actually that had been a pretty mild exchange, considering the foul language that generally flew around backstage.

Valerie quickly assessed what the press would make of their brawl should it leak out. Sleeping with quite a few men was one thing. A sexy reputation, even that of a nympho, had never hurt a gal in show business. But the idea of all those joy sticks dropping out of her did not appear either exciting or even appetizing. It would be a different and wonderful story if somebody had said it about Doriana. . . .

"You're so right, DD," she said piously, thinking that the initials also stood for drop dead, "I'm a pro, I believe, even if your friend doesn't seem to, that we in show biz have certain standards to uphold. I'm prepared to forgive and forget." She sat down in front of one of the mirrors and started to fuss with her own face.

Doriana glanced at Carol, fearing a fresh explosion, but evidently all fight had already gone out of her. She was actually smiling, a wan, downcast smile, and, nodding silently, walked out, carrying her large handbag as though it were full of lead.

And as if to give emphasis to this image of resignation, before the door closed on Carol, another image, that of Doriana's transformed secretary, appeared in its open frame —the embodiment of springtime, loveliness and exuberant confidence in all the tomorrows.

Twenty-Six

Doriana stared at the smiling Noelle for a moment, unsure of her reaction. On the one hand, Noelle's presence would unquestionably stop Val Bing from carrying on viciously behind Carol's back. On the other hand, Noelle had been explicitly told never to come to the studio.

It was not instinctive female reluctance of being seen side by side with this pretty nineteen-year-old. What made her nervous was Noelle's special kind of vitality fueled by young faith in the future. Was she, an expert showwoman, subconsciously afraid that this most difficult part to play, the part of youthful enthusiasm, would suddenly become less convincing in the presence of the genuine thing? Noelle required no talent or experience to be convincing, since for her there was no part to play at all.

"Something really important must have come up, or I'm sure you wouldn't be here," Doriana remarked, without hiding her displeasure at Noelle's disregarding orders, but trying to not sound brusque, and smiling for Val's benefit.

"Something has," said Noelle, and smiled back with her brand-new poise. Then, taking advantage of Valerie's bending to pick up a comb she had dropped on the floor, Noelle pointed to her with her chin, continuing to look at Doriana. You really would have it coming if I were to tell out loud what a mess you're in, Noelle thought.

There was a knock on the door and, without waiting even a second, a tall, good-looking usher stuck his head in the door and from behind Noelle looked silently down the still stooping Valerie's exposed cleavage. "There's a call for you, Miss Bing," he announced, when Valerie straightened up.

"So have it put through here," Valerie said, but changed

her mind when the usher's head had already disappeared behind the door. "Wait! Who is it, a guy?" she called, rushing after him.

"Yes, Ma'am, a guy," he said, again ogling Valerie's breasts.

"Tell him to hold it. I'll be there in a sec."

Looking at herself admiringly in the mirror, Valerie ran the comb through her dark hair. "They always cut you off switching the damn calls," she explained, "which means that I might lose my date at '21' in the shuffle."

Both Doriana and Noelle watched her carefully adjust her breasts and check her lipstick. Then she was gone.

"Well, what is it?" Doriana asked, as soon as the door closed behind Valerie, sitting down in front of a mirror, and starting quickly to work on her face.

"Mr. Botain called a while ago. He said his business dinner at the Union League was canceled and that he would be able to pick you up here. He asked me to get in touch with you while he was busy at his first meeting at the Seagram building."

"You could have phoned," Doriana snapped.

"I tried to, but got disconnected every time the receptionist switched the call," Noelle lied, using Valerie Bing's excuse.

"How long ago did Mr. Botain call?"

"About an hour or so, maybe an hour-and-a-half."

Noelle visibly enjoyed Doriana's predicament, but Doriana was too engrossed in removing her own on camera makeup and thinking to notice the look on her secretary's face.

This was a damn complication. After his return from Australia a couple of weeks ago, Hugh had been uncommonly attentive and was around practically all the time. Not that she minded. Actually, she had missed him during his long absence. But when he said he would be busy that evening with two important business meetings, the second a business dinner that would in all likelihood last till quite late, she had agreed to have dinner with Arlen who had been begging her for a date since Hugh's return to New York. So now both of them would be calling for her here. After months of maneuvering to keep them apart, she finally would have to confront them together. Maybe it might be a good idea to pretend one of her bad headaches and retreat before either appeared.

"Mr. Redfore is already here," Noelle said casually, but well to the point, as if she participated in Doriana's thoughts. "I saw him a minute ago, and I'm not too sure, but I thought I recognized Mr. Botain in the lobby downstairs."

Doriana glanced sharply at Noelle. How much did this girl actually understand of the situation? What exactly was the situation? Doriana couldn't swear to it of course, but Hugh didn't seem aware of Arlen. He had never mentioned Arlen's name. The only remark he had once made, watching one of Arlen's newscasts, was how pleasant Arlen's deep, somewhat husky baritone sounded. Hugh, the shrewd businessman and learned art collector, was really nothing but a country boy in his love life. And in his early sixties he still did not associate love with intrigue or sex with sophistication.

She finished working on her face. This was one thing she had learned to do fast after all these years of practice—how to remove all that TV pancake gook and to apply her own light makeup without dislodging the custom-made false lashes that blended so naturally with her own. All at once it reminded her of how many, many years ago, when she was only a hopeful starlet in Hollywood, it took her literally an hour to mascara her own lashes. And the recollection of herself as she was then, that was not unlike the picture of her unsophisticated secretary, suddenly softened her feelings toward Noelle.

"I'm glad you caught me in time. I wouldn't have wanted to miss Mr. Botain tonight," she said, realizing that that kind of shamming wouldn't fool the perhaps naive, but definitely not stupid, secretary of hers.

"How about Arlen Redfore?" Noelle fired point blank, staring straight into Doriana's eyes in the mirror.

Naive, indeed! Doriana thought angrily. So this little minx did listen in on her phone conversations on the study extension. That's why the light click when Noelle hung up after referring the call to her sounded double. The girl evidently hung up when she picked up her extension only instantly to lift the receiver up again. She tried to recall her conversation with Arlen when he called her from the studio earlier. He had called from a booth in the lobby, and felt free to talk. And she, too, not knowing that her secretary might be listening in, talked freely.

"I'm trying to find somebody to build a vibrator into my bed," he told her, "just like the one a fellow newsman got himself. He has a turntable bed like mine, but his, in addition to rotating, can also vibrate. Although, naturally, when you're in mine it vibrates by itself."

"While you're at it, why don't you also install a mechanism to make your bed jump up and down, she had quipped. "Then you wouldn't need me at all. Just ride a pillow."

How many times had Noelle eavesdropped on their conversations? Enough to know the truth.

Doriana took up the implied dare. "Yes, how about Arlen Redfore? Don't you think that he'd enjoy meeting Mr. Botain?"

"Oh, I'm quite sure he would," Noelle said, smiling sweetly but clipping her words, without lowering her eyes, "although I'm not so certain about Mr. Botain. You know how Arlen talks—he's so uninhibited."

So now the impudent girl already referred to Arlen by his first name. Life was full of ironic quirks, Doriana thought. She had always kept her secretary at a distance, and now Noelle had suddenly become an uninvited confidante of her intimacies with her husband and her lover. She put the finishing touches to her face and got up.

"You should take a course in applied psychology, my dear. Every good secretary should. You're definitely not using good psychology with me," Doriana remarked dryly, and watched Noelle's smile abruptly stiffen on her face and her lips tremble slightly.

Did she go too far? Noelle wondered unhappily. Would

her daring scheme to meet Arlen—a plan that she imagined so clever a few hours ago—backfire? She was an idiot to have expected this sophisticated woman who knew how to twist a whole generation of all kinds of people around her little finger, to fall for a transparent stratagem of a young fool like her. She bit her lip, hating herself. But the opportunity had seemed so right. When would it present itself again?

"Gee, Miss Delor, I was only trying to be helpful," she said, putting all the girlish desolation she was capable of into her voice.

"Some help!" Doriana muttered under her breath. She crossed to the door, put her hand on the knob, started opening the door, and her heart skipped a beat. There, in the narrow crack, not wide enough to let slip a mouse, she could see two men talking to each other—the two men in her life, two extreme opposites with only her in common. And walking away from them was Val, who evidently must have introduced them.

She quietly shut the door, keeping her hand on the knob. There was so little time to think, but she had to make some sort of decision. Should she use Noelle? Perhaps the girl did not mean any harm. Noelle had a crush on Arlen, or why would she have cached his framed photo in her desk drawer? Most likely so many other romantic girls all over New York swooned watching him on TV and listening to his deep baritone. Perhaps if Noelle looked at Arlen with those beautiful green eyes of hers and Arlen reacted as any young man would, Hugh, the nice and uncomplicated man that he was, would not notice behind this clever smoke screen where the real fire was. She made a quick decision.

"Noelle," she said in a suddenly cordial voice, "it has occurred to me that I've never taken you out to dinner, even though I'd been meaning to. I see you're all dressed up tonight."

I'm dressed up, all right, but next to you my best looks like dirt, Noelle thought, watching Doriana slip on her floor-length specially beige-dyed chinchilla coat over the exquisitely elegant Bill Blass creation.

"Do you think you could break your date and join me, Mr. Botain and Mr. Redfore?" Doriana continued. "I'm sure you'd like to meet Mr. Redfore, wouldn't you?"

"Would I . . . I mean, sure, thank you, Miss Delor," Noelle gushed.

Twenty-Seven

Doriana was too preoccuped with her own dilemma to take notice of Noelle's triumphant expression, even though as soon as they joined the two men it appeared that perhaps there was no problem at all.

"Did you know that a mule can't procreate?" Arlen asked by way of good-evening.

So they were obviously talking about Hugh's experiences, Doriana thought with relief. It was much better than Arlen's bragging about his motorized bed.

"Arlen, here's your blind date," she said, and saw his eyes popping.

Only now had he noticed Noelle who, momentarily shedding her brand-new self-assurance was timidly hanging back behind Doriana, and it was evident that surprise had given way to admiration.

"Noelle Martin is my secretary. I don't introduce you to her, Arlen, since she's an ardent fan of yours. Noelle keeps your photo in her desk drawer, you know."

"I had no idea you had a new secretary," Arlen said.

"New?" Hugh echoed.

"Noelle has been with me for over a year," Doriana said.

"But I am new, I was just reborn," said Noelle, and smiled engagingly.

"You're a healthy-looking, beautiful baby," Arlen said, ogling appreciatively Noelle's shapely long legs generously exposed by her short green silk dress.

Doriana could easily read his mind. The heel. She did not like at all the way things were going. To be sure, Noelle's presence had solved a touchy problem. Naturally, she had anticipated some minor complications, but sometimes later;

160

another raise, maybe, or a little familiarity that Noelle had never allowed herself before. She had not foreseen this conversation that was turning to her definite disadvantage. In the first place, age was a forbidden topic, and Noelle's remark about being reborn suggested a new, pink baby, as Arlen's reaction proved.

"Where to now?" she asked, trying to steer away from the irritating subject, " '21' or The Spacebird?"

"I have a reservation at '21'," said Hugh. His voice sounded softer than usual, and maybe he even spoke more slowly.

Doriana glanced at him, suddenly alarmed. Hugh had not been himself since his return. It was even more apparent tonight. Was it because of Arlen?

"I heard Valerie Bing mention earlier that she was on her way to '21'. That's one character I wouldn't care to run into twice in one day," she said apologetically. "Incidentally, Hugh, I didn't think you and Val knew each other. Where and when did you two meet?"

"Just now when she said that you would be out shortly," Hugh explained.

The bitch, thought Doriana, the sly bitch. Of course, merely by calling out loudly about her, Val had both men react and half-approach her, and Hugh was bound to meet Arlen. Having no idea about her intention to bring Hugh and Arlen together anyway, this was clearly Val's attempt at stirring up trouble. "So how about The Spacebird?" she asked.

"I'm sure we'll have no problem at The Spacebird," said Hugh, taking great pleasure in Arlen's unmistakable interest in Noelle.

When Valerie Bing had called Redfore by name, Hugh had abruptly felt his face flushing slightly, as usual when his blood pressure zoomed. So this was the handsome young playboy whose name was being linked with Doriana's by gossiping columnists and gossiping women. If he had had any doubt, this double date arranged by Doriana, and mostly this open attention Arlen Redfore was paying the little secretary in Doriana's presence, did away with any remaining suspicion. What crazy notions jealousy could put in a man's head, he thought guiltily. He would have to walk over to David Webb's tomorrow and get Doriana something particularly nice. . . .

Arlen was broke as usual. Although he knew that this multimillionaire would pick up the tab, there was always the possibility that he just might allow him to get stuck with it. So he had better forget about showing off. The old boy was all right, though; a bit of a bore, but okay. Doriana was lucky to have a husband like this Hugh Botain. But then, Doriana was not only born beautiful but absurdly lucky as well. It was funny that this chick of her secretary turned out to be the knockout he had noticed at one of the discos a couple of months ago, and she looked even more gorgeous tonight. Naturally, no female, no matter how young or how lovely, could eclipse Doriana with that cachet and arresting presence of hers adding a special aura to her beauty. But this girl's blooming youth did make Doriana look a mite on the mature side by comparison. He'd better watch himself and not let Doriana guess what was going through his mind.

"There's a slim chance of our being anywhere near Val Bing at '21'," he remarked.

This of course might have been a crack aimed at Hugh, thought Doriana, since Val was a celebrity big enough to be well seated. So maybe he meant that a schmo who was not decked out in a Savile Row suit, even if his pockets were stuffed with Australian wool and dripping with Texas oil, would be relegated to Siberia. And because Arlen apparently willfully overlooked that the seating was determined not by her escort but by Doriana Delor herself, who always got *the* table everywhere, she knew that Arlen must be jealous. After all, he was being robbed of his date with her, despite the consolation prize she had provided for him. The idea made her feel a little better.

"Let's go to The Spacebird?" asked Noelle. "Maybe they'll take our picture in the Cockpit."

"The Cockpit is nothing but a computerized bar," Doriana said, "nothing much really. Lots of psychedelic lights and twin recliners, a simulation of a spaceship ready for takeoff— a sort of an ancient Roman orgy atmosphere in a futuristic setting."

"The Cockpit, with all that lying around in semidarkness, is hardly right for picture-taking, it's meant for other pastimes," Arlen put in.

"Don't they take pictures at all at The Spacebird?" Noelle asked, her tone that of a frustrated child.

"They will in the Champagne Capsule while we're having dinner," Doriana reassured her.

"Fine then, let's be off to The Spacebird," said Hugh.

Arlen, still thinking about the chance of perhaps having to pick up the check, made sure that it was clear he wasn't hosting the party.

"It's up to you," he said, turning toward both Doriana and her husband.

"All right, Arturo will take care of us," Doriana said. After all, she owed it to Noelle.

As they walked into The Spacebird, Arturo, one of the finest of all maître d's anywhere, found himself with a slight problem. If it were only a question of placing this little auburn-haired cutie who clung to this young nobody newsman who couldn't fool him with his English, custom-made clothes, all would be quite simple. Or even this generous tipper, Mr. Botain, who, despite his millions, wouldn't know better or give a hang if he were seated on the "wrong" side. But Doriana Delor was an entirely different matter altogether. . . .

Arturo, always so self-possessed, always so impeccable in his well-fitting tails, the only one conventionally dressed among the rest of the personnel in fantasy costumes of interplanetary spacepeople, who invariably looked more distinguished than most of the people who made him rich by over-tipping him in their scramble for choice tables, appeared troubled for a moment.

Table Two, and the whole right row of banquettes were occupied by a big money crowd. You don't mess with the Revlons and the Seagrams, not even for Doriana Delor. In fact, you don't move or crowd anybody who rated a good table in the first place.

Doriana was quick to assess the situation, and it took her only a second to come to Arturo's rescue. Cuffs on trousers became fashionable when the Prince of Wales forgot to smooth down his pants he had rolled up because of rain. And nobody ever dared question Beau Brummel's patronizing a second-rate pub—the pub had simply become the "in" place for the snob set.

"Arturo, I'd like a table on the left side tonight," Doriana said, thinking that it was actually silly to suggest right and left in the sphere of the Champagne Capsule. She also thought that Arlen, who was faced with the same problem in his bed, should feel very much at home here.

And shortly afterward she had the satisfaction of seeing Arturo showing a party of top drawer socialites to a table on the side where she was seated, meaning that it had become the "fashionable neighborhood" now.

"Would you gentlemen please excuse us," she said, and leading her secretary by the arm guided her to the doll's-house-like elevator to the ladies' room.

It was amusing to watch Noelle almost religiously stepping into the tiny plate glass elevator suspended in the pitch-black nothingness of the staged universe, her eyes bulging at the luminous meteors streaking by and the planet earth slowly rising out of nowhere, with the familiar outline of the Americas on the moonlike face.

A bit later, Doriana enjoyed the ecstatic expression on Noelle's face even more after a visit to the bubblelike powder room, its mirrored ceiling reflecting all the accessories and creating the illusion that in this gravity-free world these upside-down fixtures could be used without difficulty by visiting earthlings. And the teenager's uninhibited delight made her think that perhaps the calculated risk of bringing her and Arlen together had been worth taking anyway. She was not sure whether her men were watching her slow walk down the spectacular Lucite staircase, actually a wide, gimmicky escalator geared to move imperceptibly up, evidently shrewdly designed to allow the descending women a little more time for showing off. She hoped that both Hugh and Arlen were watching, mainly of course to dazzle them, especially Hugh, since she was wearing the diamond necklace he had given her for their second wedding anniversary. She was walking down the slip-proof frosted stairs, carefully placing her bejeweled evening pumps in the studied motion of professional models, while Noelle was loping down the same stairway as she probably would the cement stoop of her village walk-up, rushing a few steps at a time, then awkwardly pausing to wait for Doriana.

Noelle gave the impression of being as much out of her sphere on this showplace staircase as Carol was on the panel among some of the most glamorous personalities in the world. And Doriana again felt sorry for her secretary, whose glaring lack of sophistication in this snooty milieu would brand her as an outsider from the start. Just then, however, she caught the expression of four men at a center table who, seemingly unaware of her beauty and diamonds, plunged their wolfish stares under Noelle's short "open secret" dress, and was no longer certain she need pity her young guest.

Twenty-Eight

Like all the other Spacebird rooms, The Capsule had no defined walls. A transparent dome rising from the floor around the circular dining room separated it from the simulated darkness of outer space with its animated firmament, an idea no doubt borrowed from the planetarium. The inevitable planet earth hanging on the horizon was there as a reminder to patrons that they were millions of miles away from its confining restrictions and conventions. Even the sin of overeating was inconsequential in the supposedly weightless atmosphere of the dining salon where one couldn't possibly gain a single ounce. While the colorfully decked out food-and-wine-carrying stewards and stewardesses hovered over the round tables, most of the interplanetary voyagers were already concentrating on the terrestrial caviar, served in quantities which also suggested its weightlessness.

"They should have called this place 'Sputnik'," Arlen observed, glancing at the trayful of caviar appetizers brought to their table as soon as everybody had sat down, including Doriana's manager who had joined Hugh and Arlen and was waiting with them for Doriana and Noelle.

"Actually, the U.S. had been importing a lot of caviar from Iran before their seizure of the American embassy and taking of the hostages," Hugh commented.

On her way to their table, Doriana had begun to question the wisdom of leaving Hugh and Arlen alone. Nobody could guarantee that their conversation would necessarily again turn to the genetic characteristics of mules. But Arlen didn't appear to mind Hugh's comment, and Hugh was smiling amiably, so evidently they were still on good terms.

"Iran could export all the caviar it wanted even before

the Shah was deposed, since he was allergic to it," Doriana said, completely at ease now.

Her manager, by immediately switching to a new subject, prevented any reaction to her remark.

"Before it slips my mind, here are the canceled checks you wanted," he said. "I've been dragging them around in my pocket for days. You cashed them, all right. Seven grand worth. It's nice to have so much money you don't remember when and how you spent it. If you think it was a cinch to get these canceled checks you should've heard the hassle I had with the networks."

Cy couldn't help winking at her. It wasn't the first time that she had "mislaid" her checks. She had this very expensive habit of signing over her checks to a variety of good causes, from the American Cancer Society and the National Paraplegia Foundation to the United Jewish Appeal, and what not, and then pretending that she had no idea what she had done with them, to avoid his upbraiding her for her extravagant generosity.

Noelle sat very still, feeling her hands abruptly turn clammy, and she wondered if the whiteness that must have replaced the pink of excitement on her cheeks had been noticed by anyone. Maybe she was a double-dealing secretary, but she certainly was no criminal. She felt something on her wrist and nearly jerked her hand away as if it were the cold touch of handcuffs. Then instantly realizing that it was Arlen's hand under the table, returned its squeeze, grateful for the desperately needed comfort it gave her, and gradually recaptured some of her exhilaration.

It was a little later, after they had ordered their food, that it became clear that Cy had not come to the club simply to get rid of those canceled checks.

"Uxworthy wants to dump Carol," he announced, staring at the fresh supply of caviar appetizers that had appeared on the table as if they had been served by an invisible sleight-of-hand artist.

"Over my dead body," Doriana said. "Tell Brian from me

that if she goes, I go. What are *you* so happy about? You'd lose your percentage, wouldn't you?"

"Well . . . there'd be a bit of horse-trading involved. Maybe Carol would be better off."

"She wouldn't, and she won't, and that's final! She has a contract, right?" Doriana was furious.

"Hmmm, not exactly. I sold her to Brian on a weekly try-out basis, and what with the bad ratings and all, he and the ad agency feel that she's just no drawing card. Besides, earlier tonight I saw Carol with a young guy who looked like a full-back boozing in that saloon, you know, down the street on Second Avenue. No, you wouldn't know. . . . Anyhow, Carol poured her heart out to me about how miserable she was on the show tonight and that she wanted out."

"She did pretty well."

"You should see her on the color tube—ecchh! And she looked like she was ready to drop dead any sec. She's just too used up. She would get by if she was a big name like June or Val, but she's not, and she's just too damn dull and down-and-out looking to compete with three veteran glamour-pusses."

"Well, thanks for including me," Doriana said with a twisted little smile, thinking with a sudden shudder of anxiety that today it was poor Carol and that one of these to-morrows, perhaps sooner than she imagined, *she* could easily be the shopworn has-been.

Cy grabbed a caviar canapé from a passing waiter's tray, like a frog going after a fly.

"You got me all wrong, doll. You know I couldn't have meant you—you're the baby of the show," he said. That Doriana! Always in there pitching to help somebody, he thought.

"How about a little dancing?" said Noelle. She cocked her head in the direction of the band. Its low-key rock music was quite different from the hot beat of the discos.

"That's a great idea," said Arlen, springing to his feet.

Doriana watched them strolling away, practically holding

hands, he bending down to her and managing somehow not to appear stooped, and she turning her head up to the psychedelic lights of the dome, her face still wearing the ecstatic look it had taken on the instant she walked into The Spacebird. Mixed feelings of clear-cut annoyance and vague jealousy, which was vague only because she refused to admit it to herself, momentarily made Doriana forget what she was discussing with Cy.

He misunderstood the expression on her abruptly flushed face. "You mustn't get excited," he said, trying to speak authoritatively. "Deep down you know that Carol is no match for you."

"Carol knew almost all the quotes tonight, even those I missed," Doriana kept up her defense of Carol, ignoring Cy's flattery.

"Sure. And she looked like she had crammed them till the last minute. Worn out. She's lost so much weight she looked like she might slip out of her skin any second. Like a snake."

"Anybody can feel tired occasionally. Hugh, why don't you back me up?"

"Me? Yes, of course, you're right. But you never get tired, Doriana. You always look as though you've just had your beauty nap, even after—" He interrupted himself. This obnoxious little agent of Doriana's was so insignificant one nearly forgot that he was there. One tended to talk in his presence as one would in the presence of a cat.

"Thank you, darling." She put her hand on his. If only this were true, she thought.

"Mr. Botain's got something there," said Cy, impatiently attempting to assist the disdainful waiter to pour the champagne by moving the glasses toward him. "I remember last time I saw you at Rexine's you had a killer headache and couldn't even dance, and poor Redfore had to settle on that dog of Uxworthy's kid, but you looked like you just got out of bed."

I did, she nearly said, thinking about Arlen's kinky bed,

and glanced covertly at Hugh. This idiot manager of hers had a far too long tongue for such a short body.

Hugh was gazing at her, but his expression did not give away his emotions. He did not miss Doriana's agent's remark about Arlen Redfore's escorting her to the discotheque, although he thought nothing of it. There were dozens of admirers surrounding her constantly like moths attracted by a bright flame. How beautiful she was. And how seductive. She couldn't help it if all these moths swarmed around her. And what an inexhaustible supply of vitality she had, what a driving rage to participate in everything.

"All this has nothing to do with Carol's staying on the show," Doriana said, returning to the subject. She would be damned if she let Cy or Brian Uxworthy destroy Carol.

"Well, she's out, so forget it. But don't worry. I'll get her a couple of those lucrative commercials to keep her going. Besides, she said tonight that she wouldn't come back on the show even if Val wasn't on it. That Val! The other day I overheard her telling Carol how she felt for her that because the flat Twiggy look was no longer popular Carol had to go back to her falsies."

"Val's a bitch," Doriana commented, and nearly bit her tongue.

"Darling," said Val, rushing up to their table, throwing her arms around Doriana and bussing her on the cheek in the meaningless show business gesture, "You look positively divine! No wonder you have won yourself such a handsome Aussie for a husband."

She lifted her head to look at Hugh, who stood up towering over her, his graying hair appearing whiter than usual against his fresh tan.

"Why, thank you, Ma'am," he said, and somehow also sounded a bit more Australian than usual.

So after all "21" would have been a better choice, Doriana thought wearily. There was no escaping this malicious pest. And now Val would say something about Arlen.

"I thought Arlen Redfore might be here. Weren't you together?" Val said innocently.

"Oh, he's around, all right. You've probably missed lots of people since you stopped wearing your contact lenses. Doriana said angrily, and smiled sweetly at Val, who did not give any sign of annoyance.

Noelle and Arlen came back to the table, looking bored and titillated at the same time.

"We'd like to go to some disco after we leave here," said Noelle.

"Not the kind they have upstairs on the deck, we'd like to get some real action," added Arlen.

Suddenly he noticed a strange expression on Doriana's face. But he was not quite sure whether her pique was provoked by his flirting with Noelle, or simply because of Val's hanging around their table. Maybe, just in case, it would be wiser not to leave with Noelle. It would be such fun, though, if he could at least entertain Noelle on one of those inviting recliners in the bar. But DD would not understand his yen to teach this delicious youngling how to really lift off into space.

"Well, I'd better rejoin my date," said Val, looking at Hugh. "You might know him, he's also a businessman, only he's in textiles. . . . Loved seeing you again, and think of me if you should ever start giving away your oil wells, sweetie."

"You're too late, my dear," he said, grinning. "I haven't got any oil wells left. Perhaps you've read about the big fire which is still burning over a whole section of fields in Texas? Well, those happened to be mine."

Twenty-Nine

"You think Mr. Botain is really bankrupt with all those oil wells of his ruined?" Noelle asked, after Arlen had paid the cabbie in front of one of the new discos in Times Square.

Apparently their kissing in the cab all the way from The Spacebird had not interfered with Noelle's reflecting about the bombshell Hugh Botain had dropped at the club, Arlen thought. But it didn't bruise his ego, and didn't surprise him, since he himself was wondering about it, and also about Doriana's dark look when she suggested, probably for her husband's benefit, that he and Noelle had better forget about the disco, for all of them had to go to work early in the morning.

"Hugh Botain's worth millions. He owns one of the largest sheep grazing tracts in Australia and a fortune in art treasures, among other things."

Arlen wrapped his arm around her shoulders as they started slowly down the stairs, as if to overcome the onrush of the hot blasts of the rock music from the cellar.

"I'm afraid Miss Delor will sack me for leaving The Spacebird with you," Noelle said. "And she'll be furious with you for cheating on her."

"Where did you get such a screwy idea?" he asked, his face a picture of shocked innocence. This was his standard reaction to any allusions of intimacy with Doriana made by his poker cronies at the Overseas Press Club or at The Players. He was many things, but definitely not a kiss-and-tell heel.

"I am her confidential secretary, remember?" Noelle laughed. "She will be as cross as hell about you and me. She's

172

always been jealous of me, you know. Not of my looks, mostly of my age."

They had reached a small foyer at the bottom of the stairs, and through the open doors a torrid wave of smoke-filled air and deafening noise enveloped them. Arlen spun Noelle around to face him. It was impossible not to notice the magic of youth that literally radiated from this pretty girl he was practically holding in his arms.

"You are lovely," he said, as if thinking aloud. "Let's not spoil the fun by fretting about what we might have to deal with sometime later, okay?"

For a moment she remembered the checks bearing Doriana's forged endorsement now in Doriana's possession, and again mentally felt the cold pressure of handcuffs on her wrists, but did not allow the brief panic to kill her happiness at being with Arlen.

"We'll face whatever comes when it comes," she agreed, and lifting herself on her toes placed a light kiss on Arlen's lips, and jumped back before Arlen had the time to grab her. "Try to get us a table. I'll be with you in a minute. I'd like to freshen up first."

She started down the hall, swaying her hips a little more under Arlen's stare that she could feel following her. This was something she had been daydreaming about for such a long time, this thrill of actually being with Arlen and Arlen admiring her.

When she had nearly reached the end of the corridor she saw a large sign, "Lounges" and entered the room. There were soft chairs all around it against the walls and two settees back to back in the center. A few couples were sitting here and there, talking and smoking, and nobody took any notice of her, except a bearded black youth who was pacing the carpeted floor, evidently waiting for his date to come out the door marked "Chicks" for he kept glancing intermittently from it to Noelle.

Guided by his glances, Noelle crossed to the washroom, but before she had time to open the door, felt a restraining hand on her arm. Instead of getting a table, she thought, Arlen had followed her here, and wheeled about, already smiling delightedly, and turned to stone.

Ben's square-jawed face looked very hard, with a frown cutting deeply between his eyebrows. He pulled his head in somewhat as usual when getting set to fight real or imaginary antagonists or problems, blowing out the vessels on his thick neck, and Noelle guessed what was coming even before he spoke.

"What do you think you're doing?" he asked, surprisingly calmly.

"I . . . I'm going to the john."

"Don't you play cute with me," he said in a louder voice with a flash of his eyes, his sharply pointed tongue flicking out the side of his mouth to moisten his lips in a mannerism which she knew from experience could paradoxically signify either anger or satisfaction at his own particularly apt remark, or both. "What do you think Doriana Delor will do when it gets back to her that her secretary is messing around with her guy?"

"She fixed this date herself, she's with her sugar-daddy-husband." All at once she flew into a rage at Ben. "Since you've been tailing me, you must know that we were all together at The Spacebird."

"You bet! I was pounding the beat like a goddam cop while the four of you lived it up inside."

"You should have joined us." She instantly regretted her crack, for he reddened and the veins on his forehead swelled visibly.

"Cut it out, dammit, or I'll put your nose back in the shape it used to be."

"Is this cat bothering you, Miss?"

Noelle and Ben turned to the black young man who in his pacing the lounge had come nearer and nearer to them and must have overheard Ben. In his belted suede jacket which revealed his slender boyish waistline, he looked pitifully frail beside Ben who gazed at the youth with more amusement than annoyance. But again his temper seemed to be getting the better of him.

"No, no thanks," Noelle said quickly, smiling reassuringly at the young man, who appeared relieved. Maybe he had noticed the look on Ben's face, or simply had the time to weigh the uneven odds he was risking in an argument.

"Sorry," he mumbled, and rushed away to join a statuesque girl wearing a red floor-length coat, who emerged from the washroom.

"My being here with Arlen Redfore means nothing, unless it gets in the papers because of your stupid jealousy," Noelle said.

"You shouldn't be taking any chances bugging Doriana Delor now that things are going so smoothly," Ben said, quieting down.

"Smoothly, my eye," she rejoined, glancing anxiously at the archway leading into the hall which suddenly framed a tall masculine figure. It was not Arlen, thank heaven, and she sighed with relief. "Tonight Doriana was handed some canceled checks. How long do you think it'll take her to figure out that she never got the seven grand?"

She enjoyed the changing expression on his face. In the early stages of the crooked game they were playing she was terrified by the idea of getting mixed up in a forgery, and he was so coolly efficient in working out the details. Now it was she who was rather relaxed about the whole thing. She didn't think that either Doriana or even the police, if it ever came to it, would be able to tell the difference between Doriana's signature and her simile on which she had worked so hard. And it was his turn to worry, since it was he who had engineered it all and had pocketed practically all of the money.

"You've got nothing to grin about. Don't forget, babe, it's you they'll grill. You, and nobody else," he said.

"How would I know what they were talking about? So somebody swiped the checks Doriana Delor had endorsed.

Let that somebody who's cashed them worry about the whole botch, somebody who got most of the bread."

He made an effort not to explode. "There's nothing to connect me with your doings and the checks. But you'll have plenty of explaining to do and a hell of a time justifying how a working kid can afford the two-hundred-buck dress you've got on, *and* a fur coat, even if it came from Alexander's."

"So I have a rich boyfriend who spoils me, so what?"

He raised his hand in a gesture meant to keep her quiet and stood turning something over in his mind for a few seconds.

"Where did she put those checks, in her purse?"

"You didn't expect her to stick them in her bra?"

"If you were a little bit smarter you should have figured out how to get them back right then and there."

"Just like that! 'Pardon me, Miss Delor, may I go through your handbag, please.' "

"Cut out this bullshit, damn you!"

She did not reply, although her tongue itched to put Ben in his place. Arlen might be here looking for her any minute now, so she'd better get this charming duologue over with.

"Listen—" she started appeasingly.

"No, you listen. I want those checks by tomorrow, hear? I'll close my bank account first thing in the morning, even though it's not in my real name anyhow."

She wondered at his abrupt recovery of self-assurance. "Even if I manage to get hold of those damn checks, there are some bank records, remember?" she said.

But Ben, strangely pensive all at once, evidently did not hear her.

He was thinking that the combination of an appreciative hot lay and a secretary who could forge an authentic signature of her boss, had seemed like an unbeatable sure thing. Particularly since Doriana Delor did not keep track of how much cash she was getting or spending. Yet now it appeared as though he was losing not only the newly transformed Noelle but also the bonanza that would have eventually enabled him to own a horse farm he had been wanting for a long time. Why was he such a bungler, always letting things slip through his fingers just as he was about to close his fist around the prize? Always allowing himself to get sidetracked from his main objective and because of it losing everything.

He surveyed her sharply and made himself listen to what she was saying.

"Got to go now," Noelle told him.

He studied her again. No, she was not ready to defy him altogether. Not yet. He would have time to reestablish his grip on everything, if he went about it the right way.

"Let's not be stupid about the whole thing," he said in a different tone, and noticed that he had startled her. "We're both in a jam if those checks are turned over to the fuzz. Both, mainly because should one of us be picked up, he would probably involve the other."

He shrugged when she opened her mouth to protest.

"Obviously you've little love left for me, and even less respect, but we can still remain partners. I'll make you a new deal—I won't interfere with your love life if you follow my instructions. For openers, you must get those checks to gain a little time. Next. . . ."

Noelle was thinking of how drastically her attitude toward Ben had changed. She still remembered her wide-eyed gratitude that first night when his attentions had made her feel desirable as never before in her life. In that small French restaurant that had seemed so elegant then, he had aroused her dormant femininity, pride and confidence in herself. She owed him more for all this than for just the erotic pleasures he had initiated her into and had taught her to share with him in bed. When did this gratitude vanish, leaving in its place something less than indifference? Was her feeling toward him loathing now? Did this reversal come about because he was part of a disenchanting existence that had been hers for years not so long ago? Or was it because of Arlen who had materialized out of her fantasies? Or simply because she suddenly understood that Ben, the passionately inventive lover, was nothing but a scheming liar who had used her?

She glanced again at the archway. Two women were walking in through it now. She had to get back to Arlen. She nodded silently. She would promise anything, provided he let her go.

"Okay, just get those checks," he said. "I'll be in touch." He turned abruptly and strode out, nearly colliding with Arlen under the archway.

"I was just starting back," Noelle said, sighing with relief and gazing at Arlen's handsome face.

"We'll have to join some friends of mine," he said. "There isn't a damn table in the dump to be had. Would you like us to try Studio 54? A topless joint maybe? Unless you don't mind being crowded?"

No, she didn't mind being crowded with him close to her. She would be uncomfortable for a while, until she had another chance to come here. She couldn't tell him that she never actually had a go at the john, could she? And a little physical discomfort was nothing compared with the anxiety brought on by her talk with Ben. But the prospect of the dirty job ahead of her tomorrow dulled somewhat the promise of pleasure and happiness made her by Arlen's smiling eyes.

Thirty

"Darling, why didn't you tell me?" Doriana asked Hugh for the second time.

She was already in bed, the pink silk sheet drawn up only halfway over her nude body, her arms folded under her head to raise it on the single pillow to be able to watch Hugh undress. Under different circumstances she would have enjoyed his obvious shyness about exposing himself as he stripped.

"And giving me this lovely emerald bracelet from Cartier's! It must have cost a fortune," she added.

"Now don't you go imagining that I'm wiped out," he protested.

No, of course she didn't think that. Still, not even the richest could drop millions without hurting.

"I've always had more money than I could spend," he said. "Besides, I'm thinking of selling the land in Wyoming. I paid something like forty dollars an acre for the grazing land. Now Texaco, Gulf, Exxon and the rest are all bidding to get it for a thousand an acre. It will net us a few million."

"Wouldn't it be more profitable to exploit the land yourself?" she asked and instantly regretted it. Possibly Hugh might think her too venal. Moreover, he was too shrewd a businessman not to know what he was doing. Perhaps he knew that his land was not as rich in coal or oil as the prospectors thought it was. Or maybe his idea of a huge profit was different from the currently inflated standards of the oil companies which rated people worth less than ten million as "poor" millionaires. Hugh was such a modest man. . . .

His answer startled her.

"I realize that it would be a lot more profitable. But the

179

fire in Texas has helped me shake off my inertia. Frankly, I'm fed up with the way of life we've been leading for the past two years. I've been thinking of liquidating all our holdings in the States."

Hugh had often complained about crime, air pollution and what not in New York, and had talked about their going to live in Australia. He had never really meant it, had he? All she had to do was to coax him into being a little more patient.

"And I've been thinking about adopting a child," she said. "I was hoping you would like the idea and would help me with all the formalities."

"Let's talk seriously," he said.

"Aren't we talking seriously? Adopting a child is not a joke, it's a tremendous responsibility."

"Yes, responsibility," he echoed somberly. "We are too old to think about adopting kids."

This was the first time in her life that anybody had ever told her that she was too old for anything. And the first time that Hugh, who had always treated her like a child, and who was chronologically so much older than she, talked as if he were her contemporary. He noticed the baffled expression that had turned into sadness on her face, and surmised what she was thinking.

"I know that there's quite a difference in our ages. But unless people are young enough to be sure they have time to raise a child, they are too old to adopt it."

Again he used this disturbing word. But he was right of course. This was the real reason, which she always knew but refused to confront, the thought that prevented her from even dreaming realistically about creating a family. But now that he had objected to her idea, that only a few minutes ago was hardly more than an exciting daydream, she felt as if he were depriving her of children she had been longing for all her life.

"I'm not as old as you may think I am," she remarked on a sigh.

She didn't look old at all with her face slightly flushed by indignation and her pink-nippled breasts heaving a bit faster. He approached the bed and sat down on its edge on her side, and controlled himself not to fondle her. "I know that you are still young," he said, "but to raise children is not only hard work, it is time-consuming as well."

She glanced at him suspiciously. What did he mean by "still young"? Did he know her true age? Was it possible?

"If you're so anxious to take care of kids, you can do it without killing yourself at it. When we settle down in Australia, I'll build you a place for hundreds of waifs of all ages from around the globe. A home with acres of gardens, lots of up-to-date playgrounds, and a large well-trained personnel, where you could devote as much or as little time as you wished to the kids. And this place would remain there forever."

So this time he had really made up his mind about returning to Australia to live. He must have reached this decision even before his oil wells in Texas had caught fire, on his last trip down there. And he had no doubt that she would abandon everything here and go with him to make a fresh start. This was the very last thing she expected. She thought they had gained an understanding and that he had resigned himself to their present arrangement, without her having to sacrifice or at best jeopardize her career while she was still on top. But what could she tell him that she had not already told him before that would finally convince him to wait a little longer, a few more years?

There was of course another all-important reason for her profound reluctance to leave New York, a reason she could not reveal, for she could not mention Arlen to Hugh. And being unaware of her love for Arlen, Hugh might perhaps go on believing that her fondness for children would eventually prevail over her consuming ambition. Or was he counting on her commitment to him? Maybe she was more than just committed, maybe she genuinely cared for him, for being so wise and for unerringly distinguishing right from wrong.

Yet even if she were able to give up Arlen, did she care enough for Hugh to be content with him on his "station" in the wilds of the Australian continent, in a rambling house which he had turned into a museum, and a home for children which his great wealth and her yearning for kids would make the largest family in the world? But of course, there would be no question of jetting back and forth to keep alive her love affair with Arlen, since he would quickly settle on any beautiful domestic fowl in hand rather than wait for an Australian bird of paradise to fly back to him. And as for her career, once she left the scene and became a full-time housewife and a part-time celebrity, there would be no getting back to what she was in the business now. The public was so fickle and before long talked about you in the past tense. No, it wasn't possible, not yet. Not while she could still pass for a very young woman, and be loved like one. Hugh didn't know what he was asking.

Abruptly she realized that Hugh was still talking to her, and listened to his emotional description of the peace of mind she would discover in Australia, the old plea she had heard so many times before. She fleetingly thought that perhaps if she went with him into a kind of retreat, to tranquil contentment with simpler things, she could, along with the fame and glamour, also leave behind the burden of her continuous struggle for youth and stardom. But just as quickly she shook off the idea.

By Doriana's expression Hugh knew the reply to his appeal. Actually, when he told her that he had shaken off his inertia he was also thinking of their personal relationship, although he could not blame the ever widening breach created by the void of compatibility and understanding between them on this beautiful creature who was such a foolish child at heart and the victim of the overwhelming youth cult. He, who was older and wiser, should have realized that in this age of lovers living openly together and marriage being regarded by many as an obsolete ritual, his loving and wanting her without her loving him was not enough for a stable union.

"Why don't we discuss it in the morning? Come, darling," she said, throwing her arms around his neck and pulling him down.

He did not resist her, and for some moments the desire that drew them together swept aside the growing tension fed by their conflicting idea of happiness. Yet somehow he filled her without feeling her. And she, although oppressed by his weight, had the sensation of being penetrated by a partially materialized ghost without substance.

It must be all those damn Mimosas, she thought, redoubling her frenzy, but as seconds and minutes grew longer and longer, knew that it was no use, that she couldn't get even a spark, and had the nightmarish sensation that this cadenced imitation of passion would continue endlessly without hope or release, and froze, gasping for suddenly desperately needed air.

Misinterpreting her moan Hugh was gladdened that he had at least satisfied her. He pulled himself out and lay quietly, feeling the coolness of the silk sheets against his sweating body. She did not stir when he raised himself on his elbow in a couple of minutes and observed her in the dim light of the night lamp that she always left on, like a little girl afraid of the dark. She looked lovely, but somehow different, not like the familiar voluptuous and exciting Doriana but like one of the Greek statues whose perfection and beauty were created to stimulate another kind of admiration.

It troubled and baffled him that although he did not come he was gazing at her more as an appreciative art collector than as a lover.

Doriana was asleep. How long had he lain beside her, thinking? He got out of bed as quietly as possible, and crept to the dark corner where he had tossed his robe over a chair. He swore softly when he stabbed his knee against a corner of the vanity, and moved slowly toward the door. He would spend the rest of the night in his own adjoining bedroom.

Before walking out he glanced at the sleeping Doriana once more, and tiptoeing to the bed pulled the crumpled sheet over her beautiful nude body still as cold looking as a marble sculpture, and suddenly shivered as though he were covering a corpse.

Thirty-One

Doriana woke with the eerie sensation of being lost in time. The tiny bulb must have burned out, and as usual she felt even more insecure in the dark. Through the incompletely drawn draperies on the two tall windows of her bedroom overlooking Central Park the sky was a glowing red. It was not the reassuring pastel of dawn but the glaring lights of Manhattan that never rests, only slows down. Hugh was probably in his own room, where he often spent the rest of the night after making love with her, to read or go over his business correspondence. He needed much less sleep than she.

The brief rest had not appeased her tension that had built up during the evening and had later been aggravated by that disastrous intercourse with Hugh. She felt as though every cell in her body stretched and shivered and suffered independently. She tried to review the evening. What was there about it that troubled her so deeply? Of course, it had all started with that nasty "urgent" anonymous note that she had read just as she was about to correctly identify a quotation and which had resulted in her making a damn fool of herself in front of millions of television viewers.

And she also remembered all those unfamiliar faces of total strangers waiting for her outside The Spacebird, wearing the same grinning mask with secret thoughts and emotions behind it. . . .

What was it that drove her to keep on with it all? Her passion for Arlen? But even that, this role of a young lover's mistress, was beginning to be tougher and tougher to play. Arlen, who was anything but devoted to her, had only sex in mind, and when his appetite for her faded there would be little else left. So if—one way or another—one had to pay for everything in life, she would have paid an exorbitant price for nothing.

Suddenly, thinking of Arlen reminded her that her plan to keep Hugh from learning the truth had boomeranged. She knew Arlen's predatory attitude toward women too well to doubt that he wouldn't let Noelle slip through his playful fingers. In all fairness, she had to be broadminded about his occasional "extra-marital" affairs, and she really had no right to object to his giving Noelle a free ride in his motorized bed. Although all this was in theory only. And the understanding with Arlen about their having separate lives, and her tolerating his occasional swinging, were founded on her subconscious conviction that, being loved by her, Arlen could not possibly desire any other woman. But there had been something nettling about the way Arlen's and Noelle's hands seemed unwilling to part while they were walking back to the dance floor. Could it be that Noelle, with her girlish crush on him, had him respond far more seriously than he would with others?

Presently the gnawing feeling that had started to undermine her self-assurance even while Arlen and Noelle were under her close scrutiny at the nightclub, now that both were gone, and probably were still together, culminated in a totally unfamiliar emotion she had difficulty identifying for a while. She was jealous—perhaps for the first time in her life—and she found this degrading experience bewildering and painful. How could it have happened to her?

She turned over on her side, then tossed back. Dear God, how hopeless and insecure she suddenly felt, and how terrified of every remaining second of what was left of her life. For if she had lost her spell over a man to whom she had given all of herself, how long could she sustain this fight, that was harder and harder to wage, to keep her adoring public to whom she gave only an illusion? How good it would be if she could resign herself, as Carol did, to give it all up, not for baby-sitting as Carol would have to, but for the relaxed, comfortable life of the wife of an Australian magnate, with time to devote to children, good works, to a country club, maybe, golf and bridge. And forget all about show business. And about Arlen.

That's what the damn dark did to her, she thought, when her only reassurance and strength—her beautiful, youthful face and body melted into blackness. . . . She groped for the bedside lamp, but couldn't find it and jumped out of bed and was too anxious to worry about her slippers and waded deeply in the soft carpet to reach the wall switch. The light nearly blinded her. Then the telephone started to ring. The servants had evidently forgotten to shut it off for the night.

She looked at it for a moment, thinking that it must be a wrong number. Nobody would call her at this hour of the night.

The phone kept on ringing, and she picked up the receiver. "Yes?" she muttered.

"Doriana, I'm glad you answered," she heard the faint words, spoken by Carol's voice that she scarcely recognized.

"What's the matter, are you sick?" she asked, alarmed.

"No, no—"

"Then what's the idea of calling me at this hour? And speak up, I can hardly hear you."

"Don't be mad at me, Doriana, but I wanted to tell you how marvelous I felt before the feeling was gone. I'm speaking softly not to wake him."

"Wake who?"

"A stranger who picked me up at a Second Avenue pub, or maybe it was I who picked him up. But who cares? He's a young, strong fella."

Only the eccentric Carol would think of phoning in the middle of the night to talk so freely about her private life. But then, Carol, who was such a lonely woman, needed somebody to confide in. And besides, Carol was probably still pretty high after all the boozing in that bar she mentioned. Could she be that starved for sex? Some promiscuous women slept easily with just anybody, sometimes not only because they were nymphomaniacs, but simply from bore-dom. And some prima donnas of the past, believing that it improved the quality of their singing, had supposedly used any man available before a performance.

"You're running a terrible risk, Carol," she said, thinking of the danger of catching VD. One was really asking for it, picking up a guy in a bar. But Carol was either too drunk or too excited to get the point.

"I'm not afraid, although he's the most hot-tempered guy I've ever known. But something did happen to me, some-thing terrific and terrible at the same time."

"Carol, you're talking like a nun who was raped and liked it." She started to laugh, forgetting her own dark mood for a moment.

"Don't laugh so loud or you may wake him."

She *is* drunk, decided Doriana, or why would Carol make such a silly remark, as if anybody at the other end, except for Carol holding the receiver, could hear anything. But it added up. Cy saw her drinking heavily hours ago.

"Is the man attractive?"

"Yes, although this type of guy is the last I'd ever dream of getting involved with."

"Then why did you?"

"Call it kismet. He was liquored up and picking fights, and it looked as if he might wreck the whole joint, and the bartender finally called the cops. But before they arrived, the guy noticed me leaving and followed me out on the street. There was a police car getting close, and an empty cab just happened by, and I don't know how, maybe because I had had a snootful myself, but I hailed the cab and pushed the guy in and got in myself, and we just beat the patrol car to it."

"And now you've got him in your bed."

"He's fast asleep. But before he passed out, he made love to me as nobody ever did. He acted like I was Venus herself. Please don't laugh."

"I'm not laughing, Carol dear, I just didn't understand before."

"You probably still don't get it, and maybe neither do I. But even though I realize that he was either smashed or perhaps out of his head, or both, I still feel great all over. And it's depressing at the same time."

"Now I really don't get you."

"Think of when he wakes up in the morning. I'll have to face a different look in his eyes. The look of a man who'd wandered into my bed while he couldn't see straight. I just couldn't face it."

Carol's agitated whispering betrayed her anguish even more than what she was saying, and Doriana tried to choose the right words to reassure her, words that were hard to find. It was true that Carol had a nice body, but this man, after getting out of bed, would see only her old, tired face.

"He may be gone by the time you wake," were the only comforting words she was able to come up with, yet to her great relief, they worked.

"That's it," Carol said with a sudden lift in her low voice. "I must go to sleep and not think or worry any more. I'll take a few Nembutals, and while I'll be deeply asleep and dead to the world, he'll have one look at me when he sobers up and run, and he'll never get the chance to say anything. . . . Good night, Doriana. It's helped a lot getting it off my chest. I'm not afraid any more. Just so very tired. . . ."

"Take care, Carol dear," Doriana said warmly, feeling desperately sorry for Carol. She heard a click at the other end. Poor Carol, she thought, poor, poor Carol, and only reluctantly put the dead phone down herself.

Thirty-Two

There were noises behind her bedroom door. Charles and Louise must have heard her voice and come to investigate. Then all was quiet again.

Doriana paced the carpet and mechanically went to the bedside to find her mules. Why was she so upset? Was it still pity for poor old Carol, who gave herself to a barroom pickup in return for a brief moment of happiness? Or maybe it was something quite different that had triggered this malaise? How much younger was she really than Carol whom she so often pigeonholed as an old woman? How soon would *she* be like Carol?

And to fight the intensifying sense of dread she looked into the pink glass of her dressing table. But the magic mirror refused to respond obligingly as usual. And in her imagination she suddenly saw in it her bones, arteries and articulations altered by age as if in a revealing diabolical reflection, which instead of all its past flattering lies for once was determined to tell her the whole truth.

She covered her face with both hands, and stood still, trying to take hold of herself. As much as she disliked to rely on any kind of pills, she would have to take something to settle her nerves.

She was reaching for the bottle of tranquilizers when it struck her that Carol had said "a few Nembutals." One does not take a few Nembutals. And Carol also said that she would be deeply asleep and dead to the world. Was Carol talking about eternal sleep without any waking to trouble her last-minute happiness? Was Carol thinking about committing suicide while she was asking Carol to take care? She must call Carol back before it was too late; talk to her, talk her out of it. Then she realized that she didn't even know Carol's phone number. She remembered how difficult it had once been for Noelle to find it. But Noelle had written it down in the directory, with the rest of the unlisted numbers. Where would she keep it?

Slipping on her robe, she quietly ran down the stairs, trying not to disturb Hugh. Feverishly she turned on all the lights in the study. The desk was tidy, and there was no trace of the directory, which as a rule Noelle kept on the left corner of the desk. One by one, she opened the drawers. They were all empty; even the pile of scratch paper with Noelle's practicing of her signature was gone. It was in the last bottom drawer, pushed far back that she felt a thick book and pulled it out.

It was that old edition of *Bartlett's Familiar Quotations* that she had discarded. Mechanically she fingered the pages, as though Noelle, the meticulous and orderly Noelle would do an absurd thing like sticking Carol's home phone number in it. Presently she came across a red pencil mark beside a quotation about an old, old lady and a small boy of three, that, viciously paraphrased to mock her relationship with Arlen, had been handed her at the discotheque.

She knew the worn book so well. It was the reliable life-saver that had so many years ago helped her climb out of the bed of the freckled kid who stole the quotes from the Jerry show for her; the book whose revised edition she studied diligently lately to successfully compete against the aggressive Valerie Bing, the clever June Fleming and the studious Carol Nemm on the Brian Uxworthy show.

Nervously she started leafing through the dog-eared book, looking for the other quote about the perfume, she had received at the studio right before showtime, which she knew would also be checked in red pencil. There it was, of course. She sat quietly for a moment, her thoughts now slow and lucid. Why did Noelle do it? So it was she who had set out methodically to destroy the little of her self-assurance that was still left.

Now that she thought about it, she couldn't explain to herself why she hadn't suspected Noelle all along. Her young secretary was embittered by years of frustration and exposure to a constant display of all that she didn't have and wanted so desperately. But, naturally, this was no excuse for what Noelle had done to her. It was far worse than if the girl had stolen money or jewelry. . . . And thinking about theft suddenly reminded her of the checks in her evening handbag which she had absently left in the library earlier, and she went to look for it.

Her endorsement on the checks was countersigned by an unfamiliar name, and briefly she let herself be fooled by the perfection of her signature, but only briefly.

The meticulous Noelle had made another mistake that would put her behind bars. The "e" in Delor was written the way she used to write it up to perhaps three months ago, when she corrected it because Carol had remarked that writing "e" like that was old-fashioned. But Noelle got her sample signature before then, and went on writing it as she had practiced. There were hundreds of Noelle's phony signatures, identical with those on the embezzled checks, all over the country in replies to Delor fans. Any handwriting expert could easily establish the fraud. And Carol would certainly enjoy thinking that she had played a key part in the whole matter.

Doriana jumped to her feet. How selfish and callous one became in the kind of life she was leading! She had completely forgotten all about Carol, poor Carol who perhaps had already swallowed her sleeping pills. Because she had been sidetracked by her own affairs she had neglected to find a way of calling Carol back immediately. She must find Carol's address and phone number without losing another second.

It would be useless to try the TV station where one could never get any information from the night receptionist. And so was calling Uxworthy, whose phones were shut off for the night. And Cy would still be on his nocturnal prowling rounds of joints. No, she would try to phone somebody she was certain had gone home to bed early.

She practically ran to the phone. But nobody answered for an eternity, so maybe they were still out someplace. Then Arlen's voice, sounding even lower and huskier than usual, betrayed his annoyance.

"Who the hell do you want?"

"Arlen, it's Doriana. Please let me speak to Noelle."

There was a pause, then Arlen spoke in his normal voice. "You can't be serious? Why would Noelle be here?"

"You and I both know why, but never mind. It's a matter of life and death, I mean it literally. Please let me talk to her at once." The stereotyped phrase sounded corny, not even melodramatic, just corny and probably unconvincing.

Then, after another silence, he spoke with more assurance: "You're wrong, I'm all alone, dammit!"

She didn't believe him, yet how she wished to be proven wrong after all! She was like someone gravely ill, with all the symptoms of approaching end, but still hoping to the last for a word of reassurance. She had to know if Noelle was there for her own sake, but even more, for Carol's.

"I'm trying to find the address and phone number of Carol Nemm, you know, my co-panelist on the show. I'm afraid that she has or is going to take an overdose of sleeping pills. Noelle knows her address and phone number. She has it written down in a directory, but I can't find it. Noelle told me once that Carol lived in a nice neighborhood, so she must know, but all I remember is that it might be somewhere near Peter Cooper. Maybe it's Gramercy Park? Ask her!"

There was still another silence.

"Why don't you call Noelle at home? I took her home hours ago."

"Where does she live?" she asked, trying to trap him.

More silence. Doriana stretched her neck as though it could help her to hear what was going on in Arlen's bedroom. She thought she heard some whispering.

"On Chrystie Street in the Village."

She felt blinding rage at both of them. "I don't give a damn if Noelle is at your place. But I think you two ought to be shot if you let a woman die."

Shaking with indignation and despair, she strained her ear to the silence at the other end. There was no whispering any longer, and no sound of a click, so he was still there.

"Tell your wench to call the police and give them Carol Nemm's address."

Even in her agitated state of mind she realized that Noelle would hardly remember Carol's address by heart. But she couldn't just give up, so she kept on talking, even though she knew that Noelle wouldn't come to the phone.

"And if she doesn't, and if something happens to Carol, Noelle will be an accessory to it. And tell her she's not working for me any more, and not to have any illusions it's because of you. I have more important reasons, and she knows damn well what they are."

She hung up, and it was very quiet in the room. She was no longer trembling, and not even mortified that Arlen might realize how jealous she was of Noelle. That's what that double-crossing secretary would point out to him, even if he didn't think of it himself. She suddenly felt a sickening revulsion for the girl. And the realization that she was firing indispensable help did not bring regret but merely relief at ridding herself of an unscrupulous ingrate.

Her thoughts didn't linger on Noelle. It was Carol's fate that she was still preoccupied with. She had done all she could for now, but did she do the right thing? What if this suicide notion was only her imagination? What if the police, alerted by Noelle's call, broke into Carol's bedroom only to find her with a drunken bum, both soundly asleep in her bed? The papers and other news media were sure to play up the story, justifying Uxworthy's unfair bouncing of Carol off the show. . . .

Her own distraught sigh startled her as though it were someone else's. She didn't want to think about Arlen, but she couldn't help it, and envied Carol's refuge in deep sleep.

Thirty-Three

Doriana went back to bed, and lay awake, certain that Arlen was still making love with Noelle, his hard athletic body entwined with the teenager's, and hated them both, growing more and more wretched. And she thought that her love for Arlen could not live side by side with this new bitter resentment of him, and that there were only two alternatives to end this internal conflict—let it destroy her or give Arlen up forever. And although the idea of losing him was unbearable, and no matter how it hurt, and it hurt like hell, this was the right moment to ditch him and make a clean break, rather than to stretch it out and give him the advantage of ditching her.

But the crushing realization that the choice was really no longer hers at all, since Arlen had already left her, for this was what he had actually done, fueled her anguish even more. His occasional flings with some anonymous wenches and his unmistakable yen for her own ex-secretary were two entirely different matters, for knowing Arlen as well as she did she had no doubt whatever that his affair with Noelle would turn into a lasting relationship. For such was the power of Noelle's great youth, combined with her newly-found loveliness, the sortilege she knew so well since it had once been hers. . . .

Finally, from sheer exhaustion, she fell asleep, but the brief blackout did not bring her either physical or mental rest. She rang for her coffee, without realizing how early it was, and Louise appeared so fast that she wondered whether her maid, who seemed to have made a practice of waiting behind doors, had been standing outside her bedroom with the breakfast tray ready.

She glanced at Louise sullenly, not expecting to hear her

say anything beyond the "Bonjour Madame," since this was how she always wanted it—no news to digest, no problems to solve, no unpleasantness to face, until plenty of strong black coffee had dispelled her usual wake-up blues that this morning were deeper than ever before.

But another glance warned her that her maid was going to break the rule this time, and she didn't even have a chance to speculate what had made Louise look so irritably cheerful on such an unhappy day.

"There were quite a few calls for Madame," Louise said, translating from the French, in which she was thinking, as she spoke. "Monsieur Redfore has called three times already in the past twenty minutes." She set the tray on the bedside table and went about purposefully drawing open the heavy draperies.

"Don't you know that I always like to enjoy my coffee in peace?" she snapped, blinking at the sudden light. She knew that she didn't sound stern enough to discourage her maid.

"Monsieur Redfore sounded *très impatient.*" Louise paused and, looking aside as if refusing to take notice of Doriana's displeasure, added, apparently without seeing any connection, "And Miss Noelle hasn't reported for duty yet, and quite a bit of mail has arrived already."

The piles of unattended mail she had to cope with after Noelle's plastic surgery flashed through Doriana's mind. Now she must find a suitable replacement.

The heavy cloud had lifted somewhat after the second cup of strong coffee, and instead of the unproductive brooding, she was faced with practical problems, all disagreeable.

"Monsieur Arlen said to tell you that Miss Noelle called Miss Nemm last night and that everything was all right."

I had forgotten all about Carol, Doriana thought, deeply ashamed. Thank heaven everything was fine. She would have never forgiven herself had anything gone wrong. And Noelle had done the right thing and had called Carol first and not the police.

She became aware of Louise eyeing her curiously, evidently perishing to know what this was all about.

"Is Mr. Botain up?"

"Monsieur Botain was up very early. He had coffee and left. He said he had a business meeting at the Waldorf."

So Hugh had really meant it last night. Maybe this very minute he was selling his holdings in Wyoming. Or in Texas. Or both. The maid was again staring at her and somehow she had the impression that Louise could read her thoughts as clearly as she read hers—a practical telepathy born of long familiarity and circumstances.

"Monsieur Botain is such a fine gentleman," Louise commented. So they finally had a fight, she thought. Well, it was unavoidable. How long could an older husband tolerate his woman's young lover? It would be natural and acceptable for a short while, but it almost looked as though her mistress was married to two men at the same time. She had very mixed feelings about the triangle. She liked this handsome devil Arlen Redfore, whom she knew only through his TV shows and from his uninhibited telephone conversations with her mistress to which she enjoyed listening on an upper floor extension. What a lover, *quel mâle!* But her devotion to her employer made her prefer—should there have to be a choice between the two men—the older and more dependable Monsieur Botain.

Perhaps it was rather because of Hugh than because of what had happened between her and Arlen that Doriana was afraid to face the new day. How well she understood, now that she had felt the pain of rejection herself, how unfair she had been to subject Hugh to such an ordeal. And she reflected sadly on how true it was that if Arlen did not deserve her love, she certainly merited Hugh's devotion even less, and that exactly as Arlen had been taking her for granted and using her, so had she accepted all of Hugh's love and consideration for the past two years as if it were her due, without giving him anything worthwhile in return, as though her allowing him to bask in her presence was reward enough.

And she thought wryly of how just it was that now it was she who found herself on the receiving end of deceit and betrayal, the awful, and oh how well-earned, moment of truth. . . .

And because she was thinking about it earnestly for the first time in her life, she began seriously weighing Hugh's latest plea to settle with him in Australia. Although he had added nothing new, perhaps because fate was forcing her hand, she felt herself yielding to the temptation to say yes this time.

Maybe Louise noticed some indefinable look of perplexed wonder in her face, because before leaving the room Louise turned around a couple of times and finally put her puzzlement into words:

"Is Madame considering a new film or show?"

"Yes, I'm thinking about an entirely different type of show," said Doriana.

Crossing to the vanity, which was the next step after the coffee, and before her bath, she looked in the mirror that ordinarily helped lift the gloomy cloud. Only for a second did she recall the tricky reflection. But as if the disturbing recollection could never be totally forgotten, so did the mirror seem to have retained some occult power of revealing secret things that her usually confident eyes had never seen before. It was not new eye bags, nor lines around her eyes or mouth.

It was the expression of her eyes that made her cringe as if in pain. And once again her mind went back to Carol, for this was the look that she had so often caught in Carol's eyes.

She knew only too well the logical and inexorable progression of changes wrought by aging. Some wrinkles were an early sign, and one could only wonder or guess which lines appeared first. That was nothing to worry about; it was all in the domain of cosmetic surgery, abrasion and collagen injections, although of course some things, like the creases around the mouth that expressed both laughter and suffering were easier to correct than the lines etched on the forehead by frowning, or even more so, the vertical lines of tension between one's eyebrows. Then came the chinline, and this was also a correction that Dr. Orgood or even any of his associates could easily take care of. One could also get rid of eye puffiness, provided one had the good sense to have a reputable cosmetic eye surgeon do the job.

The true giveaway, however, was not the face, nor even the tortuous arteries that marred the once smooth forehead, but the discreet pigmented spots on one's skin—the alarm signals of insidiously slowing metabolism, the stigma of age. Yet even these blemishes could be removed or disguised long after the lifeless mask of an expressionless face refused to look alive and young after too many lifts, like Carol's face after her last cosmetic operation. There was one thing that no plastic surgeon could ever correct, no makeup could ever conceal, no expression ever alter—the dispirited soul that stared dully through one's eyes.

Doriana watched herself in horror. When did it happen? How could she have missed the dreadful moment when she had started to betray her despairs, doubts and anxieties that somehow crowded out her youthful enthusiasm for life and her unfailing confidence? Did anybody suspect her defeat while she was still a winner? Who had guessed? The one man who didn't was Hugh, she hoped.

Without analyzing herself any longer she ran to the telephone and her heart was pounding so wildly when she got Hugh on the line that she could scarcely talk.

He did not seem aware of her agitation. He was only puzzled by such an early call.

"Darling, I must see you right away. Could you make it back home before noon?" she said breathlessly into the receiver.

"Something wrong?"

"No, not a thing. I have a pleasant surprise for you, but I don't want to discuss it over the phone."

Yet despite her lighthearted tone, she felt no joy when she hung up. Did she really decide, just like that in a matter of a

moment, something that had been so difficult even to consider? Did she really intend to go away with Hugh to Australia without any further vacillating and doubting and fighting him and herself? Why not? There was really nothing more
to keep her here in New York, was there? And she could still
go on making an occasional movie and do guest shots on TV
in Europe and the States. After all it took only seventeen
hours to fly from Australia to the West Coast now, and one
of these days the crossing would take considerably less with
newer supersonic jets. And who knows, perhaps she would
start a new TV career right there in Melbourne, where Hugh
owned a large town house. Hugh would probably even buy
her a jet to travel in without having to depend on com-
mercial flights.

For a flashing second she had the temptation to include
Arlen in her fantasizing about the future, but forced herself
back to reality. I have made my decision, and that was that,
I've made it, I've made it, she kept repeating to herself, as if
trying to blot out the fact that the decision had actually been
made for her.

She walked over to the dressing table and stood still in
front of the mirror, without looking in it, afraid of the same
nightmarish reflection she imagined she saw a while ago, but
when she lifted her eyes, they disclosed nothing more than a
touch of bafflement, like those of a child discovering a
whole new world. She switched on some more lights, but
her eyes remained untroubled with only a few fine lines
around them. One did not shut one's eyes in despair with
complete impunity, she thought. But the eyes of Doriana
Delor, the most beautiful woman in show business, were one
thing, and those of Mrs. Hugh Botain, the most beautiful
housewife, quite another.

The phone rang, but she did not lift the receiver. It could
be Arlen. He must have invented some plausible justification
for his behavior last night.

"Your manager is on the phone, Madame," said Louise,
appearing in the door.

"This is my third try this morning," Cy told her wearily.

"Why's everybody up so early today? What can you possibly have to tell me that couldn't keep?"

"It's about Carol. Carol Nemm."

For a moment she thought that he was again talking about Uxworthy's decision to drop Carol, and nearly lost her temper. Then her memory washed over the past hours and brought back a ghastly suspicion.

"Cy, anything wrong?"

But he remained silent. Why do some people always seem to enjoy so much telling others grisly things? He had been trying so hard to get through the busy line to be the first to break the news as gently as he knew how to Doriana, who was so impressionable, so good-hearted and such a true friend of Carol's. . . .

"Cy, for heaven's sake, say something! So she did, she did take those damn sleeping pills after all! I was afraid of that, I was afraid of it last night. I—"

"No, she didn't." he broke in.

"She didn't?" she echoed softly, more and more grateful for the reassuring words. "She didn't take the pills, thank God!"

"No, she didn't," he repeated, still stalling yet realizing that he must tell her the truth now. "No," he went on with difficulty, "but she would have been better off if she had. Poor Carol got herself murdered last night."

Thirty-Four

To have lost her job, the kind of job she would have a tough time getting again, even if she could produce a good reference, seemed like a depressing thing to have to face, especially with a stiff hangover. Noelle sleepily silenced her alarm clock, which insisted that it was high time to get up if she wanted to make it to Doriana Delor's by ten, even without taking a few minutes for the toothbrush or coffee.

"Shuddup," she told the alarm clock. "I've no job to go to."

The meaning of what she said out loud, still half asleep, suddenly became clear, and she woke up completely and lay still, evaluating her situation. No job. No salary. That was bad. No more Doriana Delor and her silly fan mail—that was good. Arlen. Her Arlen, whom she took away from Doriana—that was terrific.

She wasn't given long to savor the final tally in her favor. The determined ringing of the doorbell, which generally meant the mailman, sent her scrambling out of bed. She ran to the door and glanced through the peephole. This was one precaution she never overlooked. She had moved to the East Village because the neighborhood atmosphere with its informality appealed to her. But one never could tell when some ordinarily harmless hophead desperate for the price of a fix might all of a sudden show up with who knows what ideas.

She saw Ben's face, removed the chain and opened the door.

He brushed past her, visibly disturbed. "I've something important to talk to you about," he said, flinging himself on the chair by the door.

His face, a reliable barometer of his stormy outbursts, was

congested as if he had had little or no sleep after an all-night binge.

She nodded her head, feeling no self-consciousness about her nakedness—she slept in the raw the year round. She knew him well enough to realize that he meant what he said. Ben wouldn't be sidetracked by a commonplace sight like a girl's nude body when he had business on his mind.

Slipping on a see-through negligee he had given her, she went to the kitchenette and plugged in the electric coffee percolator on the counter. "Like some coffee?" she asked him, shaking off the unruly auburn hair that fell over her eyes. "I always set it up before turning in, so I don't have to fuss in the morning. It'll take a couple of minutes. Be right back," she said, before disappearing behind the bathroom door.

The coffee was ready when she returned and Ben gratefully accepted a mugful, moving toward the table. "It sure hits the spot." He sipped it greedily. "Remember, I asked you to get back the checks we cashed?"

"That *you* cashed," she said pointedly.

He nearly blew up, but controlled himself, managing not to raise the tone of his voice.

"Okay, that I cashed and that *we* spent. Anyway, you don't have to bother."

"That's good news. I don't know how I would've swung it. She gave me the gate by phone last night."

"How come?"

She shrugged. "She must have gotten sore, after all. You were right about that. Anyhow, she wanted me to call the cops about that old Carol Nemm dame taking some pills to do herself in. But I phoned Nemm first and she was okay."

"It sure is a small world," he said.

She looked at him with puzzled eyes. He was strangely cool now, and his face reflected more consternation than anger.

"I don't get you," she said, pouring some more coffee into their mugs. "Care for a Danish? Prune or cheese?"

He ignored her offer. "I know she didn't commit suicide, because I was with her last night. She's dead, all right, but not from pills."

She stared at him, without understanding.

"Last night I picked up a gorgeous chick in a saloon on Second Avenue. You should've seen her—one in a mil— and I let myself get loaded like a stupid punk who'd never had a drop before."

"And you passed out."

"I sure as hell did after awhile. But worse than that, when I came to, instead of her there was this old witch in the sack with me."

"You're putting me on," she said, sorry she had interrupted him. Once one interrupted Ben it was hard to get him back on the track. He again looked as though he were about to lose his temper, and she tried to soothe him. "How did she get there?"

"That's what I wanted to know. And she only grinned, and said, 'Look at me, don't you know me?!' I pushed her away and she fell out of bed and hit her head against the table, but not real hard, and lay there, and when I shook her to make her get up I saw that she was dead. I went through her purse and it had an American Express card and a couple of other credit and ID cards, all made out to Carol Nemm."

Noelle backed away as far as the wall let her, and her terrified expression infuriated him as though he could read her thoughts.

"Come on, you little nitwit, I didn't kill her! But I'd have a helluva time proving it. And that's where you figure."

"Me? What do I have to do with it?"

"You're my partner, remember, kiddo?"

"No way! Not in something like that!" She forgot to be afraid of him now. The main danger seemed to be associated with him in general.

He stood uncomfortably close to her, and looking in her eyes knew that he would not have any problems with her anymore.

"Look, I told you I didn't want you to do anything, not even get those checks. I'll take care of it myself, although I have worse things to worry about now than those goddam checks. I'll do it for your sake, for old lang syne. But I'll have to step on it."

"I don't get it," she said, and her voice trembled.

"You will. You've got a key to Delor's place. Where is it?"

She still had the key she had borrowed from Yvonne. Charles had let her keep it, because it was more convenient to let her come and go without having to open doors for her. After all, she made part of the household staff. Now she was sorry that she had bragged to Ben about it.

"What do you need a key to her place for?" she asked.

"It'll take the cops a day or two to trace me to that Nemm woman. They will, soon as they find the pretty kid I picked up at the saloon who must know that dead old dame, for how else did I end up in her pad?"

"But what does Miss Delor's key have to do with it?"

"You're a dum-dum! I have exactly twenty-three bucks and seven cents left in my pockets, and even if you have any bread left—"

"Not a penny."

"See? I've got to split, but fast. You told me that she often carries quite a bundle of cash in her handbag."

"You've got to be kidding! How do you expect to get up to her place? The doormen, the elevator men, her servants. And how about Mr. Botain?"

"One of the doormen is an old army buddy of mine, remember? And he knows about us. He'll let me through if I tell him I came for your things. And as for her servants and her old man—"

Could he be toting a gun? Could he have lied to her about Carol falling out of bed and accidentally hitting her head? And in that case. . . .

"The key?"

She didn't like the look on his face. She nodded meekly, and pointed to her pocketbook on the dresser.

Without a word he walked over to it and, spilling the contents of her purse on the table, carefully picked up the two keys.

"Which is it?" he asked.

She was thinking. Of course she could lie to him. Give him her own key. Then call Doriana to warn her. They'd arrest him as soon as he appeared. Perhaps a grateful Doriana would rehire her, letting bygones be bygones. . . .

It was curious how Noelle's feelings had changed in the last few hours. Perhaps her bitter prejudice against Doriana, who had been so good to her from the start, had been nothing but jealousy because of Arlen, jealousy whipped up by her constant eavesdropping on Doriana's revealing telephone conversations with Arlen. And now that she had taken him away from Doriana, for this is what she thought she had accomplished, mistaking Arlen's intense love-making for true passion for her, this enmity had evaporated, leaving in its wake a sense of her own triumph mixed with sympathy for her beaten "rival".

But if she made peace with Doriana she would lose Arlen. And what about those incriminating checks that Ben promised to get back for her while he was robbing Doriana? . . .

Noelle now had no concern for Ben himself. His vile temper and his risky gambles seriously outweighed the benefits they both reaped from his schemes. No. She had had it with him. With Arlen Redfore interested in her she was in another class altogether. She was on her way up. The couple of songs that Arlen would arrange for her to sing in a club or maybe even on somebody's TV show, would be a stepping-stone. She had her destiny and Ben had his. Her sole worry was to what extent Ben would implicate her, could implicate her, if he were arrested.

Hoping that he did not notice her momentary vacillation, she removed her own key from Ben's hand, leaving in his open palm the one to Doriana's triplex, and knew that she had done the smart thing.

"I saw you hesitating, baby. You've only two keys here, and one is obviously to your 'palace', the other to her co-op. I'd have tried the key you gave me on my way out, and if it fitted it would have meant that you double-crossed me. Maybe you were thinking of phoning your boss, giving her plenty of time to call the fuzz while I'd be fumbling at her door with the wrong key. If you had, I would've made you sorry."

His eyes had that certain shrewd gleam again, as always when he scored a point. One thing Ben was not; he wasn't stupid.

"Why would I?" she said, trying to steady her voice. "Haven't you promised to get me back those canceled checks?"

"Now you're making sense. I'll get in touch when things cool off." He spoke calmly now, putting the key in his pocket. "I'll mail you the key and the checks before I leave town."

As soon as he was gone, cupping her breast in her hand, as if afraid that her heart might leap out of her fragile ribcage, in the same gesture she used while watching Arlen on TV or listening to his voice over the phone and imagining that it was he caressing her, she moved quickly to the door, and with a loud sigh of relief put on the chain.

Thirty-Five

The more Hugh thought about Doriana's phone call the more it puzzled him. What kind of surprise did she have for him? Was it a particularly important movie contract or another TV series offer? Anything of that sort would stimulate Doriana, although by now she should know better than to expect him to share in her pleasure at such news, which would automatically mean her devoting still more of her life to her career and less and less to him.

And when he went down in the elevator and was slowly walking in the block-long Waldorf lobby toward the barbershop on the Lexington side, and while he was reclining in the barbershop chair, idly listening to the chatter of his barber mixing his Italian-flavored dialect with the Lower-East-Side singsong of the reedy manicurist, he was no longer thinking about Doriana's phone call but was trying to concentrate on what he intended to bring up at the unavoidable business conference.

When he returned to his Tower suite, his valet, Peter, announced knowingly:

"You had a lady caller, Sir. I invited her in, but she said she'd rather meet you downstairs in the main lobby, near Peacock Alley. She's been waiting there for a while now. It's the same young lady whom you brought here with you some time ago, Sir."

Peter was naturally not talking about Doriana, who was the only other woman who had ever been up here.

So Stephanie was back from France. And she was here to tell him that she was ready for the job in Australia. How could he have forgotten that he had offered it to her? It seemed like such a good idea at the time, to abort their

208

sudden regrettable intimacy by sending her away. But now it crossed his mind that perhaps Doriana's surprise had something to do with their last night's conversation. What if she had a change of heart about going with him to Australia? What terrible timing it would be sending Stephanie to where they would be going themselves. He shrugged. This complication he was inventing was farfetched of course. And his wishful thinking about his wife was as unrealistic as his inclination not to attend a business lunch set for one o'clock.

On his way down he wondered why Stephanie refused to wait for him at his place. Was she afraid that it might end as it had the last time?

Presently he was holding Stephanie's hands in his and eyeing her curiously, as if he were seeing her for the first time. For one thing, her hair was tinted a reddish-brown and she had on a bit of makeup. He also noticed that she was wearing one of those pant suits, definitely not something she would have worn before.

"Good to see you, Stephanie." He bent down and nuzzled her on both cheeks. "You should have waited for me upstairs in my flat," he scolded, and was amused when her face turned crimson. Suddenly she looked like the old familiar Stephanie, and he knew that he had guessed right why she preferred to meet him in public. "When did you get back? How was Paris?"

"I got back a couple of days ago. And Paris was *magnifique, formidable!*"

He hasn't noticed how much I've changed, she thought moodily, remembering how only a short time ago she felt that she had to rationalize her belated desire to improve her appearance. How superficial her contempt for the vanity of looking younger and more glamorous really was. Or perhaps it had never been a sincere conviction, but only an easy excuse for letting herself go. In that small seafood place, imagining that a man she then knew so little had a beautiful girl friend she knew not at all, had suddenly made her acutely conscious of her overweight, graying hair and shapeless clothes. And the worn morale-bolstering notion about youthfulness and glamour being important only to silly "sex objects" and not to liberated, commonsensical and intelligent women, now did not seem so valid. Besides, why the hell should she consider herself intelligent? The smart of this world were the ones who did the most with the least and not those who did nothing with something. And this intellectual drivel of hers hasn't done her any good, has it?

"Let's sit here," she indicated a few unoccupied chairs in the central square.

"How long do you think you'd need here before going to work on my collections in Australia?" Hugh asked, as soon as they sat down.

She didn't react immediately, and he couldn't figure out what she was thinking. Somehow her face wasn't as easy to read as before. Not knowing why, he remembered how he had once thought that without any makeup, except maybe a touch of lipstick, she must be looking the same early in the morning straight out of bed as she did on dates.

He didn't waste any time trying to get rid of me by exiling me to a faraway job without interference with his married life with Doriana Delor, she thought.

Perhaps it was when she had accidentally learned from an illustrated story in *Paris Match* who her "rival" was—the world-famous and dazzlingly beautiful blonde she would have to be insane to imagine Hugh would ever leave for her —that her unhappiness at his attitude toward her turned into resentment.

"I feel guilty about having to go back on my word, Hugh," she said after a brief pause, "but I won't be working for a while. In fact, I've already resigned my job here in New York."

"Are you ill? You certainly don't look it."

"Never felt better," she said, and laughed. "There are other reasons why women quit working."

He looked at her closely. Egad, was it possible? It had never entered his mind that their quickie intercourse might end up in her pregnancy. Although she wasn't the type to be on the Pill just in case, of course, and she certainly hadn't planned on having sex that evening. Still, it would be one hell of a bloody mess. And she might turn out to be one in a million who nowadays was against having an abortion.

Neither his scrutiny nor his scowling escaped her. He misunderstood me, she thought. He got the idea that I'm expecting a child. His child. He clearly took it for granted that he was the father. She had a sudden urge to confirm his suspicion. But why did she want him to believe that? What was her real motive? A subtle revenge for rejecting her? Or futile hope that it might somehow influence their relationship? Or simply to get a lot of money from him?

"I really came back to settle all my uncomplicated business here in a hurry. I have to jet back to Paris tomorrow. Jerome and I plan to be married this coming Friday and—" she interrupted herself, noticing his startled look and elaborated: "Jerome is the guy I met in Paris."

The truth was that even if Jerome wanted a divorce, which Stephanie strongly doubted, he couldn't get it anyway, so there was no question of marriage either. But since she had lost whatever illusions she might have ever had that her relationship with Hugh was anything more than a one-shot affair, she had little to jeopardize by bolstering her own ego with imaginary tales about her other conquests. Or maybe she simply lied to Hugh about her getting married to kill the persistent temptation to exploit him one way or another. But it was certainly bum luck to become involved with a millionaire devoted to a young and beautiful wife, and then have an affair on the rebound with another man, who wasn't free either and penniless in the bargain.

Hugh wondered if Stephanie had guessed what he had imagined for a moment. He felt relieved and foolish at the same time. How fortunate that he didn't give himself away. Perhaps it was because he had almost made a bloody ass of himself, but he could hardly curb his mounting irritation. Or maybe it was because she had taken him in. So that's what

she was really like. How long did it take her after their enjoying sex on his sofa to get involved with this Jerome? He
realized that their relationship didn't entitle him to any
explanation, nor bind her to a damn thing either, and that
he didn't care and that it was nothing but a touch of male
vanity. And, as for moral indignation, how long did it take
him after being with Stephanie to hop into bed with his own
wife?

"I'm very happy for you, my dear," he said.

"Let me tell you a bit more about Jerome, then you'll
understand how really lucky I am," she continued to lie.
Telling Hugh about her attractive lover, who was a younger
man, was another way of getting even with him.

He was barely listening to her account about that Jerome
chap, the successful author of several prestigious books, who
was teaching 19th-century literature at the Sarbonne, and how
they had met at the Cité Universitaire. He was thinking that
now all at once Doriana seemed closer and more important
to him than ever.

Stephanie stopped talking, and he wondered if the last
thing she said called for a reply, but she bailed him out.

"So you see, one doesn't have to be an international beauty
to be loved. By the right fellow," she added. "So beauty isn't
everything."

How different Stephanie's taking in stride her drabness
was from Doriana's fretting about the slightest line on her
face, Hugh thought. But somehow this comparison didn't
seem fair, and it wasn't because he adored Doriana and was
only casually interested in Stephanie. Something else was
bothering him, and he finally realized that it was Stephanie's
expression throughout their conversation.

He was too shrewd a businessman, and too experienced an
old hand at antique auctions, not to recognize a competing
bidder's bluff. So perhaps it wasn't his imagination when he
thought that Stephanie was leading him to believe that he
had made her pregnant. So maybe she had been lying all
along about other matters also. What was she up to? Had she

intended a little blackmail and had gotten cold feet? Or was she trying to annoy him? And her story about her French romance, could she possibly imagine that she could make him jealous? And this petty cheating, at which he was only guessing, stripped Stephanie of practically the only good points she might boast about—her honesty and common sense. Perhaps it was all for the best that she had not accepted his job offer.

"I'm truly glad for you," he said. "You must give me your address in Paris."

Maybe he is thinking of sending me a wedding present, she mused. The fact was that she didn't have any permanent Paris address, and she couldn't very well give him that of Jerome's home where his wife would receive Hugh's gift. For all she knew it could turn out to be a fat check. She'd rather starve than ask him for a loan, but a gift of cash would certainly help a lot in the circumstances. She hesitated only a second.

"We're changing apartments," she said, "but you can get in touch with me care of American Express." She would get his gift with a slight delay.

"Fine. You'll hear from me," he promised. "It's too bad that I have an urgent business conference scheduled, or perhaps we might've had lunch together," he added, mostly to keep up appearances.

"I'll take a rain check. One of these days I'll pop up in Fun City again," she said breezily, not meaning it either.

Thirty-Six

Doriana did not listen to what her manager told her after hearing from him the tragic news about Carol. She sat motionless when he had finally hung up, trying to piece together what she could recall of the disconnected bits of his account. Something about Carol leaving a small Second Avenue tavern with a disorderly boozer whom other patrons knew by sight. So Carol's killer would not run around loose for long. Poor Carol, who had given up long before her heart and breathing had stopped, wasn't even buried yet, but a replacement was most likely already boning up on quotations to fill her spot.

She shook her head sadly and got up. Her life must also go on. She was startled by a noise behind her and abruptly turned around.

It was Louise, theatrically wringing her hands—a gesture that befitted the expression of compassion on her rosy face—undoubtedly having as usual eavesdropped on her telephone conversation on one of the extensions.

"*La pauvre malheureuse!* And she was such a nice . . . lady."

Louise had hesitated before calling Carol a lady, Doriana thought. For in Louise's eyes a lady fell into one of two categories: she was either rich, or successful in getting money from men. A rich kept woman filled the qualification on both counts. Poor Carol did not qualify on either. What folly everything was . . . and yet they all went on playing this cruel game of life so earnestly. She, too, would have to shake off her melancholy for Hugh's sake. She glanced at the window, trying to guess how late it was. Sometimes it was impractical not to keep clocks in the house, even if it gave one the false illusion of arresting time. She sighed deeply, as if she could sigh away her sadness. Hugh should be home shortly. She would like to talk to him without her curious couple in the house.

"Louise, please ask Charles to take my white mink to Ben Kahn's to have it cleaned right away. There's no time to have them call for it," she said.

"But, Madame, it was cleaned only—"

"It's not as clean as I'd like it. And please get some strawberries. Mr. Botain will be home for lunch."

Aha, so that's what it was—a reconciliation lunch; they must have had a fight. Or why would her mistress want to be alone with Monsieur Botain? Maybe it was because Madame was planning to make up with her husband by again frolicking with him in that chair downstairs? No, she decided, not with that poor old dead *poule* on Madame's mind.

"I could ask Charles to pick up some strawberries on his way back from the furrier's," Louise said, playing dumb.

"You'd better do it yourself, and be sure to get the best California berries on Madison. . . . Oh, yes, and you might as well take my pearl necklace to Cartier's for restringing. Take your time, provided both you and Charles are back by noon."

So she was determined to be alone, Louise thought, pouting visibly. *Merde!* She would have liked to know about the surprise her mistress had promised Monsieur Botain over the phone.

It was always a problem to get her maid to carry out orders, but once she had made up her mind to do what she was told, Louise proved the most efficient person in the world. She was still wondering whether it mightn't be a good idea to give Louise another errand to run, to keep her out for a while, when she heard the back door click shut behind the couple. She need not worry about Charles returning too soon. Charles always took his time. He would first hurry over to the furrier's, but afterward he would loiter on a busy Fifth Avenue corner, watching the leggy girls.

It was quiet in the house now, and she walked up and

down the stairs, from room to room, trying to create an illusion of life, while Carol's dead eyes and the wistful smile she had seen on her face as she left the dressing room the other night, followed her around. She almost regretted now to have sent the servants away. How thick the walls of her apartment were, a good centrally air-conditioned building with tightly sealed windows and solid privacy. One could be screaming at the top of one's voice in here without being heard. Why didn't Carol scream for help? What time did she die? And what was keeping Hugh?

More than ever before she knew that she had made up her mind. It was Carol's dead eyes now staring at her with that dullness she had glimpsed in her own eyes earlier, which made her want to get away from everything, even if she couldn't run away from herself.

She felt cold, and the muffled ringing of the phone that was always turned down until early afternoon startled her as if it were Big Ben. She listened to its insistent, almost inaudible ringing with a sense of relief, enjoying its rattling as if it were the most harmonious sound she had ever heard. Was it Arlen again? If it was, she didn't want to talk to him. But perhaps it was Hugh, calling to say that he was delayed, that he couldn't make it? Her heart fell, and the ringing acquired a rueful note.

Just as she was about to lift the receiver, the ringing ceased and she heard the click at the front door. Hugh was finally here! More eager than she had ever been in her life, and ignoring the phone that had started to ring again, she was at the door before it opened, ready to throw her arms around Hugh.

But standing quietly in the entrance was the massive figure of a well-dressed young stranger. His dark eyebrows were almost knitted together, lending his rather handsome face a menacing expression.

The worst possible thing, she thought, if indeed he had broken in, was to show fear. She always knew how to handle men, all kinds of men, young and old, rich and poor, good or bad.

Nonchalantly letting the door slam behind him he took a step toward her and his face suddenly relaxed, and presently he smiled, flashing strong white teeth.

"You needn't be afraid of me," he said.

His voice was strangely familiar, but she couldn't connect it with the man's face.

"Who are you? Do I know you?"

"You must know quite a few guys, or you wouldn't wonder if you knew me."

There was a touch of sarcasm in his voice, and it gave his words an insulting ring.

"Your voice is familiar, but I don't recall ever seeing you before."

"You haven't, but I've seen you often, including that day in the hospital when I had a good look at you."

Now she knew why his voice was so familiar. So this was the man who had nearly raped her while she was blinded by bandages after her cosmetic eyelid operation and who had finally caught up with her here in her own well-guarded home.

Moving brusquely, he crossed to the foyer phone extension, lifted the receiver and dropped it back into the cradle.

And only in the abrupt silence did she realize that the phone had kept on humming all the time. And more and more afraid, she felt furious at herself for not thinking of it sooner. All she should have done was to dash to the phone, grab it and call for help. Or she could have run to the house phone and summoned the doorman.

He must have intercepted her look, for he suddenly broke into laughter, and like the guffaws of the studio audience at her witticisms, it again eased the tension.

Without noticing that she had regained her composure, his eyes returned to her practically naked breasts, that seemed to materialize more and more out of the sheer silk folds of her negligee, and the awareness that she was defenseless in this empty three-layer-cake of an apartment exacerbated his craving. And even the boozing, the emotional shock of realizing that he was somehow implicated in a woman's violent death, and near-exhaustion after all that sex before passing out last night, could not tame his desire.

She observed him with mounting distress. What could she do to save herself from him? "You'd better go before one of my servants comes down. My butler is armed," she attempted weakly.

He felt something approaching indignation for a moment. How important was it to this woman to deny him her celebrated body that so many men had had before? He was beginning to lose his temper. If he was prepared to gamble with his freedom by putting off leaving town, it was certainly not to waste time on talk.

"Look, you beautiful fool, you're alone here. Your slaves are out, and I haven't time to lose."

She made another desperate attempt. "I'll give you my jewelry. You can have it all if you just leave me alone." Who could resist her famous gems? she thought, trying to buck up.

"Believe me, Doriana, you're in for a treat with an exceptionally well-endowed guy. Let's not waste any more time."

Watching her changing expression, he knew that he had won. Perhaps it was this rapid disintegration of all pretense of poise and self-confidence bred by years of unchallenged success, that made her all at once look like a vulnerable child. Her blond flesh suddenly reminded him of how it felt to touch her full, velvety breasts.

And lifting her eyes Doriana instantly realized the inevitability of what was about to happen.

Thirty-Seven

Doriana lost only two or three seconds wondering what to do. There was a bolt on her bedroom door. If she could manage to dash up to the second floor and lock the door behind her, she could phone for help before he broke it down. But the library was closer, and her evening bag with the emerald ring in it was still there on Hugh's chair where she had left it. Maybe if she had the time to dangle the priceless gem before him it might change his mind. Hugh would be here any minute. If only she could stall for time.

"Let me give you my emerald ring anyway," she said. She quickly turned around and started to cross the foyer. She felt his hot breath on the back of her neck just as she entered the library. She bent down to pick up her purse, and this was a mistake.

He grabbed her from behind in his strong arms, pushing her forward into the softness of Hugh's chair and burying her face in its pliable leather.

"Don't, don't!"

There was so much anguish in her outcry that it reached him in spite of his excitement.

"Don't fight me, gorgeous," he said, but he relaxed his grip enough to allow her to wriggle around and face him.

She felt his rigid penis against her body. How long could she resist him?"

"Don't fight me," he repeated squeezing her arms with such force that she could not help screaming.

It was no use. She might as well let him get it over with.

He did not need any encouragement. He felt a mounting urge to enter this lovely body he had dreamed of, asleep or awake, for so many years. And at the moment when he

219

thought he could not bear it any longer, he suddenly felt her unexpected submissiveness and forgot about everything else.

Doriana was sprawled uncomfortably, one leg pinned down over an armrest, her head pushed into one of the corners, conscious of his weight multiplied a thousandfold by his active thrust, as if he were still fighting to subdue her.

Be done with it, be done with it, she thought. Dear God, it would never end. "Let me go!" She wasn't quite sure whether she had thought, whispered or cried out her entreaty.

In the first moments when he felt the warmth and softness of her parting body he nearly lost consciousness of all else. But somehow, despite his excitement, his coming appeared more and more remote, and gradually his craving once more began yielding to growing frustration and hot anger against this cold woman whose indifference was denying him. He felt sharp pain in his penis, a pain that grew unbearably stronger and stronger.

"I'll wake you up, you bitch!" he shouted, pinching her breast, and kept on pinching it as if he wanted to destroy it.

She let out a scream and tried to shake his body off hers. But as she fought savagely an odd thing began to happen. It was as if the desperation whipped up by pain, loathing and fear suddenly aroused all her senses. And baffled and horrified and hating herself for it, she felt her body reacting to his. All at once she did not feel the pain any longer, and didn't think about the horror of being raped. There was only the welling up of the approaching climax. And she came in endless spasmodic waves of a tidal orgasm, the kind of delirious fulfillment she had rarely enjoyed since her "nymphet" days.

She heard him curse wildly when she went limp under him, and a second later she felt a stabbing pain in her right shoulder as he brutally bit her, and she jumped up screaming.

"That's how I brand my stable," he said.

She could hardly keep on her feet. Her whole bruised, aching body, with a thousand individual hurts, seemed to be as painful as the bite which was now bleeding slowly from the deep impressions of his strong teeth.

His face was still congested, with vertical lines cutting his brow, and her fear briefly submerged by her involuntary sexual response, reappeared from the depths and turned her weak voice unsteady.

"Get out. You got what you wanted," she said wearily again.

"You mean *you* got what you wanted, you whore," he growled, staring at her.

What a big laugh the whole mess was! And it looked as if his intentional lies to Noelle would turn out to be the truth after all, and all he would end up with was those lousy incriminating checks, he thought resentfully.

"I'll take those canceled checks Noelle told me your manager turned over to you last night," he said.

She suddenly understood so many things at once. But what was there to say?

Maybe she only imagined that he laughed out loud when she turned away from him to look for her handbag that must have slipped from the now empty chair. No, she did not imagine it. He was laughing uninhibitedly, shaking the long-stemmed yellow roses in the tall Steuben glass vase on the table.

His loud laughter stopped so abruptly that she nervously spun around.

He had not moved toward her, and wasn't even looking in her direction. He was silently watching Hugh standing in the open library door.

Thirty-Eight

Not sure what to make of it, Hugh let his eyes wander from Doriana to the stranger and back again. She was vainly pulling her torn negligee over her bared breasts, and her always artfully coiffured hair hung in limp disarray over her puffy face. He couldn't figure out her expression. And the well-tailored, burly young man with dark wavy hair mussed over his creased forehead, who was laughing when he entered, did not look or act like a surprised intruder.

Doriana was pressing one of her hands against her lacerated shoulder, without realizing that this instinctive gesture would have such grave consequences.

Hugh, who could not see that she was bleeding, stared at her, waiting for an explanation, but she averted her eyes and did not rush over to him for protection, nor even call for help, but just stood there as if petrified. So maybe he had walked in on them while they were having a wild affair. But how could that be, since she had been expecting him back home?

"What's going on here?" Hugh asked, gazing at her.

But she said nothing.

Only a few minutes ago she would have given anything imaginable to have Hugh here. But now, how gladly she would pay the same price for not having to look at her husband's bewildered face that was slowly reddening with anger. She was desperately trying to collect her thoughts, but her assailant's arrogance seemed to add to her confusion. He should be stopped. Hugh would at a sign from her. But was Hugh a match for this young man with those powerful shoulders and arms? Hugh was much taller, but also much older, and he might get hurt. And the man might be armed.

Ben, who had not moved, trying to appear as nonchalant as possible and grinning confidently from Doriana to Hugh, suddenly caught the determined look that had slipped into her haggard face. Was she going to make trouble for him, after all? If so, maybe he had better change her mind for her in a hurry.

"If you think that I forced her into anything, Mr. Botain, you're wrong. Just ask her if she had her kicks or not. Go ahead, ask her, ask her," he insisted.

The sound of his name slapped Hugh like spit. He looked from the smiling young man who was casually lighting a cigarette to Doriana who gave no hint of having heard the crude remark. So it was after all an unsavory affair with this individual she seemed to know well. His face flushed to a deeper hue.

"Don't listen to him," she forced herself to tell Hugh, but she knew that she sounded unconvincing, and it made her lose the little composure she had been able to muster.

How does a woman explain that an orgasm with a powerfully equipped rapist is not an act of consent? That it does not compensate for the degradation, horror and pain? How could she explain anything to Hugh when she couldn't explain it to herself? Explain why her body that recently had so often refused to thaw out in the arms of her husband or even in those of her young lover should respond so vibrantly in the grip of a rapist? Was she a subconscious masochist?

Taking advantage of Doriana's silence and apparent indecision Ben edged past Hugh toward the door, but made the mistake of checking his fly, and his gesture triggered her almost hysterical reaction.

"Get out, get out!" she screamed at Ben.

"I was just going to," he said. And because his apprehension was now gone, he felt his short-fuse temper slowly rising again against this expensive whore who had turned out to be such a letdown and scarcely worth all the scheming and risks he had taken. Sex was sex, and she was just another lay, and not such a hot one, at that. What had suddenly become of the passion that had been swelling from his boyhood when he was masturbating dreaming of her? It had been there until the very moment he had at last screwed her down to the big leather chair, when his desire had ended in an aborted, painful erection, and had turned into resentment, as if she were guilty of a deception. Or was all this somehow his own fault? Some kind of temporary insanity?

He also remembered the embezzled checks and hesitated whether he ought to claim them, but decided against it. He wouldn't stick around to face the music, and to hell with Noelle. To hell with Noelle, he thought again, realizing that the words rhymed as if in a kind of poetic justice. Anyhow, asking for those damn checks would destroy the impression he managed to create that this old fool had just caught his wife with a boyfriend. Might be a good idea to bolster this impression by lousing the bitch up a bit more, he thought vindictively. He rummaged in his pocket and finally produced Noelle's key to the plush triplex.

"You may need this," he said, tossing it on the cocktail table. "I won't have any more use for it."

Hugh and Doriana both watched him striding hastily out of the room, and in another moment they heard the click of the door lock. They were alone.

It was so quiet in the large apartment, now frozen in a chill of suspended animation, that they both heard a new click, the faint click of the service entrance, far back in the kitchen quarters, and as though the intruder could have somehow managed to open the door without a key, for some seconds they both thought that he had come back.

Presently the cheerful face of Louise appeared in the door.

So it must be past noon, though Doriana.

"When would Madame wish to have lunch served?" Louise asked.

She knew well that she was committing a faux pas by barging in on their tête-à-tête, but her curiosity prevailed over her common sense and her professional training. And quite obviously it paid off. She stared at Doriana dumb-

founded. Well, well, they must have had a wild reconciliation just then. She looked knowingly at the big chair. That's
where they probably had their patching-up party, in this
roguish chair in which she had once seen them making love.

But as seconds passed in total silence, Louise began to
fret. Had her indiscreet intrusion so angered her mistress
that she would reprimand her in Monsieur Botain's presence?

Doriana did not even seem conscious of her maid, however. She was staring at the picture in the pink mirror on
the wall which returned her anguished look. So that's how
her husband must see her! After two years of careful groom-
ing and posturing she was forced to let him see her in this
state. Could the damage be undone? She had to get out of
his sight and do something about the mess that she was.

"Have lunch ready by one," she told Louise, who sneaked
out so fast that she forgot to acknowledge Doriana's instructions.

Hugh watched Doriana going to the door and knew that
he wouldn't wait for her an hour, after which she would
reappear with the beautiful and relaxed face of the usual
love goddess. How many men had keys to their apartment,
keys like the one this young stud had left on the table? How
many lovers had she had while he was making a damn ass of
himself and probably the laughing stock of the whole world?
So that's how it worked out. Had he come an hour later, he
would have most likely never known the difference. This was
probably all it took to transform a face bloated by promiscuous sex into that of the woman he had always worshiped
and admired.

He was reflecting on how hopeful he had been about their
future together only a short while ago. An aging man in love
could certainly be trusting and stupid. . . . It also puzzled
him that the feeling that had dominated his life for such a
long time could evaporate so suddenly. Although was it sudden, really, or had it been happening by degrees without his
realizing it?

Was he, like everyone else around her, so hypnotized by

her beauty that he had lost all perspective? And Stephanie's trite phrase about beauty not being everything came back to his mind and acquired meaning, for it also implied that there were qualities far more precious and valid in a durable relationship between a man and a woman, qualities like honesty, which, humiliated and indignant, he now thought Doriana lacked. He was skeptical at the time Stephanie had made her remark, because he suspected her of being resentful of him and jealous of Doriana, and, what's more, of being dishonest herself and of scheming and lying to him. Yet, that worn remark now was influencing his reaction to his wife's composure he found so shocking in the circumstances.

And while he was gloomily judging Doriana, who seemed to be taking for granted that he would continue playing the role of a dupe, his anger rose to a nearly murderous pitch. Perhaps it had begun mounting a while ago, as he watched her guilty embarrassment and the man's insolent smirk, but he had held it in check. And the thought that he let the man get away, made him despise himself.

"Pour yourself a drink, we'll have lunch as soon as you've finished it," she said, making sure that he heard her, looking at his still somber face. Hugh's drink would be as usual a double one, and she would have a few minutes to make herself presentable, to pull herself together, and, most important, to think of how to satisfactorily explain everything to her husband.

He no longer could suppress his instinct to punish someone for what had happened to him, and hit the target, the true core of all his troubles—Doriana.

"Lunch?" he said, without giving her a chance to leave the room. "Lunch?" he almost shouted now, allowing the built-up pressure to escape for the first time. "Did all that damn frigging give you a hell of an appetite?!"

Stunned by this outburst of abuse, she experienced a new wave of panic, as if now it were Hugh who was menacing her. But because she knew how unfair his attack on her was, forgetting that he was totally unaware of the truth, her anger also started to replace her passive despair.

"You act like an uncouth bastard!" she lashed out, and watching his congested face all at once very close to hers, thought that he was going to hit her, and turned round to walk out the door.

For a second he did want to strike her, then felt strangely numb. It was as if a spring within him that had started to tauten more and more when he found Doriana with a strange young man, after it wound up to its limit, had abruptly snapped and uncoiled, leaving him limp and weary, with no resentment left, but no forgiveness, either, just bitterness and the desire to get far away from all of it.

"I'm leaving," he heard himself say, as if it were somebody else talking. Maybe it was, for he felt that he no longer was the same man. "I'm leaving, I have a plane to catch."

For a second Doriana remained speechless, and just turned and faced him again. Was he running out on her when she needed him most?"

He took his wristwatch from his coat pocket where he had dropped it before entering the apartment. It was an old gag —no timepieces in the place, like in the Las Vegas casinos. Although he never quite understood this silly taboo, as he failed to understand her other quirks, he had always humored her.

She couldn't help noticing his impatience, and this gesture was like an omen of disaster. As if he were a total stranger who had never known the rules of the house, or maybe was too indifferent now to care to remember them.

He would have liked to add something to his brusque announcement, but really didn't have anything to say. All he wanted was to leave and try to forget her face with its abashed expression of a mature woman virtually caught in an illicit sex act, coupled with the forlorn look of a frustrated and frightened little girl. He wanted to get out without any recriminations, and before weakening at the last minute and perhaps making up with her. He just couldn't, and didn't want to, take any of it any more.

"I'm flying to the West Coast and then on to Melbourne. For good this time. My lawyers will get in touch with you about arranging our divorce settlement," he said.

Did he hear her gasp?

All those years before the cameras, the old training, came in handy in helping her to keep him from guessing how shaken she was. So they were all through. He would never learn about her news she had promised him. He didn't even remember to ask her about it.

Fleetingly she felt an urge to cry, to beg, to make him forgive her for what she was guilty of and for what she was not, but again contained herself. And she remembered how she had once allayed her fears that he might become an alcoholic, by believing that he was too strong a man to succumb to any weakness. Now his strength was helping him to overcome the greatest weakness he has ever had—his long-suffering tolerance of her senselessness, of her taking him so shamelessly for granted.

He took his key to their triplex from his pocket and didn't have the subtlety not to put it down on the table alongside the other key where the intruder had tossed it not long ago. He certainly couldn't have done it intentionally. Yet the casual, unthinking gesture cut deeply, maybe more painfully than his dry words.

Thirty-Nine

Now she was all alone. Hugh was gone, gone forever. Gone without understanding and without giving her a chance to explain. How deeply he must have been hurt.

"Mr. Botain has an emergency on the West Coast," she told Charles when he appeared to announce that lunch was served. "I'll eat alone. A little later." She wasn't hungry; she felt as if she were never going to be hungry again.

She remained standing near the door after Charles had left.

The phone rang and she crossed over and mechanically picked up the extension. "Yes? Yes, Cy."

She listened quietly, without interrupting. So the coroner's verdict was that Carol had died of heart failure, ruling out murder.

"Thanks for letting me know, Cy. The dead can't be brought back, but there's some comfort in learning that Carol did not die a violent death," she said, thinking that she had come dangerously close only a short while ago to becoming a famous violent crime statistic herself.

But Cy was already talking business, and she forced herself to concentrate on what he was saying.

"Yes, Cy, sure, Cy, it's very smart of you, Cy. We might get together at Les Girls tonight and you'll give me the list of quotes. I'll go over them tomorrow. I've got one of my blinding headaches now."

Only after hanging up did she realize that she forgot to ask her manager about Carol's replacement on the show.

Her evening bag was under the coffee table, probably kicked there by her struggling feet. She picked it up and took out the crumpled checks. Nothing could prevent her now from punishing that disloyal little cheat of her ex-secretary who had betrayed her and who was in turn betrayed by her accomplice. But even as she was thinking about it, she was already tearing up the checks into bits that fell to the carpet like dead white butterflies.

Noelle is nothing but a very foolish girl, she thought without rancor. Besides, punishing Noelle would be like punishing herself. Weren't they both branded by the same strong teeth? Both already punished, both deserving of pity?

But aside from that, what else did they have in common? Noelle was really young, so very young inside and out. No hormonal changes causing anxieties, no wrinkles crying for cosmetic surgery. Sending her to jail would be robbing her of the joy of the ephemeral, sweetest years of youth. Condemning Noelle would be like murdering youth itself, the marvelous youth one could never get back at any cost. When it was lost all one could hope for was a poor imitation—the deceptive mask of skin-deep rejuvenation. And even if it were to be made easier to attain in the future with the perfecting of new methods like cryogenic and laser-beam cosmetic surgery, it would still be only synthetic youth.

All at once it struck her that her prematurely aged mother's extravagant dreams about the then newborn cosmetic surgery were so very like her own rejuvenation fantasies not really long ago, when she herself knew next to nothing about facelifting. The only difference was that her mother's dreams had never come true and that her mother had never gotten what she wanted out of life. But was there such a great difference after all? What did she have left? For a short while longer show business with all those silly talk and game shows that proliferated like rabbits, and the adulation of men, young and old, rich and poor, who even for briefly walking in and out of her bedroom would offer whatever they had—excitement, virility, or their wealth. That's all it amounted to. And it could not and did not satisfy the deep human hunger and need for a sense of continuity, the need of being wanted and really cared about, and for the need to care and want in return.

It was different with Hugh, with Hugh only. He was the only man who truly cherished her and whose love she had slowly killed by stretching his patience and understanding just a little too far and for too long. The passing time, her eternal natural enemy which she fought so fiercely and sometimes seemed nearly to thwart had its turn by rushing events while she stood still, left behind. And as though it had waited somewhere in the wings for this particular moment to emerge, Louise Bogan's haunting poetry stood sharply out in her memory.

> *What she has gathered, and what lost,*
> *She will not find to lose again,*
> *She is possessed by time who once*
> *Was loved by men.*

And she also thought of how much, unlike all those hundreds of impersonal quotations she had crammed for her television show, this anguished lament of another lonely, aging woman so painfully applied to her. She felt futile tears clouding her eyes. Her headache was growing unbearable. God, how wiped out she felt.

Dropping the negligee off her aching shoulder, she examined the pattern of the man's teeth that seemed less distinguishable in the swollen, bruised flesh. Unless attended to immediately, it would leave a nasty scar.

She felt as desperately lonely as if she were the sole shipwreck survivor washed ashore on a desert island. Hugh was gone. And Arlen was with Noelle. And she, the Divine Doriana, the living legend universally regarded as the most desirable of women, was left alone and unwanted. What a big joke she had somehow played on herself. If only she could laugh so that she might not weep.

She lived through the next few hours in a haze, acting mechanically, trying not to think. Applying wet compresses to her puffed up face. Pretending to eat lunch Charles had to reheat twice. Going to Dr. Orgood to have him treat her lacerated shoulder that had required eight stitches, without feeling the sting of the anesthetic injection, and not caring one way or the other about his believing or not her story of tripping and cutting herself against the jagged edge of the fireplace screen.

Not until she was near home did she think about Hugh again. By now he must be all packed, or maybe had already left for the West Coast, going about doing things fast and efficiently as usual. It was only four hours since he had walked out from their triplex, and out of her life, but she felt as though she had always been alone.

Louise met her behind the front door, evidently waiting for her to return. "Mr. Redfore called again, and there's a telegram for Madame."

Doriana ignored both the message and the wire. She knew what they were about. Arlen was still trying to lie his way out, and Cy was asking to meet him at some bistro other than the one they had agreed on for tonight, as he had already done at the last minute so often before, when he had some trading in mind, maybe for poor Carol's vacated spot on the show this time. But when she had walked past Louise, and had started up the stairs, her maid called to her excitedly:

"The *télégramme,* it's from Monsieur Botain."

Louise was in a quandary. She had heard not only the shouting of the jealous Monsieur Botain, but also his cold announcement about his leaving her mistress for good. And she had to make Madame read the telegram before it was too late, even if it meant admitting that she permitted herself to open it.

Doriana turned round so abruptly that she nearly stumbled on the carpeted stairs. She rushed down the few steps and practically tore the telegram from Louise's outstretched hand. But fighting the overwhelming desire to read it, she forced herself to slowly walk out of Louise's sight into the library. There she stood still for awhile, giving herself a chance to breathe a little easier, trying to guess what Hugh had to say to her for the last time. Then she read his wire.

"Am booked flight 23 taking off Kennedy 10.05 P.M. tomorrow evening. Shall wait for you at the TWA Ambassador Club. Join me. Let's try for a fresh start in Australia together. Hugh."

That was all. He didn't conclude with the word "love," yet this was a message of love and forgiveness. And for the first time since Hugh left, she was at last able to cry. She wept without inhibition, sobbing loudly, not minding that her maid might hear her, and without giving any thought to the harm such weeping could do to her delicate eyelids. And because the message was so unexpected and so unrealistic, since it was only one day before the scheduled flight, with no time decently to step out of the show, with no time to make plans for her dedicated couple, not time enough to take care of anything else, it all seemed to be happening as if in a waking dream.

Presently, when she had regained some composure, she began to analyze the message. Hugh, who must have so rightly suspected her of infidelity with Arlen and who now wrongly believed her guilty of promiscuity with another man, had nevertheless forgiven her. But obviously knowing her as well as he did, he wasn't prepared to get back on the same old seesaw again and perhaps risk another delay. Hugh was giving her a second chance now or never to reach a decision, unaware that she had made it before he had left, without letting her tell him about it. And although his attitude toward her had changed from patient and permissive to demanding and intransigent, he was still willing to forgive her. But could she ever hope for that most difficult absolution of all to attain—to forgive herself?

She had been a liberated woman ever since she could remember, and yet had never been fully content or happy. And only now that she was at last ready to embark on a sheltered life of emotional dependence on her husband did she feel as though she were about to be truly free and on the eve of discovering that inner serenity she had been longing for and had never known.

Drying her eyes she looked around the library that only a short while ago was the scene of her destruction, and now, wondrously, of her regeneration.

And thinking about Hugh's steadfast devotion that had made this miracle possible, all that she had so carelessly called love before—physical attraction, sensual craving and its fulfillment—now seemed less important. It occurred to her that she no longer would have to fear being incapable of responding with youthful abandon to a younger man's fugue, and that Arlen had become only one among others in her past. And the knowledge that she was leaving behind her tempestuous lifestyle, made her feel at peace with herself, and the lazy sensation of not having to run, to compete, to fight for the survival of something that until now had been the very essence of her existence, and had abruptly become not worth fighting for, nearly made her forget how many immediate efforts she had to mobilize to set things in motion. She had only 24 hours to accomplish a great deal before going away with Hugh. Only one day, she said aloud, and shook her head incredulously, for even a whole week would not make her task any easier.

Cy must be the first on the list to learn about her plans. She rushed to the phone. Where did she find all this energy? Like a prisoner longing to escape from her confining world of false values and unrealistic ideas of happiness, yet afraid and doubtful of any changes, now all at once she was free of her shackles and feeling strong and confident, and eager to grasp the security of Hugh's extended hand.

Cy took so long reacting to the news of her unexpected departure and her stepping out of the show that Doriana began wondering whether they had been disconnected.

"Finding a replacement for you isn't going to be a cinch, you know. And on such short notice! What's the rush, anyway?" he finally said.

Perhaps he didn't quite understand or did not take her

seriously. "My husband and I have decided to go to Australia to live."

"But that's nutty," he wailed, "no superstar in her right mind would quit while her career's booming and she's at the top. You're acting like a child!"

Only yesterday she would have enjoyed this likening to a child, as much as she did when Carol had compared her to a quiz kid. How could she explain to her materialistic agent that, on the contrary, this was perhaps the first and the most significant adult decision she had ever made in her life. But evidently Cy must have realized the futility of his further trying to change her mind, and when he spoke again his tone was totally different.

"It's got to be awfully important to make you do this in such a hurry. But whatever it is, I wish you the best, doll. Even if it's some blow to me! I'll miss ya, we all will. Is there anything I can do?" he said, and his voice was barely audible and a bit shaky.

"No, thanks, Cy," Doriana said. "Hugh's lawyers will take care of the triplex and will have some of our favorite paintings and personal stuff shipped to us in Melbourne."

After putting down the receiver she remained sitting near the phone, thinking. How many people would regret her leaving? Not those like Cy, who profited from her success, but those who would truly feel her absence? Yet with each passing second there appeared to be less and less probability of singling out a sincere friend who cared, who really might miss her. Poor Carol would have, of course, but Carol was dead, and probably not greatly missed herself.

Looking back on her own life again, Doriana now realized that in all those years of stardom everybody had been taking advantage of her, and the painful awareness that she had always been the victim of some men's greed and of other men's lust, and also the dupe of her own gullibility, was hard to bear.

And this contemplation of giving of her possessions and of herself so freely in the past, reminded her of the great debt she had still not repaid. She must attend to it instantly—take care of Louise and Charles to allow them the alternative of either following her to Australia, or retiring comfortably in their beloved France without having to keep on working after so many faithful years of service to her.

As though taking a farewell tour of her home, she walked across the foyer to the study, but didn't even attempt to touch the pile of mail, and entered the spacious living room, where, gazing out of the ornate frame, the Bouché masterpiece, for which it seemed she had posed only yesterday, still reigned over the whole world.

She looked into the mocking eyes of the woman in the portrait, who had seen so much yet had learned so little and who went on proclaiming that there was only one thing worth having—the one thing she no longer had. But this time it did not set off either self-pity or distress, for she knew that these arrogant eyes were not telling the whole truth, that it was so very hard to grow old only for those who refused to grow up.